Distorted Loyalty

Written By
Stacy Eaton

~~~

Nitewolf Novels

Books by Stacy Eaton

My Blood Runs Blue
Blue Blood for Life
Whether I'll Live or Die
Garda ~ Welcome to the Realm
Liveon ~ No Evil
Second Shield
Distorted Loyalty
Six Days of Memories

Dedication

This book is dedicated to my two best friends. We might not always get the chance to hang out, but you both know I love you dearly!

Acknowledgements

This story came to me in a rush and stayed with me for an entire twenty-eight days while I wrote it. During that time, while I lived in the world of Rachel and Grant, my family, my friends, and just about everything else seemed distant to me. I can never thank my husband and my daughter enough for the patience, love, and support that they offer to me when I am in my writing haze. I love you both so very much.

My editors on this book deserve a great big thank you, also. This story would not be as strong as it is if it weren't for Dominique Agnew and Lisa McShea and all the effort they put into helping me shape and edit it to the final story.

A thank you to my formatter, Rachelle Ayala, for her hard work in making sure my book looks great in print and electronic form, and a huge shout out to Natasha Brown, my graphic artists who designed the cover.

My beta team has always been important to me, not just on this novel, but for supporting me through my trials and arguments with characters, editing, graphics, and preparing to release this book. A huge shout out to all of my team: Melissa Rutter, Jan Galloway, Dodie Auglis, Marie Godley, Pat Egan Fordyce, BreAnna Eichhorn, Tatiana Lammers, Fan Nichols, Jen Wolf, Ashleigh Danner, and Scott Johnson.

The biggest shout out goes to all of my readers who continue to encourage me with their reviews and their words of how much they have enjoyed my stories. It is for my sanity and for you that I write, and I thank you for that.

Chapter 1 – Rachel

Josh sucked on his straw so hard, he emptied his cup. His cheeks puckered while he drew in the last few drops. The loud slurp reminded me of the operating room. "Josh, I think you got it all." I eyed him over our almost-empty lunch tray as I spoke.

He grinned his boyish smile, and my heart tugged a bit in my chest—not that I would tell him his smile was boyish. At the age of sixteen, he was of the distinct impression that he was a man. My heart strings pulled a little tighter as I watched him eat the last of his fries. In a few years, he would be off to college, either near or far. At least I thought he was going to college, he hadn't mentioned doing anything else.

"Don't scrunch your face like that, Mom, it makes your wrinkles stand out." The surprised expression on my face must have entertained him because he belted out a laugh, "Just kidding."

I shook my head at him, "So why did you want me to come out shopping with you?" His laughter died quickly, and he glanced around the small café. I watched his nervous demeanor for a moment. "I'm not buying you anything expensive, Josh, Christmas is only a few weeks away."

He shook his head. "It's not for me."

I rested my elbows on the table and took a sip from my soda

cup. I waited patiently for him to continue, and he searched every part of the room, except for where I was sitting. Well, someone is very nervous, I thought to myself.

"If it's not for you, who is it for?" I asked. I tried to ease his unease by busying myself as I set my cup down and wiped grains of salt off the edge of the table into my hand and dropped them onto my empty plate.

Josh studied me for a long moment, and I saw the boy behind the young man hiding in his blue eyes. He leaned across the table so he could speak softly. "You have to promise not to give me a hard time."

Oh boy, this should be good. "Alright," I said and waited for him.

"Um, see, there is this girl," he glanced around the room, and I followed his gaze.

When he hesitated, I chimed in, "Wait, what girl?"

He brought his attention back to me, "Her name is Jazlyn." I nodded for him to continue. I had heard the name before. "I, um, I," he stuttered for a moment.

"Josh, spit it out, what about the girl?" I watched him sitting in the hot seat, a little pink tint to his cheeks. It was obvious that he liked this Jazlyn, whoever she was.

He blew out a quick breath and rushed to speak before he lost his nerve, "I want to buy her a gift, but I don't know what to buy her, so I was thinking that you might be able to help me pick something out." His cheeks brightened.

"I didn't know you had a girlfriend," I stated, trying to keep the surprise out of my voice that he was seeing someone.

"I don't, but I have wanted to ask her out for a while. I thought maybe I could get her something small and ask her out, or ask her out and then give her a small gift over holiday break."

This was the first time that I could remember that Josh had wanted to buy a female, other than me, a gift, and it reminded me again that he was growing up—too fast.

"What does she like?"

He shrugged, "I don't know. I don't know her that well. That's why I needed your help."

Okay, what do you buy for a girl that you don't really know at the age of sixteen that doesn't cost an arm and a leg? "Is she a girly girl or is she athletic?"

His shoulder rose again. "She plays sports, but she wears nice clothes, so she is kinda both, I guess."

I looked out the window and scanned the shops that surrounded us in the Main Street Shopping Plaza. My eyes landed on a shop just down the way. Bingo! "Come on, I have the perfect idea."

We dumped our trash, and Josh opened the door for me, and then held it open for two women and another one with a stroller as they entered. He was such a nice kid. I took a second to look at him as a stranger would. He stood about five feet eight and was lean and muscular from his swimming. His complexion was clear, his eyes bright, and he actually looked you in the eye when you spoke—a rare quality for any young person these days.

"What do you have in mind?" he asked as he caught up to me on the sidewalk.

"Well, if she likes to play sports, she gets sweaty, but girls don't like to smell bad, so she probably likes lotions and things like that."

His eyes widened, "You're not going to make me go into *that* store are you?"

I laughed at him, "What's wrong with the Body Scent Shop?"

He rolled his eyes, "Mom, don't you remember when I was younger and we went in there? I thought that purple liquid kids' soap was grape juice and drank it?"

I laughed. Oh, I remembered it, and the three hours at the hospital afterwards.

"And the next time I was in there, I knocked down a whole display of bottles and some broke. We couldn't get that nasty smell out of my sneakers for weeks."

"That smell was lavender, and yes I remember both of those times. Just don't drink anything, or touch anything, or look too hard at anything, and you should be fine." I laughed as he shook his head again.

"You know, you could go in without me, I think I'm bad luck when it comes to that place. Besides, how do you know she would even like something from there?"

I smiled and nodded towards the store, three girls about his age stepped out the door, all of them giggling and carrying small bags of goodies.

"Oh, man, I know them. Can we wait till they're gone?" he whispered as he turned his head so they wouldn't see him walking in their direction. He really thought that if he avoided their gazes he wasn't really there? Teenagers.

"No, you wanted my help, you got it." I glanced at my watch, "Besides I need to do this and then drop you off at home. I have to get to work in a little while."

"But, Mom," he whined.

I turned to him, "Do you like this girl?"

He rolled his eyes. One of these days, he was going to roll them, and they were going to roll right out of the sockets. "Yes," he replied.

"And do you want my help?" I asked.

"Yes," he mumbled and took a step toward the shop door. "Let's go." He pulled the door open, and I winked at him as I stepped past him into the store.

The holiday scents of peppermint and pine filled the air and encircled my head. I loved the peppermint, but I could do without the heavy scent of the tree. My nose tickled, and I wiggled it to hold back a sneeze.

"So what should I get her?" he asked softly as he examined the closest shelf.

"Not any of that, that's for people my age. Come on, let's go over there." I pointed to shelves on the opposite side of the room.

"You sure I can't wait outside? I feel like I'm going to slip and fall and knock something down."

I laughed at him over my shoulder and walked away. I knew he would follow me. We came to a display that had the latest body washes and lotions—fun scents that young people would enjoy. He picked up a bottle and flipped the cap open as he put his nose to the hole to smell it. He wrinkled his nose.

"Not that one," he muttered and put it back on the shelf.

A sweet female voice caught his attention, and his eyes widened to saucers as she spoke, "Hi, Josh." He spun around so fast, his earlier fear of knocking something over filled me. Thankfully, he made it around without a disaster.

"Hi, Jazzy, what are you doing here?" His cheeks reddened perceptibly, and he shot a quick glance at me. I wasn't sure if he wanted my help or for me to disappear.

"I'm shopping for a gift for my mom. What are you doing here?" Oh, the shy little smile she tossed his way told me that she returned his interest. I had to fight to suppress the grin that threatened.

I took a second to check her out for myself. She was about two inches shorter than Josh with a heart-shaped face and wide, bright blue eyes. Her cheekbones were strong and I wondered if she took after her mother or father in her features. She was definitely pretty with her long wavy hair pulled in a ponytail holder at the back of her neck. I was impressed at his selection in girls.

"I, uh, I," he began and I realized that if he was going to have any chance here, he would need my help.

"Hi, I'm Josh's mom." I stepped close to Josh but didn't touch him. I knew teenaged boys hated moms being clingy.

Jazlyn took a little shuffle back and smiled at me carefully, "Hi, I'm Jazzy."

"It's nice to meet you Jazzy. Look," I peered at Josh quickly, "maybe you could help Josh. He was thinking of buying a friend a small gift, but he's not sure what she might like."

A dash of disappointment rushed over her features, but she got control of them fast. "Sure, I can do that."

Josh gave me a wide-eyed look. "I'll just be over looking for that other thing I needed to get." I pointed to a display a few feet away as Josh nodded and then grinned.

"So, what does your friend like?" Jazzy asked him as I sauntered away.

"I'm not sure, why don't you show me what you like. She probably likes the same thing," he replied as I browsed over the table in front of me.

A deep masculine voice reached my ear over my right shoulder and caused a shiver to go down my spine. "I'm not sure I like the idea of your son buying my daughter a present."

I spun around to view the man who had just spoken so intimately in my ear and had to look up. Holy cow! This guy could be the twin to the actor who played the leader of the wolf pack on that hot vampire cable series; only this guy had short hair.

For a moment, I wasn't sure if he was being serious or joking with me, but a sexy smile slid over his lusciously-full mouth, and I realized he was very much not upset.

I cocked my head to the side, "And what makes you think it is for your daughter?"

He grinned, "Because I can see the teenaged lust in his eyes." I laughed at his comment and glanced at Josh and Jazzy. They were standing close, and she was holding bottles up for him to smell. The pure look of pleasure he wore on his features had nothing to do with what he smelled.

"I'm Grant." He held his hand out for me to shake and I placed my palm into his. His hands were huge and swallowed up my petite mitts.

"I'm Rachel." His hand spread warmth all the way up my arm. I had not realized how cold I was until I felt his heated skin.

He released my hand after a moment longer than necessary, and cleared his throat, "So that's Josh?"

"Oh, I see she has mentioned him." I absently picked up a bottle from in front of me and sniffed it. Yuck! It was pine. I blew air out of my nose to clean out my passages and found Grant chuckling at me.

"Not a fan of pine?" I took in his features as he spoke and

realized I had never seen a man quite this gorgeous before. His beard ran along his strong jaw, not a heavy beard, but one that looked soft and just full enough to want to touch. His wavy hair was tussled over his forehead, from either the wind or his own hand running aimlessly through it. My fingers twitched to reach out. "No, not at all, I'm a sweet and fruity girl." I glanced back to the kids again and saw them talking softly, their heads bent towards each other. "Ah, to be young and in love again."

"Does age really matter?" he queried.

"Well, isn't it when you are young that those first moments are the most special? You know, that first look when your heart beats out of your chest?" Like mine was doing right that second.

He stepped closer, "What about those first words?"

"Or that first touch. You know those little electrical impulses that flow through your skin?" I said softly, remembering the warmth his handshake had sent up my arm.

"And the butterflies that fill your stomach," he volleyed back as he stared me down with big soulful blue eyes.

"The same ones that take flight and steal your heart," I whispered.

"But nothing compares to the anticipation of the first kiss." He glanced at my lips and I realized that I was breathless as I flicked my tongue over my dry lips to wet them. My God! What was this man doing to me, and why was I allowing him to affect me in such a way?

I realized the moment I heard Josh yell that Grant and I had been lost in our own little world, and that the sounds of the shoppers and holiday music had all faded away. It was the sound of utter panic in my son's voice that broke through the romantic moment and planted my feet back on the hard wooden planks of the store floor.

"Mom!" Josh shouted, and I spun toward him expecting to see a display all over the floor, but the look of sheer horror on his face directed at the front window caught my attention and I turned. "I think someone just got run over by a car," he yelled and took off toward the door. I dropped the bottle I had in my hand on the nearest table and rushed to follow him.

The moment the door opened, I heard a woman yelling. I took off running between two cars parked outside the shop. I heard heavy footsteps behind me but didn't turn to look.

A woman stood in the parking lot screaming and crying, and as I made my way around an SUV to a large blue construction van, I saw the unmoving feet of a woman lying on the ground under the chassis of the van. I dropped my purse to the ground and went to my knees beside the unconscious woman's feet.

I peered under the vehicle, nothing appeared to be caught in the mechanics of the van. "Josh, grab her other leg," I instructed, "we need to pull her out slowly."

Josh wrapped his hands around her ankle while I took her other one, "On three, pull slowly until I tell you to stop. One, two, three." We moved her in slow motion, I didn't want to jerk her and cause more damage than she had already sustained. When she was out from under the van, I dropped back to my knees and did a visual assessment on her.

Blood ran from a large laceration on her forehead. Dirt consistent with a tire mark went over her abdomen and lower chest. A bubble of blood popped at the edge of her mouth and dribbled down the side over her pale skin—not good.

A man stood behind Josh, his hands on his head, "I didn't see her. I swear I didn't see her," he kept repeating.

"Someone call nine-one-one," I shouted and went about checking the woman for a pulse. She had one, but it was slow and off beat.

"Mom, is she alive?" I heard Josh ask me at the same time that I heard Grant's husky voice.

"Oh my God, Ilana!" he shouted and dropped down across from me.

"Don't touch her, Grant," I said right before I heard a girl scream. I could only guess it was coming from Jazlyn.

"Mom! Mom! Dad, that's Mom!" she began to sob as she

screamed.

"Grant, take care of your daughter," I commanded. "Josh, get down here and stabilize her head and neck." I shifted her neck up in a slow movement and twisted her chin to face front and up. As soon as Josh was on his knees above her head, he placed his hands on either side of her face at her jawline and held it still. "Keep holding it like that, Josh. If she wakes up, you need to make sure she doesn't move it."

His face was pale, and he nodded in a jerky motion. I had put him through a first aid course a year ago, so he knew what he was doing, although this was the first time he used what he'd learned in real life.

In the distance, I heard sirens. The man who had struck her was still mumbling that he had not seen her, and a crowd created a circle around us. I focused on the woman in front of me.

My God, I had just been flirting with this woman's husband while she was getting run over by a car. I am going to hell.

A police car pulled up and an officer rushed to us, telling people to move back. "What happened?" he asked as he kneeled next to Ilana on the opposite side of me.

"All I know is she was run over by this van," I jerked my head over my shoulder, "and that guy in the bright yellow shirt and jeans is the driver."

He glanced at the two things I pointed out. "Do you know what you're doing?" he asked me as he watched me check her pupils the best I could without a flashlight.

"I'm an ER doctor, give me your flashlight." He yanked it out of his belt and handed it to me. "This woman is married to that man over there." I said with another chin point as I grabbed the flashlight from him.

"Aw, shit," I heard him mumble as he stood up.

I lost track of what was happening around me as I attempted to listen to her breathing and assess her the best that I could without medical equipment. She was in bad shape, and she needed to get to the hospital.

The ambulance arrived, and I passed along all the information that I'd been able to come up with to the arriving paramedic. I helped them put her on the board and gurney before I helped to get her into the back of the ambulance.

"Josh, go grab my purse. My keys are in the front pocket, go straight home." He looked shaken. "Are you alright to drive?"

He nodded, "Yeah, just kind of freaked a little. I can't believe that is Jazzy's mom."

I wanted to take the time to talk to him, but I had to get into the back and help them. "I know. Go get the car and go home, I'll call you in a little while."

I jumped into the back of the ambulance and began to pull the doors closed. Grant stood in the same spot, his arms wrapped around his now silent daughter as he stared at me. The pain on his face felt like a scalpel cutting into un-numbed skin. I looked away and slammed the door.

"Let's go. She doesn't have much longer to live," I stated as I sat down across from the paramedic and began to better assess Ilana now that I had medical equipment to use.

Chapter 2 – Grant

"What do you think Mom would want?" Jazzy asked me as she sniffed yet another bottle of lotion.

"Something light and fruity," I replied.

Jazzy stared at me with a stern expression, "Mom doesn't like fruity."

"Yeah," I grinned, "but I do."

She scrunched up her nose, "Yuck. She doesn't wear it for you."

I blurted out a bark of laughter, "If she doesn't wear it for me, who does she wear it for?"

"She wears it for herself." She shook her head like she was the know-it-all teenager she pretended to be all of the time.

"Oh, my God! Dad!" She spun around on the tips of her toes, pure excitement flooding her face.

I stepped back, shocked at the immediate change in her mood. "What?"

She peeked over her shoulder, "You remember that boy? Josh? The one I was telling you about?" Why she had to turn sentences into questions, I would never know. "He's here!" She squealed high enough that I winced.

"Where?" I said, searching the store over her head. I was six foot five, so looking over her five-foot-four frame was easy.

"Don't look!" she gushed.

"Why not?" I asked, confused at her reaction.

"He'll see you!" she added quickly.

"I'm kind of hard not to see, Jazz," I replied dryly and planted my eyesight on the boy who had my daughter's heart doing a wild pitter pat. "Ah, I see."

"Dad, stop staring," she whined and peeked over at him again.

I checked out the kid covertly. He was about five foot six, maybe seven. His hair was cut short and he had some kind of hair product in it that helped the front stand up and look fashionably wet. His jeans actually came up around his waist and didn't hang off his hips—thank God for that. He wore a thick hoodie and either looked scared to death or embarrassed as hell to be standing in the store.

I switched my view over to the woman with him, and found her much more interesting to inspect. She was almost his height and lean. Her light brown hair hung straight down to hit below her shoulders. The soft blond highlights reflected the gleam of the light in the store. She fought back a smile, and I knew she was aware that the kid with her didn't want to be there.

They walked over to a wall display. "What should I do?" Jazzy asked and I peered down at her, totally confused by her question.

"What do you mean, what should you do?"

She got that well, duh, look on her face, "Should I go talk to him?"

I held back the laughter that bubbled inside me, "Sure, go talk to him."

She bounced up on her toes, "Okay." Before I could say another word, she high-tailed it to his side and said hello. Wow, to be a kid again, I thought as I moved closer and listened to Josh's mom encourage Jazz to help her son.

It dawned on me as she walked away that he must also be interested in my daughter. He looked like a decent kid, and she was sixteen now. I had to let go a little bit, didn't I? Well, maybe not yet.

I stepped over to Josh's mom and, without thought, leaned down and whispered in her ear.

Her eyes widened as she twisted around, and I wondered if I was about to be smacked. I wasn't normally flirtatious, but there was something about her that brought it out of me the moment I laid eyes on her.

Her irises were bright blue, like her son's, and her skin looked soft. Somehow, the initial banter between us turned sultry as we discussed the exciting things to come first in a new relationship. She drew me in with her easy smile and gentle voice.

"But nothing compares to the anticipation of the first kiss," I said as I looked down into her face and took in the little flick she did with her tongue. What kind of fire was I playing with?

It took me a moment longer than her to break out of the little fantasy we had indulged in when her son yelled to her. Before I understood what was happening, she dropped a bottle on the table, and I caught the other two she knocked off and stacked them before I followed her.

She ran towards the parking lot, her son right behind her. A large blue van sat in the traffic lane, and people were converging on the area. I heard her yell to someone to call for help just as I rounded the corner. It took me a moment to realize that the woman lying on the pavement, bleeding from her head, was my wife.

"Oh, my God, Lana!" I fell to the ground beside her, my normal calm demeanor shaken to the core. I was unable to process anything besides the fact that my wife of seventeen years was unconscious on the ground.

My daughter's shriek electrified each vertebra, setting off every nerve ending in my body.

"Grant, take care of your daughter," Rachel stated in a tone that left no disobedience.

I stood as she said something to her son and turned to Jazlyn, sobbing and staring at her mother on the ground. I wrapped my arms around her and drew her head into my chest to block out the view.

I should be doing something, I absently thought as I heard the sirens. I was the one who normally arrived at a scene in one of those cars. I had been to hundreds of calls, some much more intense than this, and I had never questioned what I had to do.

At this moment, I could not think, much less act. I stood and held my crying daughter as close to me as I could get her. I stared at Rachel as she poked and prodded Ilana. Her son was holding Ilana's head to protect her spinal column. I had no idea that Rachel knew what she was doing, except that she was doing something— more than I was. I was lost, utterly and completely lost.

Paul Robinson showed up to the scene, the lights of his cruiser bathed the area in flashing red and blue strobes. He went down to his knees and spoke to Rachel. I stared at my wife's face. Blood was not only running from her forehead, but from the side of her mouth. I squeezed my eyes shut.

Robinson came to my side, "Grant, they are going to do everything they can."

I nodded. I knew there was no way I would be able to speak. The ambulance arrived, and Robinson went off to talk to witnesses and the driver of the van that had struck Ilana. I watched as Rachel gave out commands in a voice so different than the one she had used in the store only a few minutes ago.

A few minutes ago, I had looked into her eyes and wondered how her skin would feel and how her lips would taste. I shuddered. My wife was being struck by a car as I had imagined kissing another woman. Jesus, what a bastard I was.

Jazzy stopped sobbing and watched from the safety of my arms as the ambulance crew moved her mother into the back of the waiting bus.

Rachel called her son over and spoke to him before she climbed into the bus and turned to close the door. Our eyes met, and in that moment, I knew in the center of my heart that Ilana's prognosis wasn't good.

Rachel slammed the door, and the ambulance siren wailed as it pushed through the crowd. Robinson came back to me, "You need a ride to the hospital?"

"No, I'll be okay to drive." I rubbed Jazzy's back as I spoke, needing the comfort as much as she needed it from me.

"You sure?" he asked.

"Yeah, thanks, Paul. Let me know what you find out," I said as I ushered my daughter in the direction of our car. We climbed into the cab of my SUV, and we both sat staring out the windshield.

"Dad, she's going to be alright, isn't she?" Jazzy's voice had lost the cocky teenage attitude and now sounded more like the lost nine-year-old that she used to be.

I could lie to her and tell her that everything would be fine, but I didn't lie to my family. My hands shook as I attempted to stab the key into the ignition. "I don't know, Jazzy. It didn't look good."

I turned to face her, and she swallowed and wiped her eyes. "But the van was backing out. It wasn't like he was going forty miles an hour in the parking lot. He couldn't have hit her that hard."

I reached over and ran my hand down the side of her head. Maybe she didn't realize her mother had been run over. "We can wish for the best, but I can't promise you anything, Jazlyn." Oh Jesus, please let her be alright.

She nodded and turned to stare out the side window. A crowd still stood around the scene, gawking at the blood pooled on the asphalt. I had seen more blood than that and watched the people walk out of the hospital a week later, and I had also seen a lot less blood and people dead at the scene before we arrived. I couldn't forget the look on Rachel's face as she had pulled the door closed.

I clenched my eyes for a second while I fought off the unwelcome notion that she wasn't going to make it.

We drove in silence. Jazzy didn't even reach over to change the radio station or turn up the volume. I wanted to say something, but I had absolutely no clue what to say to make this situation better. Better? Damn, I would settle for bearable! I clenched the steering wheel instead of hitting it with my fist like I wanted to.

She couldn't die! We'd been married for almost seventeen years, together for almost twenty. What were we going to do if she died?

Don't think like that. Be positive, I thought and immediately wanted to scream obscenities.

When we pulled up to the hospital, the ambulance was still parked at the unloading door. We parked, and I grabbed Jazlyn's hand as we made our way to the entrance.

I had walked into this very hospital countless times in the course of my job, but this time was different. Today, I wasn't here to interview a victim or get blood drawn for a DUI suspect. This time I had to wait in the hard plastic chairs in the sterile white waiting room with twenty other people.

I filled out the paperwork the receptionist had given me. It was slow going, as I had a hell of a time concentrating. Every time the automatic doors to the patient area swished open, my chin popped up. I finished filling out the forms and gave them back while I asked the nurse if she knew anything. She shook her head and said someone would be out soon.

Soon, how freaking soon? I stalked back to my chair. Jazzy stared straight ahead at the flickering television that hung high on the wall. I knew she wasn't watching it. I knew that, like me, the visions she saw were memories of her mother.

I sank down in the seat beside her and put my arm around her, pulling her into my shoulder. She curled up against me, and we sat there for another twenty minutes before the door opened and a nurse emerged, tension in her face.

The nurse searched the waiting room and when her eyes landed on me, they stopped. She dropped her eyes for a moment and came to join us, "Mr. Murphy, if you could follow me, please."

Fear kept me from asking what I needed to know. I took Jazzy's hand as we followed the nurse through the doors into the busy emergency room. She led us to another waiting room, but this one had comfortable chairs and couches. The lighting from the table lamps shimmered onto the beige walls, casting a warm soft glow around the room.

"If you could have a seat, Dr. Wilde will be in to talk to you in a few minutes." The nurse gestured in a welcoming manner.

"Dr. Wilde?" I asked quietly, unsure if that was Rachel.

"Yes, Dr. Rachel Wilde. She will be in to speak with you soon."

She was a doctor. Well, that gave Ilana a better chance, didn't it? Not knowing what else to say, I gave her a brief nod while Jazz and I sank down into a couch facing the door. I glanced around the room. There were telephones on the side tables, and a longer table with a coffeemaker against a side wall.

Less than ten minutes later, the door opened again and Rachel walked in. She now wore light blue medical scrubs, her hair pulled back from her face in a tight ponytail at the nape of her neck and a butterfly bandage adorned her forehead. She made immediate eye contact with me and held it before she stepped further into the room and closed the door behind her softly.

Jazzy and I both sat up straighter, and I reached for my daughter's hand as Rachel moved in front of us. I forced my shaky legs under me and stood. Jazlyn clung to my side as we waited for her to speak. Those next three seconds were the longest of my life.

"Mr. Murphy, I'm sorry. We did everything we could."

Chapter 3 – Rachel

"Give me your stethoscope, Mike." He ripped it from around his neck and handed it over.

"I'll start a central line," he said and began to rummage through one of his bags.

I grabbed the edges of Ilana's blouse and yanked it open, sending the buttons flying around the inside of the ambulance. The skin on her stomach was turning purple as if a bruise were already forming under the skin, and I knew with certainty that she had major internal bleeding.

I listened to her heart, it was slower than it should be, but that could also be from shock. "Before you put the line in, let's set up the leads so we can watch her heart. I don't like what I'm hearing."

"Her pulse ox is down at seventy-two. BP is eighty over forty-eight."

"Son of a bitch. Okay, get the line in and we need to be ready with the pads if she codes." I glanced at the young male EMT who was also in the back with us, "Get an airway, and start forcing air."

I put the stethoscope to her abdomen and could hear the blood in her abdomen pulsing with each soft beat of her heart. If we didn't get to the hospital soon and get her open to stop the bleeding, she would be dead in minutes.

I stood up to dig into the cabinet above my head to see if they had something I could use. The ambulance leaned to the side as if it were going around a corner. I lost my balance and smacked my head on the corner of the cabinet. "Shit," I called out as I righted myself.

The machine next to Mike beeped, and we both turned to the screen.

"Damn, damn, damn!" I put the side down on the gurney and leaned forward to start compressions as her heart stopped. "What's our ETA?"

The driver of the ambulance called out that we had about three minutes till we arrived.

"Drive faster and radio in to advise we have a code."

Mike put the pads up in front of him, and I leaned back away from Ilana along with the EMT so he could shock her. Mike and I stared at the machine, nothing.

"Do it again."

Mike put the paddles back to her chest, and Ilana's lifeless body jerked as the shock went through her. Nothing.

"Get that line in her so we can give her meds." I leaned back over her and started compressions again. The EMT used the resuscitator bag to force air into her lungs.

"Dr. Wilde, did you know you are bleeding?" Mike asked as he went about putting the line in her arm.

"It's not my bleeding I'm worried about," I said and kept on with my compressions. I had felt the hot liquid running down the side of my face. Obviously, I had split my forehead when I had hit it on the cabinet.

"Doc, we're pulling up," the driver called out.

"She has a lot of blood in her airway," the EMT said.

"I know, I can hear it," I said as I climbed on the gurney, straddling her hips so I could keep doing compressions while we moved her into the hospital.

The back of the ambulance opened, and I kept my center of gravity low while still pumping her chest to keep whatever blood she had in her veins flowing to her heart and brain. The gurney was pulled out and pushed in through the open doors.

Her color wasn't good. She had become a whole new shade of white in our transport. They wheeled us into a room and someone called out that he would take over the compressions. Someone else helped me off the gurney.

Three people lifted her off the gurney and onto another one. The ambulance gurney was shoved out of the way as a nurse came towards me with a gown. I shook my head; I was already messy, although I did take the gloves she held out. A tray sat out ready for me and I lifted a scalpel as Dr. Simpkins, the on-duty doctor walked into the room.

"What do we have, Rachel?" he called out as another nurse helped to dress him as they did me.

"She was run over by a van, massive internal bleeding in her abdomen; coded in the ambulance." I slit through the skin on her chest. The bright red blood oozed out through the incision. With multiple hands working on her, someone cut her chest plate and pulled her diaphragm open.

There was a collective gasp in the room from all those around the gurney. There was too much blood, way too much.

Simpkins barked out orders, while he attempted to find the source of the bleeding. I massaged her heart to keep what little blood she had left moving through it. As I worked, a nurse came up and wiped off my forehead, putting a butterfly on my laceration.

"Come on, Ilana, don't give up." I had her heart in my hands, and not an hour before, I had been thinking of her husband's gorgeous eyes and seductive smile. How was this for ironic?

The pace was furious in the room; words were only spoken as an expletive or a command.

"What time did the patient arrive?" Simpkins asked.

A moment later a nurse called out, "Five twenty-five."

I glanced at Simpkins. He was looking up at the clock above my head. "Rachel, we need to call her. We won't be able to get her back."

"No, we have to keep trying," I stated.

"Rachel, it's been over thirty minutes since you arrived," he said softly, and I met his brown-eyed gaze.

For thirty minutes we had worked on her. It felt more like ten. He was right, it was over. I nodded and dropped my eyes to Ilana's face. I'm so sorry. I tried. I really did.

I stepped back. "Time of death is five fifty-eight," Simpkins said, and I heard him rip his gloves off his hands.

I stared at her for another moment. I could tell that she had been a beautiful woman and that her daughter had inherited her looks. She was a woman in the prime of her life with a beautiful family. I lowered my chin to my chest—a family I was going to have to go and face.

I pulled off my gloves and tossed them in the biohazard bin. I glanced down at myself. My blouse was stuck to my chest from sweat and body fluids, my jeans splattered with Ilana's blood.

"Susan, would you bring her husband and daughter back to the family waiting room. I'm going to go change and then I will speak to them."

She nodded as I turned away.

"Jane, can you have someone close her up and then clean her in case the family wants to see her?"

"Sure, Dr. Wilde." She went in search of an orderly as I wound my way through the hallway to the locker room.

I sat on the bench and hung my head. What a way to start a shift. I grabbed my toiletry kit out of my locker and took a quick shower to rinse away the sweat. I pulled my hair back in a ponytail and put on clean scrubs before I picked up my jeans and blouse and tossed them in the biohazard bin in the locker room. I loved that blouse, I thought absently as I dropped the lid.

Simpkins met up with me as I arrived back at the nurse's station in the center of the chaotic mess. He was about ten years my senior and an incredible doctor. His soft blue eyes always helped to calm his patients, and the graying at the temples of his brown hair gave him a distinguished look. I was proud to work with him.

"How did you end up with that?" he asked, sympathetically.

"Right place, wrong time," I said as I walked past him toward the waiting room.

I stopped at the door and took a deep breath. I had passed along this information to a hundred people, and it never got easier. I knew that it was best to just say the words—pull the proverbial band-aid off fast.

Only, for the first time in my life, I was afraid to open the door and face these two people. My mind raced faster the long I stood there, and Susan walked up beside me, "You going to be alright?"

I nodded.

"Did you know her?" she asked.

"No, I had just met her husband and daughter. Josh has a crush on the daughter."

"Oh, yuck." She shivered, "Well, let me know if you need anything."

I wanted to say, Alright, I do need something. I need you to walk in this room and tell them that their beautiful wife and mother died—but I didn't. It wasn't her place to do that.

I turned the knob and pushed the door open. The room was set up for just this purpose. Families could sit in the silence, use the phones to make calls, and grieve in private until they were strong enough to leave. The soft lights offered what little comfort we could offer.

Grant sat on the couch facing the door, his daughter beside him. He stood as I approached, and I swallowed the bile that rose in my throat.

"Mr. Murphy, I'm sorry. We did everything we could." For a few seconds he didn't speak, didn't even blink. It was a moment before either of them moved.

"You mean—" he started to say.

"Your wife passed away, sir. I'm very sorry."

He blinked rapidly a dozen times. His eyes shone brightly.

"No!" his daughter sobbed beside him, and he pulled her into his arms as she cried. I watched the salty tears finally begin to slide down his cheek.

I stepped back to give them space but didn't leave. I knew that they would want to ask questions, but they needed a moment to digest the information.

Grant pulled himself together when I approached with a box of tissues. I handed a tissue first to him and then to his daughter.

Jazlyn sank to the seat behind her and put her head into her hands, crying softly.

Grant wiped his eyes, sniffed, and scanned the room. I could see the internal strength of the man ready to split as he forced himself to stay composed. He wiped his hands over his face and sniffed again before he sat down beside his daughter.

I took a few steps back and lowered myself into a chair that faced them. The seconds ticked off into minutes, and I could feel each grain of sand trickling inside the proverbial hourglass.

It was Jazlyn who finally met my gaze, and my heart went out to the young girl. She would live forever with the trauma of losing her mother right before her eyes.

"How did she die?" she asked in a voice that sounded nothing like her earlier friendly confident self.

"She had a lot of internal injuries." I didn't want to tell the kid that her mother bled to death in my hands.

She pulled out another tissue and blew her nose.

Grant had not looked at me yet, and I sat patiently. When he finally lifted his face, his features were contorted in anger and I flinched internally.

"Did you do everything you could?" he asked in a tone that sounded accusatory.

"Of course we did," I responded.

"You're sure?" he spat out.

"Mr. Murphy, I can assure you that we did everything that we could for your wife." I rested both hands in my lap, attempting to appear calm but feeling nothing of the sort. I felt as if he blamed me, and maybe he did. Maybe he needed to blame someone right now, and I was the one he had chosen—not the man that had run over his wife, but the doctor who had tried to save her.

"What time did she die?" A muscle ticked in his jaw.

I took a deep breath, "Her time of death was officially called at five fifty-eight."

He glanced at his watch. "That was almost thirty minutes ago, and you are just now coming to tell us." His misdirected anger pierced me.

"I asked the nurses to have your wife cleaned up so you could see her if you wanted to before you go." I forced myself not to sound defensive.

He stared at me, his brow furrowing. "And you couldn't bother to talk to us while they were cleaning up Ilana?"

I stared at him and tried not to grind my teeth. "Sir, I understand that you are upset, but I came to see you as soon as I could."

"You had time to do other things, and get changed, but not to come tell us that she died," he stated flippantly.

I was emotionally drained at that moment, and I lost my temper. I stood up, "Would you have rather I showed up in here with your wife's blood all over my clothes?"

Jazzy made a gasping sound, and the tightness around his eyes lessened slightly as he rapidly blinked.

"I'm sorry, I didn't mean to be rude." I put my hands on my hips and took a deep breath as I stared at the ceiling for a minute. "I'm sorry for your loss. I will ask the nurse to come get you when you are ready to see your wife. You are welcome to use the phone to make any calls to family, and to use the room as long as you feel the need."

He didn't say anything, and I turned and walked to the door. Before I walked out, I turned and called out to Jazzy, "I'm so sorry about your mom, Jazlyn. If you need a friend to talk to, I'm sure Josh would be willing to listen and be there for you."

I refused to look at Grant again as I turned and left the room. The arrogant prick! How dare he accuse me of not doing everything I could for his wife, and then put the assumption out like it wasn't important to talk to him? He had no idea how hard this was to do.

"Dr. Wilde, we have a gunshot victim coming in by chopper. ETA is ten, and your husband is on line three," Susan called out as I approached the desk.

"Susan, let the Murphys know when they can see the deceased."

I walked around the counter and lifted the phone, punching the extension button harder than I needed to. "Yes, Mark."

"Rachel, how is she?"

"How is who?" I stated tersely.

"Ilana Murphy, Josh told me about what happened."

"Is Josh alright?" I suddenly remembered that he had been there and witnessed the scene. I closed my eyes.

"Josh is fine. How is Ilana?" he sounded exasperated.

"How do you know Ilana Murphy?" I asked as I turned around and perched my butt on the desktop.

He hesitated for a moment. "I went to high school with her, and she works as a legal secretary. I see her from time to time."

"Oh," I said softly. "She didn't make it."

"What?" he gasped over the phone.

"She died from internal injuries." I glanced around the room and saw people getting the trauma room set up for the next victim.

"Oh my God," he stated emotionally into the phone.

"Dr. Wilde, eight minutes to landing," a nurse called out to me, and I nodded.

"Mark, I have to go. I have a gunshot victim coming in. Tell Josh I will call him later." He uttered something I couldn't understand, and I turned to put the phone down. I glanced up to see Susan leading Grant and Jazzy out of the waiting room. Grant eyed me pointedly for three seconds before he turned away and stepped into the room where his wife now lay under a white sheet.

Chapter 4 – Grant

I was stunned at her words. I knew the possibility existed, but I couldn't believe it.

"You mean—" I had to hear her say it.

"Your wife passed away, sir. I'm very sorry," she said in a voice I wish I had never heard. Compassion laced her tone; I wanted to wretch. Jazlyn fell apart, and I reached to comfort her.

Tears crept slowly down my face. A vision of Ilana lying on the ground, blood trailing from her mouth, came to the forefront of my mind. I wanted to push it away and call to mind the moment we met, the day we said our vows, the day we held our just-born daughter in our arms, but the vivid image remained a constant.

I heard Rachel move and forced myself to pull my fragile mental status back together. Rachel handed us tissues and Jazzy sat back down and hung her head. I wiped the moisture from my cheeks. There would be time to cry later. I needed to know what had happened.

Yet, as I sat there, I could not find my voice. Jazzy found hers first and asked the exact question I wanted to know. I fought not to cringe as Rachel said she had internal injuries. Had all her organs exploded when the van rolled over her?

If that was the case, wouldn't she have been bleeding more at the scene? There had only been a small trickle of blood coming out of her mouth when we'd found her.

For a moment, I replayed the whole scene, from the moment I had walked into the store until the moment I fell to my knees. A thought came to mind, and anger flickered to life like a spark on kindling. Had Rachel taken our flirtation seriously? Had she seen a man she wanted and somehow shirked her duties to help Ilana?

My common sense tried to douse the flames, but the coals increased their intensity. "Did you do everything you could?"

I refused to allow the hurt that crossed her eyes to affect me. She had no right to hurt. She was alive while Ilana was lying in some cold room waiting to be taken to the morgue.

Her assurance that she had done everything fell on deaf ears If she had bled to death, how long had she been dead?

I looked at my watch after she told me the time of death, and the flames climbed. She had left us sitting here, hoping and praying for almost thirty minutes.

What could possibly be more important than coming to talk to the family? Then I looked at her. I mean I really looked at her and realized that she was clean and smelled of soap. She had a butterfly bandage on her forehead, but I refused to feel any sympathy for her. She had taken a fucking shower while we sat here wondering if Ilana was alive or dead.

"You had time to do other things, and get changed, but not to tell us that she died." I wasn't asking a question, I was stating the obvious. Did she think that because we had flirted in the store that maybe she should clean herself up to make a good impression on me?

She stood abruptly. The burn I felt was reflected in her eyes as she responded. "Would you have rather I showed up in here with your wife's blood all over my clothes?"

I thought about that for a moment, I wouldn't have cared, but it would have affected Jazzy. She was right. I felt the need to apologize, but she forced herself to calm down and apologized for her outburst. She spoke for a few more moments and then went to the door.

She turned and spoke to Jazlyn before she left, and I felt the anger flare again. She was trying to set her son up with my daughter. The nerve of that woman, I steamed.

Jazzy curled into me on the couch and wept softly, "Honey, you don't have to go see her if you don't want to." I said as I ran my hand down the back of her head.

"No, I want to see her." She hiccupped, "I can't believe she's dead, Daddy."

"I know, honey, I know. I can't believe she is either." We sat in silence for a few more minutes and then the same nurse that brought us back to the room came to get us. Jazzy walked in front of us, and I stopped before we entered the room next door. Rachel, or Dr. Wilde as I would now call her, was hanging up the phone. She met my gaze with a hard one of her own. I turned away from her, hoping to never see her again.

The room was a small patient room and the gurney stood in the center. A white sheet was wrapped around her and tucked under her shoulders. Her face was pale but clean. No signs of blood were present now.

My earlier anger dissipated in the quiet of the room. We moved to stand beside the bed. Jazzy swiped at the endless tears falling from her eyes.

"Can I touch her, Daddy?" How long had it been since she had called me Daddy? I wondered as I told her she could.

With a tentative hand, she reached out to caress her cheek. My eyes filled, blurring the image. I blinked, and the tears flowed down my cheeks.

"I love you, Mommy," Jazlyn choked out and laid her head down on her mother's shoulder as sobs wracked her body. I put my arm around her back and held her up. I had to force myself not to do the same thing she was doing. I had to be strong for her.

Ilana, I am so sorry. Why didn't we wait for you outside? If we had waited, I would have seen the van moving. You would be alive.

Would her spirit hear my words? Would they give her any

comfort? They didn't give me any. I stared at the face of the woman I had grown up with, loved, the woman with whom I had shared good times and bad. What was I supposed to do now?

Jazlyn stood and turned to wrap her arms around me. The door opened behind us and Tom Mickens walked in. Tom and I had been partners for four years. He was my best friend. I tried to be strong, but when he took in Ilana's lifeless body, I saw the moisture in his eyes sparkle, and I couldn't hold my pain back. Tom put his arms around us both as we all cried. After some sniffing and wiping of the faces, we turned to stare at her again.

My God, what am I going to do without you? What am I supposed to do now? How am I supposed to raise a teenaged daughter alone? I stared at her unmoving form, knowing I wasn't going to get an answer but praying I would. I took a moment to memorize her features one more time before I began to turn away. Goodbye, Ilana, I love you.

"Come on, Jazzy, let's go home."

Tom held the door open for us, and we walked out. A loud commotion off to the left caught my attention, and I turned to see a door being held open. Dr. Wilde stood in a yellow gown, her hands covered with purple gloves and bright red blood. Her face was intent on the patient in front of her, but she suddenly looked up and straight into my face. Her nostrils flared and her lips tightened into a straight line.

"Clamp," she called out and turned her back on me. The door closed, and I followed Tom and my daughter out of the hospital. Would she fight harder for that person than she had for my wife?

A few hours later, I sat in my recliner with a beer in my hand. Jazzy had cried herself to sleep on the couch. Tom's wife Beth had Jazzy's head in her lap, and she was combing her fingers through her long brown hair.

"So what do you know about the accident?" Tom asked me.

I shrugged numbly, "Not much. She got run over, she died. What else is there to know? Does anything else even matter?"

Tom studied me for a few seconds. "Do you want to know?"

Did I? One minute she was walking across a parking lot, the next she was under a van, and then she was dead. The husband in me said no, but the cop in me didn't like that answer. "Yeah."

He took a long pull on his beer. "A witness stated that she saw her park her car and climb out. She was texting on her phone. The witness remembers that she was laughing at something she read and then typed something and started to cross the street." He paused. "She said she never looked up."

"Why did the witness even notice her?" The police officer in me questioned.

"She saw her pull up, liked her car. She said something about how she was looking at a similar car and she was moving towards her because she wanted to ask her a question about it. She saw the whole thing."

That was a logical answer. "I wonder who she was texting?"

"I don't know, but you can check her phone when it is released from evidence," Tom said.

I shrugged again, I guess it didn't really matter who it was. "How did you hear about it?"

"Paul called me as soon as you left." He took another drink.

I looked down at my bottle. It was getting warm and I'd only had one sip. I didn't feel like drinking. Well, actually that was a lie. I wanted to get shit-faced, but that wasn't an option with Jazzy around.

Beth spoke up, "What can we do for you, Grant?"

I studied Jazzy for a moment, her face was swollen and red from crying, and my heart ached at the pain I knew she was feeling. "You're doing it, Beth. Thank you."

"Don't thank me for this. I'd do anything for you, or Jazzy, you know that. All you have to do is ask."

I swiped at a stray tear and turned away before I got all emotional again.

"Thank you," I muttered.

"Did you get ahold of her family?" Tom asked.

"Yeah, I called her parents, her brother was there, said he

would notify the rest of her family." I thought for a moment, "I guess I will have to call her work tomorrow."

"Speaking of work, the chief said to take as much time as you needed. He put notice out to the squads, but told them to leave you alone tonight." I appreciated what the chief had done, but I was not looking forward to being contacted by anyone. I wanted to crawl into bed and pretend nothing happened.

"What funeral home are you going to use? I can call them for you tomorrow." Beth asked quietly.

I faced her again, "I have no clue." How did you pick a funeral home? Ask for references? Compare prices? What the hell difference did it make which one you used?

"You could use Wilde's, they—" Tom started to say.

"Anyone but Wilde's." I barked out quickly stopping him.

"Okay," he said slowly glancing at his wife. "What about McGee's?"

"That's fine." I picked up my beer and guzzled half of it in one turn.

We discussed details for a few more minutes, and then Beth and Tom got ready to leave. Jazzy woke up as Beth stood. Her face filled with emotions I didn't want to deal with tonight but knew I had to.

After they left, I took Beth's seat, and Jazzy lay back down. I wound my fingers through the hair that was so much like her mother's.

"What are we going to do now, Dad?" she asked, and I knew she didn't mean activities. She meant, How were we going to move forward from this and live our lives without Ilana?

"I don't know, baby. One day at a time, I guess."

Chapter 5 – Rachel

The patient in front of me would live. He would have a scar on his shoulder from the bullet wound, but he would be alive to see another day.

I'd been working on stopping the bleeding when Susan had opened the door to ask me a question. I felt his hard stare as if it were a needle piercing me. I peered up at Grant and held his emotional gaze for a moment. I had done what I could for his wife; he could believe what he wanted to believe. I had other patients to worry about. With the twist of my head, I shoved the image of him into the back of my mind.

The shift went from bad to worse, and when morning finally rolled around, I could barely lift my feet. My eyelids felt like sandpaper with each blink. I didn't usually feel this way after a shift. For eight years I had thrived on the adrenaline that rushed through me with each patient and every challenge that came through the doors of our suburban state-of-the-art hospital and trauma center.

I had lost patients before, it always hurt, but Ilana's death affected me on a different level than the others. This was the first time someone had blamed me for the death. Would Grant start a wrongful death lawsuit? I knew he would never win; I had done everything I should have and more.

I sat at the main desk, surrounded by computers and charts as I spent the early morning hours writing my reports and tried not to think about the features of Grant's face or the husky lilt of his voice from the shop. When I felt my heart melt at the memory, I would remember the anger and grief I'd seen on his face when I'd relayed the news.

I finished writing my notes for Ilana and logged off the computer as Susan approached. "You almost ready to go?" she asked me.

"Yep, give me two minutes." Since Josh had taken my car, Susan had volunteered to drive me home; she looked almost as beat as I felt.

I didn't have clothes to change into, and no purse, since Josh had it, so I stacked my files in the bin and followed Susan out of the hospital.

The sun was beginning to lighten the sky, giving the whole area a bright but hazy gray look to it.

"I am so glad that tonight is over. You're off for a few days now, aren't you?" she asked me as we put our seatbelts on.

"Yeah, I have four days off. I can't wait to fall into bed and sleep for most of them," I replied with a laugh.

"You deserve some sleep after what you dealt with tonight." She hesitated, "You did an amazing job with that woman. I've worked with you for over five years in the ER, and I don't think I have ever seen you so intense with a patient."

I shrugged and looked out the window. "I guess since I knew her daughter and husband, it was kind of personal."

"How do you know them?" she asked. We had been too busy all night to really talk, and by the time things slowed down, we were all intent on catching up on paperwork.

"Josh has a crush on the daughter. We were out buying a present for her and we ran into them. I guess her mother was coming to meet them; that's when she got hit by the van."

She nodded, "I wondered how you happened onto that."

"You know what's fucked up?" I asked as I stared out the

window.

"What?" she asked around a yawn.

"Right before she was hit, Josh and Jazzy were flirting with each other, and her father, Grant, had flirted with me."

"He did not." She spun to look at me, eyes wide, her mouth hanging open.

"He was, and I flirted back." I shook my head, "I mean it wasn't anything serious, we were only joking, but there was this little spark between us." I paused for a moment as I thought, I've never felt any sparks with Mark.

"Wow," she said softly.

"When I went in to tell him about his wife, I felt like he was accusing me of killing his wife because of those few moments of flirtation."

She spun her head towards me again, "Are you kidding me?"

"No, I'm not. I'm wondering if he is going to have the case investigated."

She patted my shoulder, "You have nothing to worry about. You went above and beyond what you should have done. We all saw it, and I know our reports reflect that."

"Thanks, I know I didn't do anything wrong, but it still hurts to be accused."

She sighed, "I bet it does. I'm sure after his emotions settle down, he will think on it more and realize you did nothing wrong."

"Let's hope so."

We talked about the holidays for the rest of the drive and groaned in unison when we spoke about having to work Christmas night together. The ER was always filled with people trying out their new tools and gadgets and not doing so safely.

Susan turned onto my street, and I stared at my five-thousand-square-foot house. Mark and I had bought it after we married, and since the day I stepped foot in it, it had never really felt like a home. It was too big, too flashy, too impersonal with its three-car garage and cold stone front.

I said goodbye to Susan in the driveway and waved as she

drove away. I didn't have my keys with me, so I entered through the garage using the keypad. I was surprised to find Mark's car still inside. I glanced at my watch, it was almost seven. He was generally at work before this time.

Mark sat at the kitchen table reading the paper and drinking coffee. He was dressed for work, his briefcase on the floor beside him.

"I'm surprised you're home," I said as I opened the fridge and pulled out the orange juice.

The newspaper rustled behind me as I filled my glass. "I was waiting for you to get here, I wanted to check on you," he stated curtly.

I stopped drinking mid-sip. He wanted to what? I turned to look at him. "Check on me?"

"Yeah, Josh was pretty upset since it was a girl he knew, and he was concerned about you." He folded the paper and set it away from him, not making eye contact with me.

"I'm fine. Actually, I'm exhausted. It was a long night." I finished my juice and put my glass in the sink.

"So, how did she die?" he asked as he stood up.

"Internal bleeding," I responded with a shrug. "I'm going to take a shower and hit the bed. Have a good day at work."

"Wait," he grabbed my arm.

I raised an eyebrow at him, "Yes?"

"Was she bad?" he asked the question but didn't look at me, although he did let go of my arm.

"Mark, why the interest?" I crossed my arms.

"I told you that I went to school with her, and I know her from another attorney's office. I wanted to know the truth so I could dispel any rumors that might go flying around. You know how people talk." He finally met my questioning gaze.

The answer sounded real enough to me, "She didn't look too bad, but what was bad was that her husband and daughter were there. A van pulled out of a parking space and ran over her." I shook my head as I remembered the scene again. I could almost hear the piercing screaming from Jazlyn. "She had a lot of internal bleeding, and there wasn't anything I could do to save her. I think her husband blames me."

Mark's face looked pale when he spoke, "It wasn't your fault."

"I know that."

He picked up his briefcase. "Get some sleep," he added before he walked out of the house.

I was too tired to worry about him. I climbed the steps, dropped my clothes on the bathroom floor, and stood under the hot water to relax my tired muscles. Ten minutes after I climbed out of the shower, I was sound asleep.

****

Two days later, I sat on the couch wrapping Christmas presents for a few of my friends when Josh plopped down on a chair across from me.

"You alright?" I asked when I saw the tense look on his face.

"No, Jazzy won't even answer my text messages." He threw one leg over the arm of the chair and kicked it up and down.

"Josh, she just lost her mother. She probably doesn't want to talk to anyone right now." I folded the end of the paper and taped it against the gift.

"I know. You are off on Wednesday, aren't you?" he asked as I cut the extra paper off the other side.

"Yeah, why?"

"I was wondering if you would take me to the funeral," he said softly.

My hands stilled. "You want to go to the funeral?"

He pulled his leg up and put it on the ground in front of him, "Yeah, several of the kids at school are going."

"So why don't you go with them?" I resumed my taping.

"I'd rather have you there. Most of the guys have parents that are taking them." I watched him for a minute. "It's a funeral, Mom. I've never been to one of those. It kind of freaks me out."

Ah, there we go. He was afraid to go. I knew a lot of people who feared death—and funerals. "If you want me to take you, I can."

He stood and leaned down to kiss my cheek, "Thanks, Mom." He started to walk away, "Do you mind if Greg goes with us?"

I turned to look at him over my shoulder, "I thought you just said the other guys were going with their parents."

"His have to work." He turned into the foyer and disappeared around the corner.

I hadn't thought about going to the funeral. Maybe it wasn't a good idea. What if Grant really did blame me and I showed up? I didn't want to make his grief any worse.

Maybe I should sit in the car, then he wouldn't know I was there. Decision made, I finished wrapping the gifts for the people I worked with.

****

Wednesday morning came, and a feeling of foreboding cloaked my shoulders. I had waffled back and forth between actually attending the ceremony and waiting outside. I finally decided that if there were a lot of people, I would go into the service. Grant and his daughter would be sitting up front, and they would never see me.

I drove the two boys to the church and had to park down the street. Hundreds of people had come. I knew I would be safe to slide into the service and get lost in the crowd.

Josh and his friend sat in another pew with a few other kids from school. I sat in the next to last pew on the outside by the wall. The pews were filling up fast, and I knew I wouldn't have a problem hiding, even though I thought the pounding of my heart might give me away.

I read the pamphlet commemorating Ilana's life. I ran my finger over the photo on the cover of the beautiful woman I had tried to save. I would never wish death on anyone, especially a mother. Her eyes sparkled with the vitality of life in the photograph, unlike the dull unresponsive pupils that I had checked over and over again. How I wish I could have saved you, Ilana, I'm so sorry.

Music began to play, and the family walked down the aisle and was seated. The sanctuary was huge, and with several hundred people filling the space between Grant and me, I felt more comfortable and sat back to listen to stories of Ilana's life. I knew that if I had met her, we would have gotten along, maybe even been friends. The antics that she pulled while growing up, and into her adulthood, brought small smiles to my lips and soft chuckles from my chest. There were also a few moments when moisture pooled in my eyes, and I was not alone. Sniffles could be heard throughout the church.

When the service ended, I had intended to slip out the side and wait for the boys by the car. An elderly gentleman somehow beat me to the aisle and I shuffled along behind him, cutting through an archway when I could manage to slide past him.

I was searching for a side door when I turned a corner and bumped into a tall man. We both sucked in shocked breaths as he grabbed my arms to steady me. Our eyes met, and for an instant I saw pain and need, but it quickly turned to anger.

"What the hell are you doing here?" he seethed. "I brought Josh and a friend." I pulled back out of his reach. My forearms ached from how hard he had gripped me. "I'm sorry. I meant to slip out before you saw me. I don't mean to cause you any more pain, Mr. Murphy." I took another step away from him and clutched my small purse to stop my trembling hands.

His jaw clenched, "Get out of here, and if I ever see you again, I will have you charged with harassment."

"Excuse me?" I gasped. "I'm not harassing you, I'm attending a public ceremony and I told you the only reason I am here was to bring my son and his friend," I clenched my teeth, "and, trust me, I have better things to do then to stalk or harass you, Mr. Murphy." I burst around him and walked down the hall as fast as my heeled feet would carry me.

What a prick! How could he possibly think I was harassing

him? I didn't slow my pace until I reached the car. I climbed inside and gripped the steering wheel so tightly I felt like I could have bent it. The gall of that man! Arrogant son of a bitch! I came to pay my respects and he thought I was stalking him!

I calmed my nerves with deep cleansing breaths. By the time Josh and Greg got back to the car, I had my anger under control.

"Mom, we want to go to the cemetery," Josh said as he pulled his seatbelt on.

I stared at him, "Are you kidding me?"

The surprise on his face was almost comical. "Why, is there a problem with that?"

How could I tell him that I wanted to get as far away from this family as I could? I couldn't. I was proud of Josh for wanting to do this to show his support for Jazzy and her family. It showed how much he had matured in the last few years.

"Fine, but I'm going to stay in the car." I think Grant seeing me once today is enough, I thought to myself.

We joined the procession of cars heading to the cemetery. I was surprised by how many police cars were in the area and had roads closed or were blocking traffic for the convoy of mourners.

We snaked through the narrow roads in the graveyard and came to a stop behind the other cars. Josh and Greg got out and followed the crowd. I leaned back in my seat and watched the people follow the casket up the hill. From where I sat, I had a good view of the surrounding area.

Josh and his friends stood off to the left, all of them looking slightly uncomfortable. Maybe they would realize they were not immortal after all.

I scanned the surrounding areas, taking in the different designs of the tombstones, when I noticed a man standing off from the group. My eyes strained harder to get a better look.

What the hell was Mark doing here?

Chapter 6 – Grant

"What if I don't want to go, Dad?" Jazzy asked for the fiftieth time.

"Jazlyn, you are going. You have no choice," I stated sternly.

"I don't want to watch them put her in the ground," she mumbled.

"Jazzy, I don't either, but we have to go. I need you there beside me. Grandma and Grandpa need you there with us." I pulled her into my arms, "Honey, in a few hours, it will be all over."

"And then what?" she murmured into my suit jacket.

I felt my shoulders droop, "And then, we take it one day at a time." I couldn't count the number of times I had either thought or said that these last few days. We just have to get through one more day, and then one more. One foot in front of the other, that is what we had to keep doing.

"Fine," she crossed her arms and dropped herself down on the sofa. Well, at least her teenage attitude was coming back.

"We are leaving in a few minutes, so go finish getting ready." I stood in front of the hallway mirror to tie my necktie. I hated these things almost as much as I hated funerals.

Jazz stomped her way up the stairs.

Thank God for Beth and Tom. They had been lifesavers in

what needed to be done. My parents were both alive, and I didn't have any brothers or sisters, so I had no idea what to do when it came to planning such an event. My grandparents had passed away when I was young, so my only memories were of sitting through a long service and watching people cry.

I twisted my neck to loosen the knot I'd made and buttoned the top button of my sports coat. Tom and Beth would be here soon to collect us. I stared at my reflection. I didn't look any different on the outside, but I sure felt a lot different. Confusion rattled me constantly. There was so much to think about, so much to do, and I kept finding myself turning to ask Ilana what comes next, only she wasn't there to ask.

I thought she had life insurance, but I had not found the policy yet. I didn't even know anything about the bills. She had taken care of all of that and I had no idea who, what, or how things got paid.

I stood in the entranceway and looked at the family room. We had lived in this house for ten years, and everywhere I looked, I saw Ilana's touch. Photographs of us were scattered around the room. The book she had been reading lay untouched on the table next to her favorite chair. A pair of discarded earrings sat beside the book.

I looked at the couch where I had slept since her death. I remembered the day we bought it when we first moved in and how just a few months ago we had talked about buying new furniture. I'd been unable to face lying in our bed alone. The only time I went into our room was to get dressed. I would have to figure out what to do with all her things. Maybe Beth could help me.

How long did you have to wait? Was there a time limit as to how long you were supposed to mourn before you could begin to pack up someone's life? The thought of going through her things one at a time and deciding if we should keep it, donate it, or throw it away seemed daunting.

I glanced toward the kitchen, it was the only room we had really changed. Ilana loved to cook, and just two years ago, we had redone it to create the dream kitchen she had always wanted. Now, I didn't even want to step foot into it and only out of necessity.

One day at a time. One day at a time.

A knock on the door pulled me from my mantra, and I opened it to find Tom and Beth on the front step. "You know you don't have to knock. You are both welcome here anytime, just come in."

"Are you two about ready?" Tom asked as he followed his wife into the foyer.

"Yeah, let me get Jazzy."

I yelled up the steps and waited until I heard her door open. I grabbed my keys off the hook and waited for Jazlyn to come down the stairs. Beth pulled her into a hug and held her for a few moments.

I sat up front with Tom, while Beth and Jazzy sat in the back talking softly about school. Jazlyn had not been back yet and planned on staying a few more days. A friend had dropped off her schoolwork, and she got good grades, so I wasn't concerned about her missing a week.

The church loomed larger than life in front of us, and people were already arriving. Fleetingly, I wondered if Rachel would come. I brushed it aside when the familiar flames of anger ignited. She had better not show her face. If I didn't want her here, why did I even think about her?

I had already talked to Tom about his thoughts of looking into my wife's death. Not that I didn't believe Ilana was injured enough to have died, but why had it taken so long? What was done to try to save her? Had Rachel, I mean Dr. Wilde, done anything wrong?

My God! When did I turn into this person that questioned everything someone did?—Oh wait, I'm a cop, that's my job—yet, I'd never had to question a doctor about the care of someone. Was it normal to wonder if there was something else that could have been done? Would I always feel anger when I thought about Ilana's death? Would the mere memory of talking to Rachel in the store always make me feel like slamming my fist into a wall?

"You alright over there?" Tom asked as we pulled up.

I peered at him, "I'm as fine as I'm going to be, why?"

"Because you just let loose one of the biggest sighs I have ever heard." He put the car in park and pulled the keys out of the ignition.

I stared at the hearse parked on the street in front of the church. My stomach rolled, and the acid that churned ever since the incident threatened to erupt.

"I'm fine, let's get it over with." I pushed the door open and helped Jazlyn from the car. We held hands as we crossed the street and entered the church. Ilana's parents were there already, along with my own. Jazlyn hugged everyone and managed to keep the tears at bay. She had my strength, and she was using it now.

The service started, and I barely heard a word that was said. I kept staring at the golden oak casket that had the lid open. I could see Ilana's face from where I sat. She looked so peaceful that it didn't seem fair that I felt so much turmoil.

By the end of the service, I had to get away for a moment. I needed a few seconds to gather my thoughts and prepare myself for the drive to the cemetery. I cut off to the side after we left the sanctuary and wandered down a back hallway. I turned a corner and slammed into none other than the woman who filled my every other unwanted thought. "What the hell are you doing here?" I saw red as I stared down at her. How dare she show herself here and bring her son, too. I threatened her, even though in the back of my mind I knew I was overstepping my bounds. I was beyond furious to see her. Her last biting comment cut into me. I turned to watch her walk away, hoping once again that it was the last time I would ever come face to face with her, and arguing with myself because somewhere deep inside, I didn't want it to be.

I fumed while I sat in the back of the limo following the hearse to Ilana's final resting place. My mind stuck on the scene at the church. Was she stalking me? Or was I going crazy? By the time we arrived at the gravesite, I had convinced myself I was going nuts.

The family all sat on one side, and, while the pastor was giving the final prayers, I searched the crowd. I saw Josh standing with some friends, all their heads bowed and hands clasped in front of them. I saw tons of people that I didn't know, and a lot of people I did, but I did not see Dr. Wilde. She might be sitting in her car or skulking behind a tree, for all I knew.

The service wound down and I stood to place a single red rose on her closed casket. I love you, Ilana. I am so sorry. I'll take good care of Jazlyn for you.

I bowed my head as I stepped away and allowed Jazlyn to set her rose atop mine. We walked arm in arm back to the limo.

"Do we have to go to the luncheon, Dad?" Jazzy asked when we were back inside.

"Sorry, sweetheart, I don't want to do it any more than you do, but we have to. I'd much rather go home and have a beer."

"Me, too," she muttered, "minus the beer, yuck."

The rest of the day was even more draining than the funeral. People came up to us one after another and paid their respects.

"She was a wonderful woman."

"She's going to be sorely missed."

"I'm so sorry that Jazlyn won't have her mother with her as she grows into a woman."

By the time we were allowed to sneak out, I could barely drag my feet toward Tom's car. "What a long day," I stated.

"I know. It's not easy. You remember me telling you how much my brother's funeral sucked, don't you?" he asked as we walked in front of the women.

I nodded, "Yeah, I do."

The ride home was quiet, and the moment we walked in the door, Jazz took off upstairs. I had said goodbye to Tom and Beth in the driveway, so I yanked off my tie and tossed it and my coat on the back of the couch. I dropped down next to them, exhausted and emotionally drained.

In all of my thirty-five years, I had never had such an emotionally exhausting day. I wanted a beer, but I didn't have the energy to get off the couch. With my shoes kicked off, I grabbed a blanket off the back of the couch and pulled it over me. I stared at a picture that sat on the bookcase from our last vacation, two years ago. Had it really been two years since we'd taken a vacation?

I closed my eyes and laid my head back. I could use a few minutes of peace and quiet.

I awoke with a start. The room was dark, and the house was quiet. My heart throbbed in my chest, and I leaned back again to calm myself. The dream that had woken me had shaken my core.

I was back in the store again, except this time, instead of looking down at Rachel's lips, I had leaned down and kissed them. A woman laughed and I looked up to see Ilana pointing and laughing at me. Then I woke up.

I wiped my face with my palms and looked at my watch to see it was after midnight. My nap had been longer than most of my night sleeps recently.

I checked on Jazzy and found her curled up with a stuffed animal, still in her clothes from the funeral. She must have done the same thing I had done.

In the kitchen, I made a ham sandwich and finally grabbed a beer. I leaned against the counter eating and glanced down at the mail on the counter near the phone. The electric bill was there. I guess now was as good a time as any to start figuring this stuff out. I picked up my food and the mail and walked upstairs to the extra bedroom we used as the guest room and office.

There were neat little stacks of papers all over the desk, and a bin under the desk.

I turned on the computer and took another bite of my sandwich while I flipped through the other envelopes. The cellphone bill was there, too. I tore open both envelopes and looked at the amount due. The cellphone bill felt a lot thicker than I would have expected, so I flipped through the pages. Good God! How many texts did that girl send to her friends? I looked at the listing of the hundreds of text messages. I put the phone bill down. Luckily, it appeared we had unlimited minutes for texting, so we weren't billed for each piece of teenage drama. I shuddered to think what the bill might be if we were.

The computer came to life and I stared at the sign-on screen. I assumed that the information I needed to know would be in her profile, but I didn't know what her password was. I tried a few things she might have used, but none of them worked.

Shit! How am I going to figure this out? I took another long pull off my beer and stared at the bin under the desk. Might as well start there, I thought. I pulled out a notebook to make some notes and then started sorting through the things in the bin. There were bills, medical notices, and insurance policy information, although they were for the cars and the house, not life insurance.

I made notes about the accounts, the last few bill amounts, and phone numbers to contact the companies. I didn't know if she did banking online or sent checks. Did we even have checks? I glanced over the desk but didn't see any. I found a bank statement and put that to the side. I would need to find out what the passwords were to access the account.

The list grew, and I realized that we had three different credit cards. When did we get the other two? I had only been aware of one. I looked closer at the bills and took in the balances. "Are you kidding me?" My thoughts began to reel as I read the numbers. They were all maxed out!

I ended up finding three store cards, too, again all at their limits. I found the latest bill from each of the cards. Over the last six weeks, the cards had been maxed out. Purchases for clothing, jewelry, hotels, and restaurants filled the pages.

Were we victims of identity theft? Did someone get our credit card numbers and make all these purchases? If we were, then it was someone local because all of the places were within thirty miles of our home.

That question began the second page of my list. I lifted my bottle to find it empty and went to get another one.

Upon my return, I leaned back in my chair and stared at the filing cabinet. It was a plain old boring four-drawer tan metal filing cabinet, the same kind I had at work, but for some reason I was afraid to go through it.

Would I find more bills I didn't know about? I knew how much I made, and I had come across a few paystubs from her, so I knew what she was making recently. I wasn't a math major, but I had a pretty good concept of how to add and subtract, and the numbers weren't reconciling. Well, they were, but they were adding in the negative column.

If that were true, why hadn't Ilana said anything? And why the hell would she go out and spend a fortune and rack up the bills?

I pulled open the top drawer and found medical and school records. Our paystubs were in there, too. Each folder was labeled in her neat handwriting. I scanned the tabs but didn't see anything that I would need immediately.

I opened up the second drawer and found all the bills. I started flipping through the files and found two more credit cards that I didn't even know we had—both opened in the last six months—and totally maxed out. Something told me that we weren't a victim of identity theft. I was getting the distinct impression that my late wife had a shopping addiction.

How the hell was I supposed to pay all these bills with my own income? I was a freaking public servant; I didn't make big money even though I was a detective.

I stared at the numbers and realized that my problems were just beginning.

Chapter 7 – Rachel

Three weeks later, life was back to normal. Christmas was only a week away, and the thirty patient-treatment areas of the emergency room were constantly filled. An unexpected snowstorm had blown into our region, and an endless number of patients had shown up at our doors from car and sledding accidents. We also had our share of people who never did any physical exercise coming in with back and shoulder problems after shoveling the heavy snow.

"Dr. Wilde," I looked up from the report I was working on, "your son is on line two," Jane called out to me.

I hit the button and lifted the receiver. "What's up, Josh?"

"Hey, Mom, do you mind if I go with a few kids to a late movie tonight in King of Prussia?"

"What time?" I asked as I tapped my pen on the desk.

"The movie is at eleven, and we thought we would see the movie and then get something to eat, so I wouldn't be back until around two."

"That's pretty late, Josh." I leaned on my elbows.

"Yeah, I know, but it's the first night of vacation. We wanted to celebrate."

He was a junior in high school, got good grades, was involved in sports, and even worked on a few committees at school. I could trust him, right?

"Who is driving?" I asked as I thought about it more.

"Todd is going to drive. We are taking his mom's SUV."

Todd was a good kid from a good family, and they swam together on the swim team at school. "Okay, but I want you to check in with me when you get home."

"Okay, I will do that. Thanks, Mom! I love you!" he gushed into the phone line.

"Love you, too, kiddo. Be careful." We hung up and I went back to my report until two ambulances showed up with victims from a motor vehicle accident.

At twelve-thirty, I finally had a moment to take a breather and sat down in the break room with a cup of coffee. Susan came in to grab her dinner.

"It amazes me what people do to themselves, you know?" she said as she sat at a small table in the center of the room.

I kicked my feet up on a small wood coffee table. "I know." I leaned my head on the cushion behind me, exhausted.

"What about that woman who came in with that bottle in her who-ha?"

I laughed, "Don't remind me of that. It always blows my mind what people stick into orifices."

Jane stuck her head into the door, "Heads up, another couple of people coming in from an accident. I just heard that it started sleeting outside, and the roads are icing up."

"Oh, damn! Josh is out with his friends. I should give him a call and check on him," I said as I stood up.

"Didn't you say he was going to a movie? You won't be able to reach him."

"I'll send him a text message," I said as I left the room to get my cellphone. I sent a message and slipped my phone into my white lab coat pocket before I went to wait for the new patients about to arrive.

Almost an hour later, I felt my phone vibrate in my pocket. I slipped it out a few minutes later while I walked back to nurse's station.

Just got out of movie. Only raining here. Going to eat. Will let you know when we are on our way home.

I thanked him for letting me know and reminded him to be careful.

It was two hours later when my cellphone rang again, and a number I didn't recognize showed up on my screen. I swiped over the button to send it to voicemail and felt a tingle go down my back. Maybe I should have answered that.

Two minutes later, Jane came into the patient room I was in, "Dr. Wilde, you have a call."

"Can you take a number?" I asked her, as I looked over a hand laceration from a knife.

"Dr. Wilde, he said it was important." I glanced at her, and saw a look of fear in her eyes.

"I'll be right back," I said to the man watching me, and he nodded.

Tension tightened the muscles of my shoulders as I walked to the desk and glanced at Jane who stood just behind me as I picked up the phone.

"This is Dr. Wilde, how can I help you?"

"Dr. Wilde, I'm sorry to bother you. This is Officer Arnold," my heart skipped a beat and I grasped the edge of the desk. "Your son was involved in an accident and was taken to Seven Oaks Memorial Hospital."

I swallowed the fear that lodged in my throat, "Is he alright?"

"I'm not a doctor, ma'am, but I think he will be," he answered.

"What about the other kids in the car?" I asked, staring at Jane as her eyes widened.

"I'm sorry. I can't give that information over the phone. I will explain the details when you arrive at the hospital."

I told him I would be leaving in a few moments, and he reminded me to drive slowly because the roads were icy. I hung up the phone and closed my eyes. Jane rubbed my arm, "Is he okay?"

"The officer said he would probably be alright, but you know officers don't know anything. He wouldn't tell me about the other kids." I shook my head, "I gotta go."

"I'll let Dr. Sherman know, and we will get someone else to come in. Don't worry about it. Go." Jane turned, "Let us know how he is." She walked off to find the other doctor, and I practically ran back to the locker room to grab my things.

It took me thirty minutes longer than usual to make the twenty-mile drive. The roads were slick, and cars were driving ten to twenty miles an hour in most places. I forced myself to drive the same speed, reminding myself that he was in capable hands and I couldn't do anything to help him if I was hurt—or dead. Oh God, please let him be alright! A shiver raced down my spine at the thought that he could be seriously hurt.

I focused on the road and pulled my thoughts away from everything else. I expelled a huge sigh when I arrived at the hospital and slipped on an ice patch just outside my car door as I stepped out. I almost went under my car and gripped the door frame and my seat to keep myself steady.

After getting my footing, I managed to get to the emergency room door without any spills. I walked to the window, "I'm Dr. Rachel Wilde, my son Josh is here."

"Dr. Wilde, come on back." She pushed a button and I moved towards the doors that were opening, but when I turned to scan the large waiting room, I froze.

Grant stood on the other side of the room. His eyes drilled into mine, and his face was pale. I looked back at the receptionist behind the thick glass and held up one finger. I moved towards Grant, afraid that he would say something hateful again, but willing to take the chance to find out why he was here.

"Grant, are you alright?" I asked as I stopped a few feet away. For just a moment, his eyes held so much pain that I wanted to pull him into my arms. I expected to see anger in his eyes at my presence, but there was only fear.

"What are you doing here?"

"Josh was in a car accident." My voice shook as I spoke, and I stared at him. I had no idea that something was wrong with Jazlyn, and then it dawned on me, Josh said friends were going out. Had he had a date with Jazzy? "Jazlyn was in the car with Josh?"

He blinked, "Your son was in the car, too?"

"Yes, I think they all went together."

He hung his head for a few seconds before he lifted it and met my gaze, "I'm sorry. They won't tell me anything, and I'm going nuts! It reminds me of when—" His voice was full of pain as he stopped at that last word. He didn't need to say anything further.

"Of when Ilana died, I understand. Let me go see what's going on, and I'll let you know as soon as I can." If I could do anything to relieve some of his stress, I would do it. I stepped closer and reached out to touch his arm, "I promise I'll be back as soon as I know something."

He glanced down at my hand and nodded. I let go and went back to signal the receptionist that I was ready to go back.

The emergency room was set up similar to ours with the nurse's station in the center. I heard my name called, "Rachel," and turned to see Bill Watkins coming towards me.

"Bill, it's good to see you, where is Josh?" We shook hands. I had known Bill since med school. We had even done our emergency rotations together and had remained friends over the last few years.

"He's alright. He's got a broken arm and a small concussion, along with the standard bumps and bruises." I felt relief course through my body until I remembered Grant standing in the waiting room.

"Bill, what about the other kids?" I was afraid to say her name.

Wrinkles lined his forehead, "Two of them didn't make it, a boy and a girl. They were killed on impact."

Oh, God! My legs threatened to go out from under me, and Bill took hold of my arm and walked me over to a wall so I could lean against it. Please, don't let it be Jazlyn.

"One of the other girls is unconscious right now, but I think she will pull through."

I looked up at him, so afraid to ask the question, but knowing I had to. "Is Jazlyn the girl who died or is she unconscious?" I held my breath, begging him to say she was alive.

"Jazlyn Murphy is in room four. She is very much alive right now." My head fell back against the wall with my eyes closed, so damn thankful that she was alive.

"She has a concussion, that's why she is still unconscious. She was sitting in the front seat and hit her head on the window. Luckily, she was wearing her seatbelt, or she might not be alive."

"Thank God." Then I thought about the fact that two children weren't alive. "Oh shit, that means Todd didn't make it. Who was the other person in the car?"

"No, Todd and a girl by the name of Marie, I think. They were both pronounced at the scene." I hung my head. Todd had been Josh's best friend for years. Memories of the two of them hanging out and swimming together for years raced through my mind. My heart hurt at the thought of what the parents were going through. No child should die before a parent, and there was one parent right this moment that needed his child more than anything.

"Bill, can you please allow Jazlyn's father to come back and sit with her?" I asked him as I pushed off the wall with my back.

"We are still running tests," he started to say.

"I understand that, but Mr. Murphy lost his wife three weeks ago when she was run over by a car. He's sitting out in the waiting room wondering if he is going to lose his daughter, too."

"Ah, Jesus, yeah go get him and bring him back. I'll let Josh know you are here. He's getting his cast on right now. Tell Mr. Murphy I'll be with him in a few minutes."

I thanked Bill and hit the large silver plate on the wall that would open the electronic doors. Grant stood as soon as he saw me.

I moved quickly to stand in front of him and without thinking took both his hands in mine, "She's alive, Grant." He squeezed my hands briefly before he sank into the chair behind him. His hands dangled between his open knees and he bowed his head.

"Thank you, God," I heard him mutter.

I sat down beside him, "Grant," I paused. I was so tempted to wrap him in my arms. Instead, I put my hand on his bent back and saw him stiffen.

He turned to me, fear spilling from his eyes. "Don't you dare tell me she's going to die."

I shook my head and grabbed his arm with my other hand, "Bill, her doctor, said she should make it, but she hit her head and she's unconscious right now."

"She's unconscious," he repeated solemnly.

"Yes, but that could be a good thing. She hit her head, and it knocked her out. Being unconscious is a way for her body to heal."

"But she could die?" he asked, raw emotion in his words.

I swallowed, "Yes, she could, but the doctor doesn't think she will." I stood up, "Come on, I'm going to take you back to see her. Bill gave me permission to bring you back to sit with her even though they are still doing tests."

Grant stood up and looked at me, "Thank you."

He looked broken, and I couldn't imagine what he must have been going through after losing his wife just a few weeks ago. The thought of Josh dying was enough to drop me to my knees. If I'd had to contend with the loss of Mark on top of it, I probably wouldn't be any better than him.

"You're welcome." I turned to walk away, and he stopped me by grasping my wrist.

"I forgot to ask, is Josh alright?" His words told me that he was sincerely concerned.

"Josh is going to fine." I paused, "Did you know that there were two other kids in the car with them?"

"Yeah, Todd and Jazzy's friend, Marie." He glanced around the waiting room. "I don't see their parents here."

I placed my free hand on his forearm. My heart thudded in my chest as I once again thought about the pain the parents would feel at the loss of their children. "They didn't make it."

"Oh, God." He dropped his head back on his shoulders and let go of my arm.

I studied him as he tried to comprehend what I had said, "Let's get you to Jazzy." I took his hand and led him to the curtained area where Jazzy lay.

Grant stiffened when he saw her, his hand tense in mine. "Go to her, hold her hand," I said softly, and he glanced my way before he stepped forward. Tears ran down his face as he reached for her. I felt my own tears on my cheeks as I watched the scene in front of me.

I felt a tap on my shoulder and turned to see a nurse, she spoke softly, "Dr. Wilde, your son is one curtain over." She pointed to the next curtain, and I thanked her and moved to see Josh.

Chapter 8 – Grant

All I wanted to do after my day was suck back a few beers and pass out. The holiday season brought out every crook you could think of. We had bank robberies, burglaries, and thefts galore, and I was beat from the last week.

I sank down on the couch with a cold brew in my hand and glanced at my watch, it was after one in the morning. I picked up the remote and flipped on a news channel, not that I really cared what the hell was happening in the world. I had enough to dwell on in my own private hell, but I needed noise.

Jazzy had called me earlier and said she was going out with friends. While I wasn't happy about her being out this late, it was the first time she had asked to do anything since her mother had died.

The sleet was changing over to rain, and hopefully by the time the movie let out, the roads would only be wet. I wouldn't allow my mind to worry about things it didn't have to. It wasn't like I could lock my daughter up in her room to keep her safe.

I finished my beer and set it on the side table. Ilana's book still sat there, a thin layer of dust now covering it. I guess I was going to have to clean this place. I rested my head on the back of the couch.

Even with the television on, the house was too quiet. Maybe

we should get a dog, I thought absently.

My mind began to wander, and without trying, it brought back thoughts of what Ilana had been doing before she had died. I had called all the credit card companies and cancelled the cards after I explained the situation to them and supplied them each with a copy of her death certificate. Of course, they all reminded me that I would be responsible for paying the bill.

Of freaking course!

At least she had a small life insurance policy through her employer. It was enough to pay off her credit card debt and expenses for her funeral. If she hadn't racked up so many bills, that money could have gone into the college fund for Jazz.

At times, I found myself angry with Ilana for what she had done. How could she have been so irresponsible with our money? What came over her to purchase all those things? And where the hell were the things that she'd bought? I glanced around the room, I didn't see anything new, but one of the credit cards had been at a home furnishing store. I wondered each day if I would come home from work to see new furniture sitting on my front lawn.

My thoughts of Ilana brought back the memories from the hospital and the ugly way I had treated Rachel.

I sighed and thought about how a week ago I had been working on an assault case, and I ran into the medic who had responded to help my wife. He had offered me his condolences. His words caused the pain I tried to hide to bubble back to the surface, but I pushed it aside and decided to step out on a limb and ask him about that day.

"It's Mike, right?" I asked him as we shook hands.

"Yeah, I'm really sorry about what happened. It makes it worse that you and your daughter were both there, I know that wasn't easy."

"No, it wasn't easy. Still gives me nightmares." I looked around the scene we were on now. The injuries were minor and the paramedic wasn't needed, "Can I ask you a question?"

"Yeah, sure," he said.

I took a deep breath, not really sure what to ask now that I had a chance to question someone. "It's about Dr. Wilde."

"She's an incredible doctor. You're lucky she was there at the scene," he said right away.

I stared at him, "Why am I lucky?"

"If she hadn't been, your wife would have been pronounced dead before she even got to the hospital," he said in a serious voice.

"Is she that good of a doctor?" I asked skeptically.

He looked at me intently. "Detective, why are you asking?"

Why was I asking? Because I needed to know, that's why. "I'm just wondering if she did everything that she could have done."

Mike's mouth dropped open, "Do you think that Dr. Wilde was somehow at fault for your wife's death?"

I shrugged and looked away from him. Yeah, that's exactly what I had thought, but I didn't want to voice it.

His voice was hard when he responded, and I found myself staring into his face as I listened, "I'll tell you this, Detective, Dr. Wilde is an incredible doctor. She did more for your wife than any other doctor would have, trust me. I have never seen her so possessed to help a patient."

"Why do you say that? What did she do?" I crossed my arms over my chest, finding it hard to believe that she treated my wife the way he said she did.

"Do you really want to hear what she did?" he asked carefully.

No, yes, "Yes," I said after a second.

"Fine, you want to know, and maybe you need to know." He glanced around the scene. An EMT was wheeling a man with a broken arm into the ambulance.

"Rachel jumped right into that ambulance and started giving out orders faster than a drill sergeant. Did you know that she split her head open on a cabinet in the ambulance when she was looking for something and never once thought about the fact that she hurt herself? She was one hundred percent focused on your wife."

I glanced away. I didn't know how she had cut her head. It didn't make a difference to me.

"Your wife went into cardiac arrest before we reached the hospital. She immediately started compressions, in fact when we got to the hospital, she climbed right up on the gurney and kept doing them until we were inside and someone took over. She didn't even suit up, but immediately went to work on her as another doctor came in. She cut open your wife's chest while Dr. Simpkins tried to stop the bleeding, and Dr. Wilde stood there for twenty minutes holding your wife's heart in her hands and massaging it to keep what little blood she had in her body moving. She begged your wife to hold on, to fight, and it was Dr. Simpkins who decided it was time to call her time of death. He is the one that made her stop working."

I swallowed the bile in my throat as I pictured Ilana lying on a table with her chest cut wide open.

"Normally, I drop off my patients and leave, but I couldn't take my eyes off of her. She was so focused on what she was doing, and everyone there knew it."

"Why did it take so long for her to tell us?" I asked, trying to hold on to the anger but finding it slipping away.

"Dude, seriously?" He shook his head, "She had just cut your wife's chest open, and worked on her like a woman possessed for over thirty minutes. She was covered in blood and sweat. She had to go clean up, and she probably needed a personal moment to compose herself."

I blinked, and I was back in the now, sitting in my living room staring at the picture of Ilana, Jazz, and me on the shelf. I had been wrong about Rachel, and I felt like shit for speaking to her the way I had. I groaned as I remembered the way I'd threatened her at the church.

I was an ass.

I closed my eyes and tried to relax, I would have to find a way to apologize to her. Maybe I could stop by the hospital and see her one night at work.

That thought reminded me of the conversation we'd had in the store, before the shit hit the proverbial fan. "Jesus," I spouted as I got up off the couch. My wife wasn't even dead a month and I was thinking about the sexy eyes and lips of another woman.

I was about to crack open another beer when my cellphone rang. I didn't recognize the number, but it could be someone from work, so I answered it.

My heart almost stopped beating when they told me Jazlyn had been in an accident, and for the life of me, I don't know how I managed to get to the hospital in one piece. I didn't even remember getting behind the wheel of the car. My only thought the whole way was a prayer to God that he would not take Jazzy from me, too. I couldn't live through losing her.

I sat in the cold sterile waiting room, once again frustrated at the amount of time it was taking to be notified of anything. The sight of Rachel walking into the hospital dressed in scrubs and wearing an alarmed look on her face calmed me just the slightest bit.

They were going to let her into the back, and I wanted to yell, What about me? But she scanned the room as she headed to the door and her eyes locked on mine. Did my eyes hold the same fear in them as hers?

I was surprised she came to my side and asked how I was and shocked to find that her son had been in the car with my daughter. My concern grew because suddenly as I looked down at Rachel, I saw not only a woman who cared about people, but a parent scared to death for her child.

"I'm sorry. They won't tell me anything, and I'm going nuts! It reminds me of when—" I stopped and was about to apologize to her for my behavior when she surprised me by taking my arm and finishing my sentence.

I watched her walk away, and felt the beer I had consumed revolting in my stomach. What if she came out here and said Jazlyn was dead? Stop! Stop thinking like that! She's not dead!

The next ten minutes seemed like forever, and when Rachel emerged from the back, my heart stuttered in my chest. Her features looked more relaxed, but I was afraid to hope. She reached for my hands as soon as she got close enough, "She's alive, Grant."

Thank you, God, thank you, my heart called out through every ounce of my being.

When she said my name so seriously, I was expecting her to tell me that while she was alive this moment, she was probably going to die anyway. Rachel explained the situation to me and stood to take me back.

It was then that I remembered about her son being in the car, and I was thankful he was going to be alright. When Rachel took my hand and led me to the back, I marveled at the strength she was allowing me to gain from her simple touch. I knew that it meant nothing other than support, and I would never forget it.

Jazlyn looked pale lying on the hospital gurney, and my knees locked at the sight of her hooked up to monitors. I wanted to scream, run away, pretend like this wasn't happening, but Rachel encouraged me to go to Jazzy.

The moment I touched her hand, nothing else mattered. I let the tears of fear fall from my eyes. I sank down into the chair beside her bed and rested my head on the thin mattress as I sobbed silently.

I never thought about Rachel standing there or what she might think about me, and I never heard her leave. Once I had composed myself and sat up cradling Jazzy's hand in mine, I could hear Rachel's soft voice talking from the other side of the curtain I heard a male voice and figured it was Josh.

I listened to them talk about the cast he had on now, and how his test results had come back with a minor concussion, but no other major injury.

Rachel asked Josh what had happened, and I stood up and moved to the edge of the curtain. I paused for a second before I pulled it slowly back.

Josh and Rachel turned to me, and I wondered if they would be upset that I interrupted. "I'm sorry, I heard you ask Josh what happened, if you don't mind, I'd like to hear it, too."

Josh sat up straighter on the bed, "How is Jazzy, Mr. Murphy?"

I glanced over my shoulder at my daughter, and then pulled the curtain back further so he could see her. "She's still unconscious."

Rachel reached for her son's hand. "Honey, she's going to be alright. Her brain needs a little bit of time to heal, that's all." Rachel met my eyes over the bed and I wanted to believe her.

"Yeah, but Todd and Marie aren't," he said softly and swiped at his face with his forearm.

"I'm so sorry, kiddo," Rachel whispered and placed a kiss on the top of his head. "Josh, honey, I know it is hard, but can you tell us what happened?"

He sniffed, and I handed him a tissue. It reminded me of when Rachel had done that to me, and I lifted my eyes to her, I knew she remembered it, too. She looked away, but not before I saw the pain in her eyes that I hadn't seen before.

I studied the toes of my shoes for a moment, knowing that some of that pain was my fault. I really needed to apologize to her.

Josh took that moment to speak, "We went to the movies, and when we got out, the roads were slippery, so we walked to the restaurant on the other side of the parking lot and got something to eat." He paused and thought for a moment, "When we came out, it was only raining, so we thought it would be safe to head home."

Rachel held her son's hand, and I stepped closer to hear his soft words. I noticed a shadow of a bruise forming on his cheek and wondered how badly Jazlyn would be bruised up.

"Todd was driving, and he was driving slow," Josh looked up and took us both in. "He wasn't driving crazy or anything."

Rachel nodded for him to continue.

"Jazzy was sitting up front with Todd, I was sitting behind her, and Marie was behind Todd. Marie took her seatbelt off to lean up and give something to Jazlyn." Josh stopped and stared off into space for a few moments.

Rachel glanced at me and then back to her son.

"It all happened so fast. I had my arm up on the back of Jazzy's seat, I had been pulling her hair, teasing her." He peered up at me, and I tried to smile. "I don't know why Todd slammed on the brakes, I couldn't see out the front window, but Marie started to fly forward and it felt like the car spun. Then we hit something, and it got really quiet."

Josh got silent too as he relived the moment. "I called out to Jazzy, but she didn't answer. Marie wasn't even in the car anymore, and Todd's side of the car was completely caved in. He was almost sitting in the same seat with Jazzy. I managed to get my seatbelt off and reached over to Todd, I couldn't find a pulse, but I found one on Jazz." He shuddered. "I think I called nine-one-one after that. I don't remember. I was too freaked out, and I didn't know where Marie was." His eyes landed on his mother and tears leaked down both of their faces.

"It's okay, Josh." Rachel wiped the tears from his face and pulled him into her arms.

I fought to control the emotions that swirled in my mind. So much sadness for the loss of those two lives, but Josh and Jazzy were alive, and I was thankful for that.

"I did what I was taught, Mom. I moved as close to Jazz as I could and I held her head stable and talked to her to keep her calm—just like I did with her mom."

At his words, I lost control of my emotions and let the tears fall unchecked. He had been scared to death and did all he could to save my daughter, just like his mother had done for my wife.

Chapter 9 – Rachel

My heart ripped to shreds as Josh explained what happened. He had been through hell, and yet he'd kept his thoughts straight and did all he could do for Jazzy.

I studied Grant as I held Josh. He was staring past the curtain to his daughter. Grant had surprised me tonight. I had expected to see anger in his eyes, but instead he seemed embarrassed. I was confused at the change in him, not that I minded, but it surprised me.

"Josh, I need to go call your dad and let him know what happened."

"Mom, don't call Dad, it will only worry him. I'll call him tomorrow."

"He's going to flip when he finds out I didn't call him when this happened," I said as I stared down at Josh.

"Yeah, like there is something he can do about it? I'm fine. It's not going to kill him to learn about it tomorrow."

He was right; there was no sense in waking him up this late. We would be leaving to go home soon, and we could tell him later.

"Rachel, would you mind keeping an eye on Jazlyn for a moment? I need to go call her grandparents. I didn't even think about it until you mentioned his father."

I stared at him, he trusted me to keep an eye on his daughter even though he thought I killed his wife? I was very confused, but I wasn't going to say no.

"Of course, keep the curtain open. If there is any change, I'll come find you."

Grant nodded to me and planted a kiss on his daughter's forehead before he disappeared around the other side of the curtain.

I moved around Josh's bed so I could stand next to her bed. Her color was good and so were her vitals. This poor child had been through so much, I prayed she would wake up with all her faculties. I heard Josh climb off his gurney and join me by my side.

I reached down and lifted her hand, squeezing it gently. Josh moved to the other side of the bed and took her other hand.

"Jazzy, wake up, it's Josh," he said softly to her. "Please wake up."

I felt her fingers twitch in my hand. Josh's eyes opened wide and I knew he had felt it, too.

"Josh, keep talking to her."

"That's it, Jazzy, come back to us, you can do it, open your eyes. Come back to me." Her head turned toward the sound of his voice, and my heart sped. "Your dad's here, Jazzy, he's worried about you. You gotta wake up."

Her eyelashes fluttered.

"Josh, keep talking to her. I'm going to find her father." I whisked out of the curtain area and searched for Grant.

"If you're looking for that tall good-looking man, he is over there." A nurse pointed to Grant who held the phone to his ear and had his back to me. I started toward him, and he turned when I was halfway there.

He pulled the phone from his ear mid-sentence. "What's wrong?"

"Nothing. She's waking up, Grant."

"Mom, she's waking up," Grant said quickly into the phone. "I'll call you back." He grabbed my hand as he reached me and took such long strides towards the room that I almost had to run to keep up with him. Our hands released as we reached her treatment area. I stood back while he entered.

Josh was brushing the hair from Jazzy's forehead and leaning over her, whispering. Her eyes were open and she stared at him. My heart swelled. Oh please, let her be alright! For Josh, for Grant, for everyone, let her be alright.

"Jazlyn," Grant's voice cracked as he stepped to the side of the bed and took her hand.

She turned her face to him, "Daddy."

I blinked back tears and reached for Josh. "Come on, honey. Let's give them some time." We stepped back into Josh's area and pulled the curtain closed.

A nurse discharged Josh but told him he wouldn't be able to swim for eight weeks because of his cast. He groaned. I knew he was thinking his chances for making the state team this year had just washed down the drain. Poor kid, I thought.

"Can I say goodbye to Jazzy?" Josh asked when we were finished.

"As long as it's alright with Mr. Murphy." Josh peeked around the curtain, and Grant's deep voice responded.

Grant stepped to the side where I could see him, and Josh bent over the bed to speak with Jazlyn. Grant turned to look at me over his shoulder, a look of relief on his face.

"How is she?" I asked as I moved closer to him. Now that the urgency was over, and the kids were alright, I took the moment to really look at him. His lack of sleep manifested itself in dark circles under his eyes and I wondered when the last time was that he had slept the entire night

"She's doing good." He smiled and it brought a shine to his eyes that reminded me of the first time I had met him. "She remembers everything right up to the accident and even remembers Josh talking to her. They want to keep her overnight for observation since she was unconscious for so long, but they expect a full recovery."

"Good, I'm glad." I took a step back, turning away from the sparkle of happiness I saw on his face. My heart ached to see it. "Come on, Josh, it's time to go home."

Josh leaned over and gave Jazlyn a kiss on the lips, and I saw Grant clench his jaw, but he didn't say anything. Josh blushed as he stood up and tried to make eye contact with Grant. "Sir, is there any way you can call me when she gets home? I'd like to know that she's alright."

Grant reached out and put his hand on Josh's shoulder. "I'll do you one better than that. When Jazzy gets home, I'll even let you come over and keep her company, maybe watch a movie with her since you both have to take it easy for a while."

Josh beamed up at Grant.

"Oh, Josh," Grant called out as we turned.

"Yes, sir?" my son said as he faced him again.

Grant peeked at me for a brief second, "Thank you, for what you not only did with Jazlyn, but with her mother."

I didn't know if Josh could hear the emotion in Grant's voice, but I did.

"You're welcome, sir, my mother always said that I should do everything I can to help someone else." Josh slid a glance my way and winked.

Grant focused on me. "Your mother is a good woman." My heart stopped at his words, and he turned back to Josh, "Drive safe."

Josh said goodbye. I gave a brief wave and moved to the exit.

What change had come over Grant that he didn't hold me in contempt for his wife's death any longer? I dwelled on the changes in him on the ride home. When we got home, I gave Josh a pain pill and sent him off to bed. I tossed off the medical scrubs I still wore from earlier that night and climbed in bed. I stared at Mark's wide shoulders. How come when Mark looked at me, I never felt that sudden rush of adrenaline through my heart that I did when I saw Grant? I tried to think back to when we had dated. I couldn't remember those feelings.

Things with Mark had always been comfortable. As I looked back over our time together I wondered why we had ever decided to get married. Maybe it was just a marriage of convenience since we had busy careers, and he did a lot of traveling. I attended some of his events, but mostly we had our separate lives. Mine focused on my job, taking care of the house and spending any amount of time I could with my son.

The fear I had felt earlier struck me. What would I have done if I had lost Josh? The horror of what those other parents were feeling chilled me. I moved closer to Mark to steal from his warmth.

He shifted in the bed to put space between us. I stilled. He had never pulled away before. I stared at the outline of his head.

When was the last time he had even taken me in his arms? Months? I slid back to my side of the bed and rolled over. We had been drifting apart for a long time and we didn't even really talk anymore. Where had my mind been that I hadn't noticed it before?

I was still awake when his alarm went off at five. I climbed out of bed, and he turned to look at me, "What are you doing home?"

"Josh was in a car accident last night," I said as I pulled on my robe.

"Is he alright?" He sounded worried, and I was glad that he at least still cared about Josh.

"Yeah, minor concussion and a broken arm. Let me go check on him, and I'll explain."

He grunted something as I walked out. Josh was sleeping soundly, and I hated to wake him, but I needed to. I rubbed his arm and called out his name. He blinked a few times and looked at me.

"What time is it?" he asked.

"It's still early, go back to sleep. I was only checking on you." I kissed his forehead while he snuggled under his blankets.

When I got back to the bedroom, Mark was pulling clothes out of the closet.

"Todd and another girl were killed in the accident last night," I said as I plopped down onto the mattress.

"What?" Mark spun around and looked at me.

I nodded. "Remember your friend, Ilana Murphy?"

He visibly tensed, "Yes, what about her?"

"Her daughter was in the accident." The blood drained from his face.

"Did she—" he started to say, but didn't finish the sentence.

I shook my head, "No, she's alright. She and Josh survived, but Todd and a girl named Marie were killed."

Mark sagged back against the door, and the hanger holding his suit slipped from his hand to the floor.

I didn't move from where I sat, "Are you alright, Mark?"

He shook himself and leaned down to pick up his suit, "Yeah, just shocked. Poor kid, to watch her mom die, and then have two friends killed."

I didn't know how to respond to that, so I said nothing.

"She's going to be alright, though?" he asked.

"Yeah, she will." I stared at him and wondered why he was more interested in Jazlyn than Josh.

"Good," he responded and went into the bathroom, closing the door behind him to get ready for work. I stared at the closed door for a while wondering about my husband's strange response

Chapter 10 – Grant

"Jazzy, baby, you're going to be okay." I fought to hold back the emotion, but I was just so grateful, that I didn't really care.

"I'm so sorry, Dad. I know I probably scared you so much." She squeezed my hand.

"Honey, don't worry about that. I'm just glad you're alright." I caressed her cheek softly. She had a few small cuts on her face, but nothing bad enough to have required stitches. One cut on the side of her forehead was taped shut with a butterfly, and it reminded me of Rachel.

"I'm glad Josh is alright, too. What happened to Todd and Marie?" she asked, and my heart broke.

I took a moment to think of how to tell her, but there was no easy way. "Sweetheart," I started and I saw her features change, maybe she didn't know, but in her eyes, I think she already did.

"What?" she breathed softly.

"They were both killed in the accident." I grasped her hand firmly.

She blinked and large tears spilled down the sides of her face. She turned away and appeared to be thinking, her eyes looking around the room, "I knew that."

"You did? You must have heard us talking about it." I wiped a few tears from her face.

"No, I saw them." She turned back to me, "They were with Mom. I saw Mom, Daddy." I stared at her for a few moments wondering if she had damaged her brain. "Mom was there, and she told me I had to come back." Her words came out in a rush, and I felt the hair rise up on the back of my neck. "Mom said she would take care of Todd and Marie, but that I had to come back to take care of you." She squeezed my hand, "Mom said that you needed me."

She looked away, and I stared at her profile. I didn't know if I believed in all of that, if there really was life after death, but if she was saying she saw her mother, how could I refute her?

"I know Todd and Marie's parents are going to be really upset, but maybe they will feel a little better knowing that Mom is there watching out for them."

"Yeah, maybe," I said softly. "Why don't you rest now? You need to get some sleep so you can come home."

She gripped my hand hard, "You believe me, right, Dad?"

I didn't hesitate, "Of course I do." It didn't matter if I didn't believe her. She was alive, and I would believe anything she wanted me to.

I sat on her bedside and watched her sleep. We had moved to a room in the juvenile wing of the hospital. Soft murmurs from other patients, parents, and staff filled the hallway. I moved to sit in one of the lounge chairs in her room, one that was larger and more comfortable than in other patient rooms. They knew that parents would be staying with their children and sleeping while they could.

Did Jazz really see her mother? Did she get close enough to death to cross that line? "Thank you, Ilana, for sending her back to me," I said softly before I drifted off to sleep.

I woke a few hours later when the doctor wandered into the room. He was an older man, a few inches shorter than I was with a full head of gray hair and glasses perched on his nose.

"How are you feeling today?" he asked Jazlyn as he stood beside her bed.

Her color had improved dramatically, even though a few bruises colored the right side of her face.

"Actually, I feel really good. When can I go home?" She pushed the button on her bed to raise it.

"That's good. We want to run one more CATScan on you and do a few more tests, but if everything goes well, we can release you right after lunch."

We spoke for a few more minutes with the doctor, and then the nurse came in with two breakfast trays. I called Tom to let him know what had happened, and to ask him to let the chief know that I was going to be off today. Tom berated me for not calling him and having to learn about the accident in the news.

"I'm glad you're feeling alright today," I said to Jazz as I took a sip of my lukewarm coffee after I got off the phone with Tom.

"Actually, I hurt all over, but if that is the price to be alive, then I'll take it."

I winced at her words and set my coffee cup down. "Well, you will hurt for a while. I wonder how Josh is feeling." I had thought about Josh and Rachel several times through the night—of course, Rachel more than Josh, and for different reasons. I felt guilt spear my heart as I remembered that Ilana had not been dead for a month and I was thinking about another woman, a married woman at that. I had noticed a simple plain band on her left ring finger last night.

"Can I give him a call?" she asked as she took a bite of her blueberry muffin.

I shrugged, "You could, but I don't know where your phone is."

"Can I borrow your phone, I know his number." She talked around her food.

"You know his phone number by heart? What person memorizes a phone number in this day of technology? I couldn't even tell you what mom's cellphone number was."

She laughed, "He gave it to me in gym class one day; I didn't have a pen, so I memorized it real quick. I haven't been able to forget it." She blushed and I was so damned happy that she was there to blush that I pulled out my phone and tossed it to her.

I watched her dial and then lean back on the pillow. "Hello," she seemed puzzled, "is this Josh's phone?"

Her confused look vanished quickly, I could just barely make out the sound of a woman's voice from where I sat, "Oh, hi, Dr. Wilde. Is Josh there?"

She listened again for a few more seconds, "Yeah, I'm going to be going home around lunchtime. I'm sore, and I have a headache, but I'm not feeling all that bad."

I watched Jazzy nod and pull a small piece of her muffin off and pop it into her mouth while she listened to Rachel talk.

"Actually, this is my father's phone." She glanced at me and smiled, "I don't know where mine is, he let me borrow it. Josh can call me later on this phone when he gets up."

I suddenly realized that Rachel now had my phone number, well Josh had it, but Rachel could easily get it from him. Why did that thought excite me? I gulped down the rest of my cold coffee. Because I'm and idiot and lonely, and was scared to death—and the two times that I have been in the most emotionally-draining moments of my life, she was there with me.

"Here, Dad," she tossed the phone back to me. "Josh is still sleeping. She said she would have him call me later. You don't mind that I told him to call your phone, do you?"

"It will be kind of hard for him to call your phone since we don't know where it is."

"True." She shrugged and resumed eating her muffin.

An orderly came to take her to get her CATScan and I waited in her room for her to return. My cellphone rang, and I didn't recognize the number, but I answered it anyway.

"Hi, Grant?" Rachel's voice sounded sultry over the phone. Sultry? Really, dude! Get ahold of yourself!

"Rachel, hello, how's Josh doing today?"

"He's alright, he wanted to call Jazzy back, but he felt uncomfortable calling your cellphone, so he asked me to do it." Her laugh sounded nervous, and I realized my heart was beating faster.

I joined her in the laughter, "Actually, Jazzy is getting another scan, and then they are going to release her if they don't find any problems."

"That's good. Hopefully her tests will come back clear. She sounded good on the phone earlier." I heard Josh say something in the background, and she told him Jazz was getting a test done.

"She seems to be feeling pretty good. I'm surprised that she is in such a decent mood. I expected her to be emotional and grumpy." I stood up and went to look out the window at the traffic on the roadway below.

"It's probably the medicine she is on. Give it a day or two, and she will probably be a mess."

"I hope not. I'm not sure I can handle more emotional teenager." I heard her chuckle over the phone.

"Well, I'll let you go. Can you have Jazzy call Josh back later?" I didn't want to hang up the phone yet.

"Actually, I have an idea. Would you two be interested in coming over this afternoon when we get home? I know that Jazlyn would like to see Josh, and I'd like to speak with you."

She sounded hesitant when she answered, "You would?"

"Yeah, I'd really like a chance to talk to you." I didn't want to tell her I was sorry over the phone. I wanted to do it in person. "Maybe we could order a pizza for the kids."

The silence on the line grew heavy, and I rushed on, "I'm sorry, you're probably busy tonight, and your husband probably wants you home."

"No, actually, he's traveling tonight. I'd like that. I would like to talk to you, too."

I released a pent-up breath from my lungs, "Okay, why don't you guys come over around four?"

I gave her my address and we hung up. For the first time in weeks, I was looking forward to something.

"What are you smiling about?" Jazlyn asked me as they rolled her back into the room.

"Nothing, just got off the phone with Josh's mom. They are going to come over around four for pizza. That is if they spring you from his joint." I tossed my phone up into the air and caught it before sliding it into my jacket pocket.

"Cool," she said as the orderly locked the wheel of her bed and left the room.

I sat down and found her staring at me. "What?"

"Do you like Dr. Wilde?" she asked, watching me carefully.

"Dr. Wilde is very nice," I replied, staring at her. What the hell was she asking?

"I know she is nice, that's not what I asked you." She crossed her arms over her chest.

I scanned around the room as if the politically correct answer were somewhere in plain view. I sure wasn't going to tell my daughter that I was lusting after another woman, a married woman, just weeks after her mother passed away. "I was kind of harsh on her when your mother died, Jazlyn. I wanted to talk to her and apologize to her for what I had said."

She tilted her head, "You did kind of accuse her of hurting Mom."

I slapped my hands down on my knees and stood. "I did, and that's why I invited her to come over. I wanted to apologize for that because I was very wrong."

"Good, because she's really nice." She let the conversation go at that, and we made small talk and watched the television until the doctor came back and said everything looked alright.

By one-thirty we were home and I was tucking Jazlyn onto the couch to take a nap before they came over. I stood over her while she snuggled into the cushions, and I bent to brush some hair from her face before planting a kiss on her cheek, "I love you, baby girl."

"Love you, too, Daddy," she whispered in a sleepy voice.

I stood and looked around the room. It was dirty, but I wasn't going to clean it while Jazz rested. Rachel might think we were pigs, but whatever. I did stop and pick up Ilana's book and earrings. I tossed the book and earrings into a drawer in the kitchen and went about putting a few dishes away.

I wondered what Rachel would think of my home. She was a doctor and probably lived in a big house. I glanced around the kitchen and dining area. I had nothing to be ashamed of; I had a nice older two-story house. It was all we needed.

Why was I even worried about what she thought of my house? Because, you idiot, you like the woman—and that right there was the problem.

Chapter 11 – Rachel

"We're going over to the Murphys' for dinner," I told Josh when he walked into the room.

"We?" He stopped in his tracks and stared at me, wide-eyed.

"Yes, we. You have a problem with that?" I asked him.

"Why did he invite you over?" He moved to the kitchen table and sat in a chair across from me.

I laughed, "Maybe so he would have someone to talk to while you keep Jazlyn company."

He grinned, "Good, you can keep him busy."

"Excuse me?" I said and raised my eyebrows at him.

"Come on, Mom, she just got out of the hospital, I'm not going to take advantage of her, but it would be nice to visit with her without her father breathing down my neck."

Oh yes, the protective father watching out for his daughter. "Well, you better be respectful of her, especially in her house with her father around."

He stared at me, "Mom," he drew my name out for two full seconds, "I'm not going to have sex with Jazlyn with you two in the next room."

"You better not be having sex when we are in a different location either," I replied. Okay, I wasn't a prude, I knew kids his age had sex; after all I hadn't been much older than he when I had gotten pregnant.

"Really, we're going to have this talk now?" he groaned. "I know all about the birds and the bees, Mom, don't go there."

"I'm not going there, and yes, I know you are of the age where that's what you think about. Been there, done that." I fluttered my hand through the air as if I were wiping away a pesky fly. "I just want you to remember to respect the young ladies. If they say no, it means no."

"I know what no means," he rolled his eyes, "and I know to wear a condom and protect myself and her."

Okay, good one, son. "Do you have any condoms?" I forced myself not to flinch while I asked.

He stared at me wide-eyed, "Really, Mom? You want me to answer that?" He shifted his right arm and cradled it to his cast.

"Yes, I do. I want to know that if you think you are old enough to have sex, and protect both yourself and your partner, that you are mature enough to walk into a store and buy some."

"I have one that they gave me in health class, but I have never bought any," he said quietly.

"Health class, as in, last year's health class?"

He nodded.

"Don't trust it, they have expiration dates. If you plan on having sex with anyone, you need to go purchase new ones."

"What, you're telling me it's okay to have sex?" He sat back in his chair and gawked at me.

"Josh, I'm not an idiot. I know kids your age have sex. I see girls as young as twelve coming into the ER who admit they are sexually active. You're sixteen, your hormones are raging." I shrugged.

His face grew bright red, "Okay, I guess I will have to buy some."

"Okay, good idea, and for the record, and because I'm a parent, I have to say this. No, I don't think you are old enough to have sex, but if you are going to, be careful," and if you do, I'll be jealous as hell because I can't remember the last time I had sex, and I'm married.

I walked out of the room to do some cleaning. While conversations like that embarrassed us both, I was glad that we could at least have them. I felt for the kids who didn't have someone to talk to about that stuff.

I was scrubbing the bathroom when I thought again about the fact that I hadn't had sex in months. It reminded me of the distance that had grown between Mark and me. Maybe this weekend when he was home, I could talk to him about it. Maybe Josh could go spend a night with his friends, and I could seduce my husband.

Images of Grant filled my mind, and I wondered what it would feel like to hold him in my arms. The fact that I was fantasizing about another man a second after I thought about seducing my husband should have probably concerned me, but whatever.

One kiss from Grant's full sexy lips would probably bring me to climax. I had held his hands, although it wasn't for purposes of anything other than support. I knew how warm and strong they were. I could only imagine what they would feel like moving over my body.

Holy crap! That conversation with Josh had put my mind on a highway, and every road led right to thoughts of Grant. I needed to get laid, and my husband had better be ready to put out this weekend.

Josh came to find me around three-thirty, and I told him I was going to jump in the shower real quick. I had spent the afternoon working up a sweat and felt dirty.

Just to prove that I wasn't taking the shower for Grant, I pulled my wet hair back in a ponytail holder and wore my oldest jeans and a sweatshirt over a t-shirt.

Josh and I left the house ten minutes before four and, as we drove down the street, I made a rash decision and pulled into a parking lot.

"What do you need from here?" he asked as I parked.

"I don't need anything," I reached into my purse and pulled

out a twenty-dollar bill. "You need to go buy something."

"What?" His voice cracked and his eyes bugged out of his head. "You're kidding right?"

"Nope, I'm not." I pushed the money towards him.

"Mom, come on. I'm not planning on having sex today. I don't think I need condoms."

"No, you're not going to have sex today, but if you are mature enough to think about it, you are mature enough to go in and buy them."

He stared at me. "I can't believe my mom is giving me money and making me go buy condoms," he muttered under his breath. Josh grabbed the money from my hand and undid his seatbelt.

I fought the smile that threatened to spill forth until he had his back to me walking toward the store, his cast shoved under his hooded sweatshirt.

Five minutes later, Josh came rushing back out of the store, his head down, his hand shoved in the pocket of his hooded sweatshirt. I didn't see a bag.

He slammed the door closed and gave me an angry look.

"What? Not ready to buy them?" I asked him.

He yanked a small box out from his front pocket. "I bought some, and I'm keeping the change." He opened the glove box and threw them in. "You owe me that much for the humiliation." I laughed as he stared out the window and mumbled, "I can't believe you made me do that."

I continued to laugh at him for another moment, "It won't be so hard the next time."

"Next time, my mother isn't going to be paying for them, or driving me to the damned store!" he stated, and then we both burst out laughing. "I can't believe we just did that."

"I can't believe I just made you do that." I wiped the tears from the corners of my eyes.

"Thanks for being such a cool mom," Josh said when he finally calmed down.

I reached over and grabbed his left arm, the one that wasn't in a cast, "Thanks for being such a cool son."

We arrived at the Murphys' a few minutes after four. I could tell Josh was nervous, and I hoped he couldn't tell that I was, too.

Grant answered the door, and he took my breath away when he smiled. It was the same smile he had given me that day in the store. Damn, girl, he just lost his wife, and your marriage is on the rocks as it is, control yourself.

"Hi, glad you guys could come over," Grant said as Jazlyn walked up behind him.

"Hi, Josh. Hello, Dr. Wilde."

We both said hello to them, and Grant took my coat and hung it on a peg by the door.

"Dad, Josh and I are going to go downstairs to the family room," Jazz said and grabbed Josh's sleeve to pull him away.

"Okay, but remember the doctor said no television for a few days. It's not good for your concussion."

She rolled her eyes, and I hid my smile by turning away and glancing around the living room.

One glance around the room and I felt immediately comfortable just from the earth tones. The coziness of the room warmed me in a way that my larger room could never do. What I wouldn't do for a room that made you feel at home.

"Can I get you something to drink? I have wine, soda, water, or beer."

"I'll take a beer if you're having one." I glanced in his direction and saw him nod before he walked away. He looked as nervous as I felt.

I walked into the living room and stood in front of the bookshelves. There was a picture of Ilana, Grant, and Jazlyn on the shelf sitting on a boat. Jazzy sat between them, grinning, and I studied Grant's face. He looked calm and happy. My eyes moved to Ilana, and I could see her daughter in her perfectly. She was the mirror image of her mother. Except for Jazzy's dark hair color and brighter blue eyes, she didn't have many of Grant's features.

Grant cleared his throat as he entered the room, and I spun

around, feeling guilty for being nosy.

He handed me a beer bottle, "That was down in North Carolina two years ago." He pointed to the picture. "It was the last time we took a vacation."

He sat down on the sofa, and I moved to the other end of it and mimicked his seating pose by turning myself towards him and bending my knee on the cushion to see him better.

I realized that his sofa was a lot smaller than mine when he put his arm along the back of it and his hand came to within inches of me. His hands were clean, his nails neatly trimmed. I thought back to when I was scrubbing the bathroom and shoved the thought aside. When I knew I had myself composed, I lifted my head to find him watching me.

I licked my lips nervously and took a drink from my bottle.

He looked at the photograph again, "I've been thinking of a lot of last times recently."

"I'm sure you have, that is natural when you lose someone." I saw the left side of his mouth tip up briefly.

"Yeah, it's amazing what you learn about a person when they die." He took a pull from his beer. "Like, how much they do that you take for granted."

"Like what?" I hoped I wasn't being rude asking, but he seemed to want to talk about it.

"The bills, the paperwork, the doctor's appointments, and school stuff. There was so much I didn't know about that she took care of." He took another sip, "I had to learn things quick, and some of them I didn't want to learn." He shook his head with a thin laugh.

"Paying bills sucks, no matter who does it," I added.

"Yeah, well," he quieted, "I found out she had opened several credit accounts and racked them all up."

Whoa, I had never asked what he did for a living, or how much he got paid, but that was never a good thing, for anyone. "Ouch."

"Ouch is right. Luckily, she had life insurance that covered the debt." He looked me in the eye, "I just have no clue what she spent the money on."

"You didn't notice new clothes or jewelry?" This was none of my business, and I felt a little awkward talking about this, but if it would help him, I was willing to do it.

He shook his head, "One of the cards was furniture. I have no idea what she bought because we don't have any new furniture."

Why would you buy furniture if it wasn't for your own place? I wondered.

He shrugged it off, "Sorry, that has nothing to do with what I wanted to talk to you about."

I picked at the label on my bottle, "What is it that you wanted to speak about?"

He turned his hips so he sat further into the couch and could face me more easily. "I wanted to apologize."

That was the last thing I expected him to say, and the next words out of his mouth surprised me even more.

Chapter 12 – Grant

"You don't owe me an apology," she said, and I saw the tension in her face relax as she spoke.

"But I do. The day Ilana died, I stepped over some major boundaries. I stood in the store and flirted with you and then an hour later, I basically accused you of killing my wife."

She kept eye contact as I spoke, and I was thankful that she did. "And now, you've changed your mind?" she asked me.

"Yes."

A bubble of laughter burst from her lips.

"What's so funny?" I asked as I watched her try to compose herself.

The ponytail at the back of her neck whipped back and forth as she shook her head. "Nothing."

"No, tell me why you laughed." I found myself smiling, wanting to know what she had thought was so humorous about what I had said.

"For a moment, I wasn't sure if you had changed your mind about flirting with me or me killing your wife." She stared me down as she spoke.

I grinned at her. "Not the flirting." What the hell was I doing? I was right back to doing it again—a married woman. I was waiting for the bolt of lightning to strike me down where I sat.

She didn't take the bait. "What made you change your opinion of me?"

I turned away from her and scooted to the edge of the couch, resting my elbows on my knees. "I'm pretty much always in control, that night I wasn't. I felt guilty for flirting with you."

"And you wanted someone to blame," she said.

I nodded but didn't look at her. "Yeah, I wanted someone to blame. I had it stuck in my head that for some reason you were interested in me, and that you didn't do all that you could for her, so that you would have a chance with me."

"Arrogant much?" she asked as she laughed.

"Not normally, but that night, I guess I was." I rolled my bottle between my hands, "When I saw you in the waiting room all cleaned up, I thought you had done that for me." I felt her move on the couch and saw from the corner of my eye that she was sitting on the edge of the couch. "When I saw you at the church, I was so pissed off, but it wasn't really because I thought you killed my wife, it was because I couldn't stop thinking about you." I turned to her and saw her surprised expression. "It made me so angry that I had flirted with you, and then I was thinking about you when my wife was dead—and someplace in my mind, I blamed you for it all."

She opened her mouth to say something but closed it and looked away for a few moments. "I'm not sure what I'm supposed to say to that." She cleared her throat and stood up. I watched her walk to the window of the living room and stare out the glass at the darkening sky.

She didn't turn to me when she spoke next, "When did you change your mind about me?"

I stood and set my bottle on the coffee table before I moved to stand behind her. "I ran into the medic that had been with you when Ilana was hit. He is the one that told me all that you did to try and save her."

She turned her head to the side to look over her shoulder, "He did?"

"Yes, and once I heard how you fought for her," I wiped my hand over my face, "and how you held her heart in your own hands and tried to keep her alive, I couldn't blame you anymore." She turned to face me and I had the crazy urge to pull her into my arms and kiss her. I put distance between us instead, "I knew then that I was wrong, and I wished that I had a way to tell you I was sorry."

"Ironic how things turned out, isn't it?" she took a wide step around me and returned to the couch.

"Yeah, it took Josh and Jazlyn getting in the accident for me to finally apologize. I could have easily stopped by the hospital and spoken to you there."

"Speaking of the accident, have you spoken to either of the kids' parents?" she asked as she leaned back. I took the conversation change in stride. What I had said had made her uncomfortable. I let it go.

"I called Marie's mother today, but she wasn't taking calls. I did leave a message that we were thinking of her and that Jazlyn wanted to speak with her when she was ready."

"I talked to Todd's father today. His wife is under sedation, and I'm not surprised. I would probably be, too, if I had lost Josh."

"Can I ask you a question?" I sank down next to her, close enough that I could touch her, but I kept my hands to myself. I felt her tense, "It's not about us." I watched her face, and it appeared to relax slightly.

"What is it about?" she asked softly.

I wondered if she would think I was crazy. "Do you believe in heaven?" She blinked. "I mean, do you believe in that whole tunnel of light and family waiting on the other side?"

"Yeah, I guess. Some doctors don't, but I guess I do. I have had patients tell me they had seen the light, and family members that they had lost sent messages back with them for others. Why?"

I took a deep breath and released it. "Because Jazz said she saw her mother. She said that her mother told her it wasn't time, and she needed to come back and take care of me. She also saw Marie and Todd, and Ilana said she would take care of them."

Rachel set her bottle down on the table and rubbed her arms. "You just gave me goose bumps, Grant."

"I got them too when Jazz first told me. I'm not sure I should believe it, but she does."

"Grant, if it helps her to deal with the situation, then let her believe. It's not up to you, or me, to tell her that it is true or not, she needs to determine that on her own." Rachel reached out and laid a hand on my arm, "If it helps you to deal with it, then that is okay for you to believe, too."

I looked at her hand and then into her bright blue eyes. She was so close that I could easily lean over and kiss her. She must have thought the same thing because her lips parted and she flicked a look at mine.

A knock on the front door pulled my attention away from her. I stood up and found Tom walking into the house, a large manila envelope in his hand.

"Oh, sorry, Grant, I didn't know you had company," Tom apologized as he and Beth stepped inside.

"That's alright, come in. Beth, Tom, this is Dr. Rachel Wilde. Rachel, these are my friends Tom and his wife Beth."

Rachel stood up and met them midway to shake their hands. "It's nice to meet you."

I saw all kinds of questions in Beth's eyes and needed to put a stop to them, "Rachel is Josh's mom." I stressed that last part. "She brought him over to visit with Jazz for a little while. We were about to order pizza. You guys hungry?"

"Sure, if you're sure we're not in the way," Tom said with a raised eyebrow.

I slapped him on the shoulder, "Of course not." It would be so much easier not to pull Rachel into my arms and kiss the hell out of her with witnesses here. "I told you that you were welcome anytime, and Jazlyn will be happy to see you."

I took their coats and hung them up before I went to order the pizza. In the kitchen I rested my palms on the counter and hung my head. Damn it! Wanting to kiss Rachel was wrong on so many levels, but why couldn't I stop thinking about doing it?

Tom startled me when he spoke, "So that's the doctor, huh?" I leaned back against the opposite counter and crossed my arms, "Yeah, that's her."

"Nice-looking woman, but I noticed she's wearing a wedding ring." He stared at me.

"I know. We're just friends, Tom."

He raised his eyebrow at me, "You were sitting awful close on the couch to be just friends."

"We were talking about the accident, it was no big deal." I noticed he still had the envelope in his hand. "What's that?" I pointed my chin at it.

He lifted it and dropped it on the counter with a loud whap. "It's Ilana's cellphone records and her text messages."

I stared at it for a few seconds, "How did you get the text messages?"

"I asked one of the tech guys to download them for me. I didn't think you'd mind." He put his hands into the pockets of his slacks. "We are the only two that have read them." His voice held a tone that concerned me.

"Do I not want to know what they say?" I stared at the envelope again.

"I don't think you will be very happy when you do, but I think it might explain a few things." He moved to the fridge, "If I were you, I'd forget about them for tonight and enjoy your company." He unscrewed the cap on his beer, "In fact, I'm going to put that envelope upstairs in your office." He reached for it, and I grabbed his hand.

"It's that bad?"

"It's not good," he said slowly. I nodded and let go of him. I watched him walk out of the kitchen. So Ilana had probably been having an affair. That would explain some of her behavior, but not all. I yanked the pizza menu out of a drawer and called to order a few pies to be delivered. I decided to wait and read the messages after everyone left.

For the moment, I needed to live my life and enjoy company. I could dwell on the past later.

Chapter 13 – Rachel

Thank God his friends showed up when they did. That was three times since I had arrived—what, forty-five minutes before—that I had wanted to kiss him. I needed to keep my distance, but watching Grant open up to me and talk about the money issues and thoughts on death only snagged my heart and pulled me one step closer.

Tom and Beth both eyed me skeptically when they arrived, but within a few minutes the tension eased. Obviously, they had known that Grant thought I was responsible for his wife's death. I had moved to a side chair, allowing Beth and Tom the courtesy of sitting beside one another on the couch. It was safer all the way around. Beth was talking about something that happened at the school where she worked, and we were all laughing when the pizza man delivered dinner.

Grant called the kids upstairs and we crowded around his kitchen table. It sat six in cozy comfort, and I tried to remember the last time Mark and I had done something like this. I stared at my slice of pizza dumbly. I couldn't recall a time that we had ever sat around with friends laughing and having a few beers over pizza.

I helped Josh as much as he would allow me to. His cheeks were pink, but he muttered a thanks to me that came more from his eyes than his mouth.

Everyone was in one stage or another of eating when Jazlyn spouted out over the table, "So, Josh's mom made him buy condoms today."

Beth, who sat directly across from me, stared at me mid-bite. I saw Tom set his pizza back on his plate from the corner of my eye. Josh and Grant both choked on what they were eating, sputtering to swallow and breathe at the same time. Oh, crap!

"What?" Jazlyn asked as everyone took turns looking at her, then at Josh and me.

"I was making a point," I stated as I looked at Grant.

He wiped his mouth with his napkin and stared at me, "Your son better not be having sex with my daughter."

Josh was beet red, but he spoke up before I could, "Mr. Murphy, I would not disrespect you or your daughter that way." He glanced at me and I knew he was looking for encouragement. "My mom knows what kids think about, I won't deny it. She wanted to make sure that I was mature enough to make the decision, and she said if I wasn't mature enough to walk into a store and buy them, I wasn't mature enough to even think about it."

Grant considered what he said then focused on me for a few seconds before he finally turned to Jazlyn. "And do you think about these things?"

Jazlyn's eyes grew wide, obviously embarrassed the conversation had come back to her, and color shot into her cheeks. "Um, I guess."

Grant sighed and scrunched up his napkin in his fist. "Shit," he mumbled, and Beth and I both hid smiles behind our napkins. Tom picked up his pizza and took a bite as if nothing was going on.

Grant sighed heavily, "Josh's mom is right. If you are going to think about these things, you should be mature enough to go buy them," he pointed a finger at Jazlyn, "and you should be on birth control, just in case."

"I already am," she replied back hesitantly.

Grant sat back in his chair, "Since when?"

"Mom put me on it when I was fifteen. She didn't want me to get pregnant young like she did."

"She didn't get pregnant at fifteen. She was seventeen, almost eighteen when she got pregnant," he stated and peered sideways at me.

Jazlyn shrugged, "Same difference, she was still young."

I looked at Jazlyn, "Your mom was smart to do that, condoms don't always work, Josh is proof of that." I turned to Grant, "I was seventeen when I got pregnant."

Grant and I were locked in a gaze for a few moments until Beth finally spoke, "And you still managed to go through med school with a small child?"

"I had a good support network. My parents were awesome about watching him. He spent more time with them the first six years of his life than with me."

Just like that, the conversation moved on, and I answered question after question about the things I had seen in the emergency room. The kids got a kick out of the strange things people did to themselves, and I managed to keep most of the stories clean and non-dramatic. There had been enough drama in the last month for us all.

After dinner, I told Josh that we needed to get going. I was afraid to stay and wear out my welcome, but I was also concerned that if Tom and Beth left, it would leave Grant and me alone again. I had found myself more than once over dinner wondering why I couldn't have met him when I was seventeen. Would I have been as interested in him back then as I was now?

Josh and Jazlyn said goodbye shyly, and he gave her a quick kiss before he peered at Grant. Thank God Grant hadn't freaked out over dinner. That could have been such an ugly scene.

"Mr. Murphy, I want you to know I was serious about not disrespecting your daughter," Josh said as we stood at the door. He held his shoulders as tall and straight as he could. I knew by the tension in his face that he was in pain and had probably overdone it today, but I was so proud of him for standing up like this.

Grant held his hand out and realized Josh wouldn't be able to shake it with his cast, so he set his hand on his shoulder, "I believe you, and thank you. She's all I have now, so please don't hurt her."

"Dad," Jazlyn groaned.

"'Night, Jazzy," Josh turned and walked out the door, and I faced Grant. Jazlyn said goodbye to me and went up the stairs.

"Thank you, Grant. I'm glad she is doing so well, and thank you for dinner." I held my hand out to shake his, and he took it and stepped closer.

"I'm glad you came over, and thank you," he leaned down, and the air in my lungs froze as he placed a lingering kiss on my cheek, "for everything."

I didn't know what to say, so I gave him a nervous smile and nodded before I turned and walked out the door. My cheek tingled the whole way.

I felt his eyes on my back even when I reached my car, and when I climbed in and glanced at the door, he was leaning on the frame watching. My heart leapt in my chest—and then crashed.

I felt things for him that I shouldn't feel. I was married, and while my marriage sucked, it was what it was and I had a vow to stick to. I needed to stay away from Grant, that was all there was to it. I put the car in drive and didn't look back.

"I can't believe Jazzy said that at the dinner table," Josh snickered from the passenger seat.

"Nothing like a little dinner conversation," I chuckled with him.

"That was nice. How come we never do that at home?" Josh asked and I knew exactly what he meant.

"I don't know. I guess we just have such busy schedules that we never get around to it," I answered him with a shrug.

"Yeah, well we should make time." He put his head back against the seat.

"You hurting?" I asked him, totally changing the subject.

"Yeah, a little bit."

I reached over and rubbed his arm, "I'll give you a pain pill when we get home to help you sleep."

Josh went right off to bed when we arrived home. I walked into the living room, the bright beige couch and tan side chairs looked too big. The walls were a bright apricot on two sides, and even with the darkness behind the windows, the room was still too bright.

Maybe I could redecorate the room, make it warmer, more comfortable to sit in. I turned the track lighting off and went upstairs.

Mark was out of town on business. He traveled at least twice a week, and tonight I was glad he was gone. I picked up the book I had on my nightstand and sank into my pillows to lose myself in someone else's drama for a little while.

****

The next morning, I had some last-minute errands to run to finish up the Christmas shopping. Josh was watching television, and I headed out.

The temperature was cold and I huddled under my jacket. The weatherman said we might have a white Christmas. I was not a fan of snow, but there was always something so peaceful about waking up on Christmas morning to a winter wonderland.

I stepped into the first store and shook the cold from my body as the heat blasted onto me from the overhead grates. Loud Christmas carols played from the speakers and people either had a harried look on their faces or a peaceful one.

In my opinion, the holidays weren't worth stressing over. You either bought a few gifts for people, or you didn't. It amazed me how many people turned into total scrooges at this time of year, and then how many negative people seemed to be so much more content. I exchanged holiday greetings with an employee and wound through the racks of books. I loved hiding in the book store. Sometimes I would come here just to escape reality. I smelled the rich scent of coffee drifting through the air from the coffee bar and decided I would indulge in a peppermint mocha once I had my purchase.

I was browsing the newly-released mystery novels, looking for something else for Mark, when I felt someone stop behind me. I glanced over my shoulder and up to find Grant grinning down at me. My heart skipped a beat. If this kept up, I was going to have to go see a cardiologist to make sure I was alright.

"Grant," I turned and gave him a smile. I was happier to see him than I should have been. "Now, who is stalking whom?" I stated playfully.

He laughed and his eyes crinkled up. My hand itched to reach up and touch the creases beside them. I shoved my hand in my pocket.

"You got me. Are you finishing up your last-minute shopping?" He glanced at the books behind me.

"Yeah, I needed to get Mark one more thing." I glanced away from him.

"Mark?"

"My husband." Why was I uncomfortable talking about the man to whom I was married? Oh, I know, because I was talking about him to a man I flirted with and wanted to flirt with even more. I felt like banging my head on the shelf behind me.

"Ah, yes, I forgot," he lowered his voice said shifted away from me.

How could he forget? It was like the elephant in the room. "So, who are you shopping for?" I asked to change the direction of the conversation.

"I wanted to get Jazlyn one of those electronic book readers, and Tom told me about a book that Beth wanted. I thought I would get her something for all the help she has been giving me."

"That's nice of you. She seemed like a really good woman."

"I don't know what I would have done without her or Tom these last few weeks." He paused for a moment, "Can I buy you a cup of coffee?"

I looked at the floor so I wouldn't blurt out that he could buy me anything he wanted—or have me for free. "Grant, I don't think that is such a good idea."

"It's only coffee—in public." He bent down to look in my face, "I promise I won't flirt."

Oh, but you are flirting right this second and I want to take you up on it. Who was I kidding? I loved the attention. Who wouldn't with an absentee spouse? "Okay, a cup of coffee, but that's it."

"You sure I can't talk you into sharing a slice of cheesecake with me?"

"What are you trying to do to me," I laughed as we moved towards the coffee bar, "seduce me with calories?"

He threw his head back and released a deep laugh, "Tempting idea, but even though I didn't eat breakfast, the slices are too big for even me."

"I think you can handle a whole slice yourself." We ordered our coffee, and he got his slice of creamy heaven. I eyed the plate and could feel the saliva pooling in my mouth. We sat at a small table near the windows, and I watched him dig into his cheesecake. We made small talk about the kids, and I spun my coffee cup around on the table to keep my hands busy. I watched the fork leave his plate and move to his mouth. I closed my eyes and shook my head when he put the morsel between his lips.

"If you keep that up, I won't be able to keep to my end of the deal," I snickered.

"Here."

I raised my chin and found him holding his fork out to me, the metal tines covered in chocolate raspberry cheesecake.

I wanted so badly to refuse but found myself leaning forward and taking what he offered. He cleared his throat and shifted in his seat. How did taking a bite offered on someone else's fork suddenly become so erotic?

"So," he put his fork down and took a sip of his coffee, "I found out something interesting last night."

"Yeah, what's that?" I said as I leaned my elbows on the table and took a sip of my minty mocha.

"Ilana was having an affair," he stated matter-of-factly, "and that's not the worst of it. She was planning on leaving me."

Chapter 14 – Grant

Rachel's lips covered the fork I held out to her in such a way that I had to adjust my seating. Those luscious lips—I had to give myself a mental shake—they must have been the reason I opened my own to blurt out the truth.

"Oh, Grant!" Rachel reached over the table and grabbed my wrist. "How did you find that out?"

"Tom brought her cellphone records home. The day she died, she had been texting someone. Tom had someone look at the text messages, and they were able to print them all out." I took a sip of my coffee, wondering why I was telling her.

Why? Because I was comfortable with her.

"She was texting with him when she got hit by the van. She never saw it coming because she was so focused on the new life that she was planning." I heard the hard edge in my voice and felt Rachel squeeze my wrist again.

"What did she say? I mean you don't have to tell me, but if you want to." Rachel let go, and I grabbed her hand as it slid back to her side of the table, grasping her fingers gently.

"I want to tell you, I need to tell someone." I shook my head. "After everyone left last night, I opened the envelope that Tom had brought over. There were pages and pages of text messages that were printed out." He laughed roughly, "The funny thing was, when I first saw the phone bills, I thought it was Jazlyn who was doing the million texts, I never would have thought it was Ilana."

The anger and betrayal that I felt as I had read the text messages returned, and I tried tamp them down. "She was talking to a guy named Tom, at least that is what the name said that was programmed into her phone." I scanned the busy store as I spoke, "Anyway, she was talking about how they were going to be together soon—and get this," I focused back on Rachel, "that the furniture had been delivered to their new place."

The rage flared in me, and I let go of her hand and leaned back in my seat. My neck cracked as I rolled it from side to side.

"Jesus, Grant, I'm so sorry. I can't imagine finding that out about my spouse, whether he was alive or dead."

"I know. What makes it worse is that she was planning on taking Jazlyn with her. She kept saying they would be a family finally."

"Oh, my God." She glanced around the room. "I don't know what to say. I don't know what I'd do if someone took Josh away from me."

"You can say what I feel: I'm glad she's dead and can't take my daughter away from me now." Rachel's face flipped back to mine. I didn't care if I sounded like a Neanderthal. No one was going to take my daughter, and the more I had learned since Ilana had died, the less I missed her.

"You don't really mean that you're happy your wife is dead?" she asked somberly.

I lifted a shoulder, "Yeah, actually I do mean that." I wanted to bang my head on the table, how could I have not seen the signs before that Ilana was having an affair?

"Wow." She wrapped her hands around her cup and stared at the lid. "Alright, I can understand that."

"What I can't figure out is how long it had been going on, and why she never said anything to me."

"It sounds like she was about to tell you about it."

"Yeah," I took a large gulp of my coffee, "after she had packed up her shit and stolen my daughter from me."

"I'm sorry, Grant, I know that was a shitty thing to learn about the woman you loved." I saw the sympathy in her eyes, but there was more there that I couldn't understand.

"Thank you." I watched her eyes dart around everywhere but to me. "What's wrong, Rachel?"

She stared at her paper cup again. "Grant, I can't do this." She leaned back in her seat.

"Do what? We are only having coffee."

"Do you think that is all we are doing? That's not what it feels like to me." She inhaled deeply, "You just told me that you were glad your wife was dead because she was having an affair. Yet we continue to flirt, and you and I both know we almost kissed yesterday, a few times. I'm married. What does that say for me, for us?" She had leaned forward as she spoke, to keep her voice low. "We are acting no differently than your wife."

Her words were a smack in the face of reality. "I'm sorry. I guess I am putting you in a pretty tough position. I didn't mean to do that."

"I know you don't, but circumstances being what they are, I think it would be best that we don't see each other anymore." She leaned away, and I felt like I was losing someone else in my life.

I hadn't known Rachel long. Shit, I barely knew her at all, but her presence had been a comfort to me through everything, and there was a connection that ran so much deeper. She had already admitted she felt it. She acknowledged the fact that we had almost kissed yesterday, and even with everything that she had said, I wanted to pull her over the table and kiss her, right here and now.

Instead I reached for her hand that twisted her cup on the table. "Rachel, look, I don't see why we can't be friends."

She snorted, "I'll tell you why we can't be friends, Grant. I want to be more than friends." She flexed her fingers to release my hold and stood up. I had to lean back so I could see her face.

"I have to go. Take care of yourself and Jazlyn, too." She

100

leaned down and placed a soft kiss on my cheek, her fresh clean scent wafted around my face. "Merry Christmas, Grant. I wish you all the happiness in the world, and," she paused, "I wish that I could be part of it, but I can't," she whispered in my ear before she turned and walked away—taking a piece of me with her.

****

Christmas had come and gone, and Jazlyn and I had celebrated a quiet morning at home. Both of us took time alone and together to travel through our own memories of holidays past. She missed her mother, and I pondered how I could have had no idea that Ilana had been preparing for another life. Some detective I was.

Neither of us was in the celebrating mood, nor did we want to be in the deathly quiet of our house, so we spent the afternoon with Tom, Beth, and a few other friends.

Jazlyn recovered quickly, but she still suffered from headaches once in a while. For the most part, though, she was back to her healthy, teen girl attitude with lots of eye-rolling and heavy sighing.

I couldn't say the same for me. I went to work to lose myself in something besides the drama that had unfolded since Ilana had died. Every day I read over the messages she had sent to the Tom guy, and his phone number was ingrained in my mind. A few times, I had even picked up the phone and dialed the number but had never put the call through. I couldn't figure out why I was torturing myself.

I could have easily done some research to find out who the number belonged to, but this wasn't a police case, it was personal. I refused to cross the lines in my job and put my professional integrity at risk. Instead, I just wondered.

What would I say if he answered the phone? Would I ask him if he was hurting as bad as I was? Would I ask him why he had done it, where he had met her, where they were moving to, and how he could have even thought about taking my daughter away from me?

As much as I wanted the answers, I didn't want them, and I

always hung up the phone before hitting the connect button.

It didn't help that I thought about Rachel every time I was alone. I knew she had done the right thing. At least one of us had been thinking. There was something between us, and I was no better than my cheating wife to want to spend more time with her, to feel the need to talk to her and to get to know her–but I refused to break up a marriage.

I stood in the doorway of my bedroom and scrutinized the room. It was time to clean house. Jazz was at a friend's, and I had a few hours to go through things. I needed to rid myself of every memory of her because of the betrayal, but reality told me that I couldn't do that. Even if I did, the debilitating pain would still hide in the recesses of my mind—but this was my room now, and I could remove her from it. I could remove the traces of her life from this small bedroom that we had once shared and reclaim it as mine. Determination gave me the strength to pull out the first drawer and scoop up the contents. I dropped the clothes into a plastic trash bag that I would pass off to charity. The more drawers I emptied, the faster I worked, as if chased by a demon that I needed to conquer.

With the drawers emptied, I yanked open the closet door. I didn't think, I didn't feel. I just reached in and grabbed her clothes and ripped them from the hangers and shoved them into bags. There were so many memories that threatened to flood me as I saw each piece of clothing, but I refused to let them inundate my mind. Sometimes her perfume would waft off a piece of fabric and cause me to swallow the ball of emotion that filled my throat. I didn't like the newer perfume she had worn; he probably did, though.

I didn't stop until the metal bar was empty and hangers littered every inch of the floor. I tied off the last bag and then grabbed a large cardboard box for her shoes.

She had them stacked neatly at the top of her closet, and I began pulling them down. I grabbed too many at one time, and several of them toppled to the floor. "Shit," I bent down to pick them up—and froze.

One of the boxes had tipped and the lid had popped off. There were no shoes inside, and I lifted the box slowly, realizing that I was about to get a glimpse of the life my wife had hidden from me.

I slid to the floor with the box in my hand and reached under me to move the plastic hangers away. My hands shook as I removed the lid completely. The box was filled with pictures and letters.

I lifted the picture on top and looked into the captured eyes of the man who had stolen my wife from me. He was dressed in a suit, and he had his arm on the back of a chair at a restaurant with Ilana seated beside him. Her hand rested on his knee.

Then it hit me. I knew the son of a bitch! He was a lawyer. I had seen him around the courthouse, but I couldn't remember his full name. I shifted through some more pictures, and my hands stilled on one while my heart skipped a beat.

The picture was taken at Ilana's office and Jazlyn was in it. Fury ripped through me as I realized Ilana had brought our daughter around the son of a bitch! I threw the box with the pictures and the notes across the room, and they scattered all over the floor. In a frenzy, I tore the picture into little tiny pieces, then rested my head on my arms and began sobbing.

I had lost so much: a marriage that I thought would last a lifetime, and a wife that I had thought loved me and cherished our life. What had gone wrong? What had I done to drive her away? What hadn't I done to keep her happy? It had been an illusion, but how long had they been together?

I wanted so badly to scream, to destroy everything in my path, to hunt down the son of a bitch and pulverize him.

Instead, I wiped my face and stood up. I boxed up the rest of her things, tossed the pictures and the notes into another trash bag, and carried all of it down to the garage.

When I returned to the bedroom, I looked at her jewelry box. I lifted the lid. I had put her wedding ring there after the funeral. I stared at it in disgust. It had meant nothing to her and so much more to me.

I remembered what Rachel had said in the bookstore. She was

the smart one, I would have never wanted to come between her and her husband.

I closed the jewelry box and lifted it off the dresser to place it on the top shelf of the closet, the one that had held all her shoes and the damaging photos. I cleared all the hangers from the floor and hung them back on the empty bar. Then I turned and shut the door. It was time to close off my heart from the memories of our life. It was over, she was dead—now even more so.

****

A month later, I was able to make it through the day without vicious thoughts taking my mind hostage. I could enter my bedroom and lie down without haunting memories. I had effectively put Ilana in the past and would not allow her to come out, unless Jazlyn brought it up.

There were times when Jazzy would start talking about her out of the blue, and pain would slice through my heart. There were other times when she would mention her, and I would fight to keep the anger out of my voice. I wondered, once in a while, if Jazzy knew about her mother's other life, but I didn't have the courage to ask her.

I was at the courthouse to attend a late afternoon plea agreement with a defendant on a burglary case I had investigated. It was a big case involving several residences and I was glad the suspect was taking the plea, so I didn't have to bring in forty-something witnesses to testify. As I stepped into the courtroom, I froze.

There in the galley sitting at the defense table was the man who had tried to steal my family. Venom seeped through my veins and my knees buckled. I had to sit on the back bench so I wouldn't jump the half wall and pulverize the man.

As I watched him wheel and deal on behalf of his client to the judge, his name came back to me, Mark Thompson. That was the name of the dirtbag attorney. I couldn't have taken my eyes off him if the place had been on fire. I wanted to see his face when he saw me. I wanted him to know that I knew.

While I watched him, I realized he was sweating. Perspiration poured off the sides of his face, and he reached for his tie several times, adjusting it as if it were too tight. He must have seen me enter the courtroom, I thought with some amount of unholy glee.

The judge made a remark that the client didn't like, and he burst out of his seat to yell at the judge. Thompson turned to calm his client, but instead of speaking to him, he opened his mouth, clawed frantically at his chest, and collapsed.

The courtroom went ballistic. There wasn't a jury in the box, but there were thirty-odd people in the room for different reasons. Two of the sheriffs grabbed the prisoner while another one ran to Thompson. I vaulted over the short wall to help the sheriff. In all the cacophony of voices, all I could comprehend was that my wife's lover was dying on the floor of courtroom six, and the sheriff was looking for a pulse.

Someone brought over an AED, and between the sheriff and me, we did CPR and attempted to shock him with the AED to revive him. Medics arrived after a few minutes, and we were pushed aside. One of the sheriffs had removed Thompson's wallet out of his jacket pocket.

The medic looked up at me as he strapped Thompson to the gurney. Several people were still working on him to get a pulse back. "He's wearing a wedding ring. You might want to send someone over to his house. Don't think this guy is going to make it." They brushed past me as they wheeled the gurney out of the courtroom.

"Detective Murphy, do you know where this is?" The sheriff held out Thompson's driver's license. I ground my teeth when I saw the address.

"Yeah, it's in my jurisdiction." I reached my hand out for the license. I definitely wasn't going to allow some other patrolman to go knock on this door. I was going to do it. I wanted to look into his wife's eyes and see for myself what woman couldn't keep her man happy.

The judge dismissed everyone for the day, and I stalked out of the courtroom, license in hand.

Chapter 15 – Rachel

"Hey, Mom, do you mind if I go over to Gary's?"

"What are you planning on doing?" I asked as I sifted through the mail.

Josh grabbed a soda out of the fridge. "We're gonna hang at his place, play video games, maybe watch a movie."

I looked up at him, "You're not planning on going out at all, are you?"

"No, why?" He pulled up a stool at the kitchen island and straddled it.

I went back to the mail, "The snow has been melting, and it's going to freeze once it gets dark. I don't want you out on the roads." I didn't add that I was afraid for him to be in a car with his friends.

"Don't worry. After what happened with Todd, I'm not taking that kind of chance." He jumped off the stool and put a kiss on my cheek. "You working tonight?"

"Nope, I'm off."

He stopped before he left the room. "You want me to hang out here? We could watch a movie."

What a great kid I had. "No, thank you, honey. You go have fun with your friends. I want to take a nice long bath and read. I'm beat."

"Alright, if you're sure."

I winked at him, "I'm sure. Give me a call in the morning and let me know you're alright, okay? I have to work at noon tomorrow."

"Okay, will do. Thanks, Mom!" he called out before he slurped a big sip from his can and left the room.

I dropped the mail on the counter and sighed. It had been a long couple of weeks. Work was nuts with all the storms and accidents we were having, plus things at home had gone from bad to worse.

Just as I had thought to do for that weekend after we had dinner with Jazlyn and Grant, I made a point of having Josh out of the house, and I planned a romantic evening. Mark had come home late, and when he saw the candlelit table adorned with fancy dishes, he'd stared at them like he had seen a ghost.

I had worn my sexiest dress, a see-through gauzy number that he had purchased for me while we were traveling in Paris a few years back. He turned to find me standing in the archway from the kitchen with two glasses of wine in my hands. His eyes had flashed briefly as he'd scrutinized me from head to toe, but instead of approaching me, he did an about face and walked right back out to the garage.

I waited to see if he would come back in, but after two minutes, I opened the door to the garage and found it empty. He came home two days later, drunk, and didn't say a word.

Now Mark came home less and less. The number of words we had spoken to one another could fit on an index card in a number twenty-two font.

For the last few days I had been considering calling an attorney and filing for divorce. I had no doubt that our marriage was over, I just didn't understand how it had happened.

I wasn't really angry, the feelings I had towards Mark had always been more friendly than wifely. Our marriage worked for us with our hectic schedules. He liked telling people his wife was a doctor, and I was happy knowing my husband was an attorney.

Why didn't I realize back when we married that it wouldn't be enough?

I decided to spend a few minutes playing on the computer and found myself sifting through photos on one of my social networks. Most of my photos were of Josh and me, or Josh and his friends. I clicked over to Mark's page. There were only a few photos, and most of them were ones he was tagged in by me—except for one.

I clicked on the image and enlarged it, my heart beat faster as I stared at Mark and Ilana standing side by side at a cocktail party. They leaned into each other, and I saw comfort in the way they stood beside one another.

Everything dawned on me in a flash. Mark was the man having an affair with Grant's wife. He was the one she was going to leave him for. I felt sick to my stomach as I stared at the screen.

It all made sense now. Ever since Ilana had died, Mark had been mourning her and slowly going to pieces. I remembered that Grant had said they were texting each other when she was killed. Did he feel guilty for that? But Grant had said his name was Tom. I smacked my forehead into my palm. She had abbreviated his last name to hide his identity.

I turned off the computer and poured myself a glass of wine. Instead of putting the bottle back in the fridge, I carried it with me to the sofa and plunked it down on the table. For a second, I considered putting something under the bottle so it wouldn't leave a ring, but then decided I didn't really care if it did.

I gulped down the wine—faster than I ever had in my life— while I mulled over everything and tried to decide if I should tell Grant or not. I reached for the bottle and missed it the first time. I grabbed it the second time around and realized it was empty. I upended the bottle over my mouth to get the last few drops. When I realized I wasn't going to get anything more from it, I tossed it aside and attempted to stand to go get another bottle.

The room spun and I grabbed the arm of the couch. Good job, Rachel, you got yourself smashed! The doorbell buzzed, and I stared towards the front of the house. I glanced at my watch and had to blink a few times and hold my hand steady to see that it was almost five-thirty.

"Who the hell is at my door?" I murmured as I went to answer it. I sure wasn't up for any guests right now.

I pulled open the door—on my second attempt. I forgot to unlock the deadbolt the first time. "Freaking locks," I slurred as I opened the door.

I must be dreaming, I thought, because Grant and his friend Tom were standing on my front porch. "Grant?"

"Rachel?" He looked as surprised as I felt. Tom and Grant exchanged a look. "Rachel, do you live here?"

I laughed, "No, I just get drunk in strangers' houses. Yes, I live here. What are you doing here?" I blinked, "And why is Tom wearing a police uniform? It's not Halloween."

I heard Tom chuckle, and Grant stepped forward, "Rachel, how much have you had to drink?"

I thought about that, "Not enough, I'm still standing." I looked up at him and found myself swaying towards him.

Grant gripped my forearms, "Rachel, let's go inside. I need to talk to you."

I shrugged and turned to walk into the house. I went straight to the kitchen and opened the fridge, intent on getting another bottle of wine. I heard Grant talking to Tom at the front door.

"I think you have had enough." Grant pushed the door closed when he walked up behind me.

"Says who?" I glanced around, "Where's Policeman Tom?"

Grant sighed, "I told him he could leave. Rachel, I need to talk to you." He led me over to the kitchen table, "Have a seat."

"Fine," I plopped down and came eye to eye with his waist. For the first time I saw the gold police badge on his belt. "You're a cop?" I reached out to touch it; the cold metal felt good on my hands. I stared beyond the badge to his black leather belt and the buckle I wanted to undo.

"Yeah," he pulled out a chair and moved it closer to me, "I

am." I was disappointed that his belt wasn't in front of me anymore.

"How did I not know that?" I stared at him, and his image wavered in front of me. Maybe he was right, and I had had enough to drink.

"There are a lot of things that we don't know about each other."

I snorted, "Ain't that the truth."

He looked at me weirdly, or maybe I thought he was looking at me weird, my mind was spinning along with the room.

"Rachel, what is your husband's name?"

"Mark."

"His name is Mark Wilde?" he asked me, and I laughed and waved a hand in the air.

"No, his name is Mark Thompson. I kept my maiden name when we got married because I was already a doctor."

"How long have you been married to Mark?"

I blinked the alcohol-induced blur out of my eyes again so I could attempt to focus on his face. "I don't want to talk about Mark." I stood up in the V of his legs and found myself trapped between them and the chair.

Grant tilted his head back and looked up into my face, while putting his hands on my hips. My heart raced at his touch.

"Rachel, sit down." He guided me back to the chair and took my hand.

"What's wrong? Why are you here asking about Mark? Wait!" I yanked my hand back and covered my mouth. "You know."

"Know what?" he shook his head and it made me dizzy. "I have to tell you something."

"No, I already know. You don't have to tell me." I tried to stand again and this time pushed the chair out of my way to move away.

"How do you know? It just happened." The chair scratched across the floor as he stood.

"Grant, they were having an affair for years, but I just figured it out tonight. I'm sorry. My husband was screwing your wife." I crossed my arms over my chest to protect myself from the wrath I expected to come out of his mouth. Yet, it didn't come.

"I know about the affair, well I knew who he was, but I didn't know he was your husband until you opened the door," he stopped in front of me, "but that's not why I'm here."

I stared at his lips, I wanted to kiss him. Mark had screwed his wife, my marriage was over, and I had this hunk of a sexy detective standing in front of me. Yeah, maybe the wine was giving me liquid courage, but I was going to take advantage of that.

I stepped closer to him and brushed the palms of my hands up over his chest and wound my arms around his neck.

"Rachel," he grabbed hold of my forearms to untangle my arms, "what are you doing?"

I locked my fingers around his neck and stood on tiptoe to reach his lips, "I'm going to kiss you, Grant. I have wanted to kiss you since the first time I saw you."

"Rachel, your husband went into cardiac arrest today in court and died."

I froze. "What?" I whispered across his lips and leaned back to look into his eyes.

"Mark was in court, he collapsed. They weren't able to bring him back." Grant tugged on my arms again, and they fell to my side. He guided me back to my chair.

I stared at him. "You came here to give me notification, but you didn't know it was me you were giving it to, did you?"

He shook his head. The buzz I had going began to swirl in a sickening vortex in my stomach as he spoke. "No, I didn't know it was you. All I knew was that the man who had destroyed my marriage and killed my wife was dead."

I jumped from my seat and ran to the powder room down the hall. I barely made it to my knees before the alcohol came rushing back up.

Grant's cool hands on the sides of my face calmed me as he pulled my hair out of the way. I wretched over and over again, purging my system of the wine and the anger.

Grant knelt beside me, and water ran in the sink. He gently placed a cool, wet cloth on my neck, and I swiped at my mouth with the back of my hand.

"I think I'm done," I said as I reached up with a shaking hand and flushed the toilet.

Grant stood up and pulled me to my feet. "Are you alright?"

"I'm not going to barf again if that's what you're asking." I stepped around him and went back to the kitchen for a glass of water. I leaned back against the sink and looked up at him. He was watching me carefully. "I'm alright; I probably would have thrown up even without the news."

"You don't drink much, do you?" He had his arms crossed over his wide chest, and he leaned against the fridge.

"No, I don't." I took another cool sip of water and hoped it wouldn't try to come back up.

"Why tonight?" he asked after a few seconds of silence.

My shoulders rose as I inhaled deeply, "Because I figured it all out tonight."

He nodded but didn't say anything for a while. "I figured it out a few weeks ago. I just didn't know exactly who he was—that he was your husband. I found pictures of them together."

"I'm sorry you had to find pictures."

"At least now I know why she was buying all the furniture. They had a place together somewhere."

I turned and poured the rest of the water down the drain. "Explains why he was never home."

Grant put his hands on my shoulders and turned me around to face him, "I'm sorry Rachel, this is all so messed up."

"Tell me about it. I'm not sure it can get more ironic than this."

A gentle smile lit his face, and my heart did a double beat. "Let's hope not." He ran his thumb over my bottom lip. "Rachel," he took a step back, "I need to take you to the hospital to do the identification."

"Will you stay with me?"

"For the identification, of course I will." He placed his palm on my cheek.

"No, I mean after." Surprise flickered over his features, and he glanced at me lips.

"Let's go ID him first, and then we will talk about that."

"Give me a minute." I stepped out of his grasp and went to the stairs. I couldn't believe that I had asked him to stay with me. I had just lost my husband, and here I was ready to climb into another man's arms.

My God! My husband wasn't even cold, and I wanted to wrap myself around Grant. Shame on me. Shame, shame, shame on me.

Chapter 16 – Grant

When I walked out of the courthouse, I ran into Tom on the front marble steps. "How did the plea go?" Tom asked.

"It didn't," I stated.

"What do you mean?" His police radio crackled on his hip.

I took a deep breath, "You know the guy who was having an affair with my wife?" Tom nodded, "I told you I knew him. His name was Mark Thompson, he's an attorney."

"Mark Thompson, yeah, I remember him. He defended a guy I arrested on an assault a few years ago. What does he have to do with anything?" Tom asked.

"He had a heart attack in court. The judge called a recess for the rest of the day. I'm on my way to give notification to his wife," I stated gruffly.

"You planned on doing that alone?"

"Of course, I retorted. "It's not like I've never done them alone before."

"Jesus, Grant." He muttered, "I don't think you should be doing the notification."

"Why? You think I'll say something?" I replied tersely.

"I don't think. I know. Grant, this has been eating you alive. Now you know who the guy is—and he's dead. Don't ruin his

115

memory to someone else to get even."

Is that what I was going to do? I thought about it. Would it change anything if I walked in on some poor woman and told her that not only her husband was dead, but he had cheated on her with my wife? Yeah, probably not a good idea.

""I'm going with you." Tom turned to walk down the steps beside me.

"Don't you have court?" I asked.

"No, I was going in to see if I could find someone. I can do it later." When we reached the bottom of the steps, he put his hand on my shoulder to pause me a moment and asked, "Are you going to be able to do this professionally?" The seriousness of his voice matched the responsibility of the job.

"Yes, I will be professional," I growled.

He nodded his assent, and we walked in silence the rest of the way to the parking lot. From there, he followed me in his patrol car to the residence.

The house was huge, and a few lights shone through the windows onto the excessively-manicured lawn. The house was a sprawling two-story with almost two dozen windows on the front. I'd hate to have to clean all of them. I climbed out and met Tom at the sidewalk. With a house this large, he most likely had a family, which meant kids. Damn.

"You sure you can do this?" He put his hand on my shoulder, and I nodded.

We walked up the sidewalk, and I took a deep breath before I rang the bell. It was never easy to tell someone that he or she was all alone in the world. I remembered the moment Rachel walked into the waiting room. I turned from the door to compose myself as the sadness threatened to crush me. I told myself I would not be sad over her death anymore.

I turned back to the door as it rattled in the jamb, then the lock turned. My jaw dropped open, and I shuffled back a step. I jerked a look at Tom. Was I imagining this? The look on his face said I wasn't.

"Rachel, do you live here?" This couldn't be right. I had double-checked the address on the license when we arrived and this was the right house.

She swayed in the door and commented on being drunk. That was easy to see. I ignored Tom as he laughed and put my hands on Rachel to steady her.

When she stepped inside, I turned to Tom, "I think I got this."

"Oh, yeah, this one is all yours. Good luck with that." He gave me a mock salute and went back to his car.

I followed the noise and found Rachel reaching into the fridge for another bottle of wine.

I finally got her to sit down, and that's when she saw my badge. I wasn't sure why I had never told her I was a cop, maybe because I didn't think I was good enough for her.

Rachel was slurring her words and weaving in her chair. I asked her a few questions to make sure that I had the right person. Damn, I never asked her about her husband—and why is that? Maybe because I wanted to pretend he didn't exist. Ya think, idiot?

"I don't want to talk about Mark." She stood up abruptly, and my hands went on their own to her tiny waist. It fit so perfectly in my hands. Crap.

"Rachel, sit down."

Rachel went off on a tangent, and trying to figure out the mind of a drunk was difficult enough without the stress of having to tell her about her husband, knowing that he had cheated on her.

I was confused about how she'd learned that they were having an affair, but now was not the time—as it was also definitely not the time to share our first kiss. I had imagined kissing her lips so many times, but I was not going to do it while she was drunk, and upset.

"Rachel, your husband went into cardiac arrest today in court and died." Her body stiffened and a myriad of emotions raced over her features. Every single one of them I understood all too well. How ironic that I was giving her the notification of her husband.

I held her as she threw up and wished there was more I could do for her. The fact that I had to ask her to go identify his body weighed heavily on my mind, but it had to be done.

"Will you stay with me?"

My heart began to gallop in my chest. What was she saying? I didn't want to get my hopes up, but I cupped her cheek in my palm anyway and told her we would wait till later to talk.

She left the room, and I dropped into a kitchen chair. Could it be any more ironic? I didn't think so. At least I no longer had to feel guilty for flirting with her.

I swiped a hand over my face. Her husband had been sleeping with my wife—and they both died within two months of each other. I looked up at the ceiling, "Hope you two are happy together."

"Who are you talking to?" Rachel said as she came back into the room.

"No one important," I took her by the elbow and escorted her to the door. "Is Josh home?"

"No, thankfully he's at a friend's house tonight." She pulled the door open and stepped out.

"Do you want to call him? I could stop by and pick him up." She locked the door and shook her head. "No, I'll tell him tomorrow."

The drive to the hospital was quiet. She stared out the front windshield without moving. The streetlights flickered shadows over her features as we passed under them.

"Are you alright, Rachel?"

She didn't answer immediately. "Yeah, I'm alright," was all she said the entire drive to the hospital.

She pointed to another door off to the side of the emergency room, "Park over there."

She pulled her keycard out of her jacket pocket as she approached the door that read: ER Employees Only. She swiped the card, and the magnetic lock released.

A woman saw her and went to speak; Rachel held up her hand and turned the opposite direction. I nodded at the woman and followed Rachel down a hallway to an elevator, she punched the down button.

People behind us were whispering, and I knew if I could hear it, she could, too. The doors slid open, and she stepped inside and punched the button for the floor below. She stared straight out the elevator while the door slid closed. The people who had been watching her looked away when she met their eyes.

When the elevator stopped, she hesitated. I placed my hand on her lower back to offer support. She walked out of the elevator and turned right. We went down a series of hallways, and through two more doors before she came to the morgue. She stared at the biohazard sign on the door.

"I've been down here a hundred times with other people, but I have never been here for myself."

"I'm sorry, Rachel."

She turned and looked up at me, hurt and sadness mixed in her eyes. "No, you're not. You're glad he's dead." She pushed the door open and stepped into the office.

My feet stuck to the floor, and the morgue door started to close. I stepped forward and took her arm, "No, If it hurts you, I am not glad he's dead." I put both my hands on her face and tilted it up. "I would never wish hurt on you—never."

She closed her eyes tightly and pulled her face from my hands. She moved to another door and knocked.

"Come in," a man's voice called out from the other side.

She pushed the door open. "Dr. Caldwell," she stated as she stepped inside. There were two silver body bags in the center of the room on metal gurneys. She glanced at both.

"Dr. Wilde, to what do I owe this nice surprise?" He stepped around the gurney with a clipboard in hand.

"Dr. Caldwell, this is Detective Murphy. He brought me here to identify the body of Mark Thompson, my husband."

"Oh, damn, Rachel." He set the clipboard down and came to her. I stepped back a half step. "I'm so sorry. I didn't know he was your husband."

"It's alright; he wasn't a very good one." Dr. Caldwell's eyebrows rose. "He'd been sleeping with his wife." She threw her thumb over her shoulder and pointed at me. The doctor stared at me. "But she died a few months ago, you probably did her autopsy, massive internal bleeding from being run over by a van."

The doctor looked alarmed at the amount of information that he received. "Let me just see which one of these is him." He turned away, flustered, and pulled at the tag on the first bag. "Not this one; must be the other one."

Before he could move to the next gurney, Rachel stepped to it, lifted the tag, and then tore the security tab away to unzip the bag.

"Yep, that's the bastard, Mark Thompson, Esquire." She turned and walked out of the room.

"Thank you, Dr. Caldwell," I said as I moved to follow her. The doctor stared in shock at Rachel's retreating back.

I caught up to Rachel in the hallway and grabbed her arm. "Rachel, stop."

I felt her body tense from head to toe. "Stop what?" The rage inside of her threatened to unleash, and I felt her body tremble.

"Stop running away," I said softly.

She tried to jerk from my grip, but I grabbed her around the shoulders and pulled her to me. Her body vibrated with anger and grief, and she tried to fight me. "Stop fighting me, Rachel. Let it out, let it go."

She fought for another few seconds before I felt her hands claw into my chest and knot my shirt in her palms. I felt the trembling stop and the sobbing begin. I pulled her with me until we were in a corner and out of the middle of the hallway and rocked her as she cried.

I fought back the tears from my own pain and whispered in her ear that it would be alright. It didn't matter if she heard me or not.

I heard a door creak open and glanced over to see Dr. Caldwell with a box of tissues. He held them out as he came closer, and I pulled some from the box and nodded a thank you to him. He dropped his eyes to the floor and went back into the morgue as quietly as he had come out.

After a few minutes, Rachel calmed in my arms. I continued to hold her tightly and allowed one hand to slide down the back of her head to soothe her. She sniffed, and I handed her a few tissues.

She pulled back while avoiding my gaze and blew her nose before leaning against the wall beside me, "I feel like I've been hit by a truck." She winced, "Sorry, bad analogy."

"No, actually, that is a pretty good one." I took her hand, "Come on, let's get you home."

"I have to stop upstairs and let them know I'm going to be out for a few days."

I pushed the elevator button when we reached it. "Do you want me to tell them?"

She shook her head. "God, I must look awful."

"You look fine." I lifted her chin, "In fact you look as beautiful as always."

She snorted, "Yeah, okay, and next you are going to tell me I smell delicious."

"Well, actually," I thought back to the coffee shop right before Christmas when she had leaned over and kissed my cheek, her fresh light scent had filled my nostrils for hours, "you have smelled better."

She laughed, "What, you aren't into wine and barf?"

"Not exactly."

"Thank you, Grant," she said and squeezed my hand as the elevator door opened for us.

"No need to thank me, I'm just doing my job."

She raised an eyebrow and gave me a skeptical look, "Really? If you tell me you do that for all the ladies, I might get a little jealous."

"Jealous, huh?" I wasn't a fan of jealousy, but coming from her, I might actually like it. We stepped inside. "Well, you will be happy to know that no, I don't do that for all the ladies."

"I'm serious, though. Thank you."

I stepped closer to her and cupped her cheek. "You're

welcome, Rachel. I'm glad I was able to be here for you, and I'm sorry that I had to be the one to tell you, but at the same time, I'm glad that I was."

"I'm glad it was you, too."

Chapter 17 – Rachel

We stepped out of the elevator, and I clutched Grant's hand as we entered the emergency room. The usual organized chaos reigned, but the minute Jane saw me she made a beeline my way.

"Rachel, I'm so sorry." I let go of Grant's hand and allowed Jane to pull me into her arms.

"Thanks, Jane. Can you tell Dr. Simpkins I'm going to need to take some time off?"

"Of course, he actually already knows." She looked embarrassed for a second, "I called him as soon as I heard."

"Oh, alright then." I turned to leave feeling as if I were on auto-pilot.

"If you need anything, let us know," Jane called out as Grant escorted me out of the building.

We were in the car and almost back to my house when Grant spoke again, "How's your head?"

"I feel like have a giant bell inside, and someone won't stop pulling the rope."

"We'll find some Tylenol when we get back to your house." A few minutes later he pulled in my driveway. I stared at the house.

"I was never a fan of this house; it's too big. Mark was the one that wanted this huge monstrosity. He said it fit his image, but I

123

never liked it. Guess I have a good reason to sell it now, huh?"

"Don't make any rash decisions right now, Rachel." He got out of the car and came around to the passenger side. I took his hand as I climbed out and stared up at him.

"Do you want me to go?" he asked softly.

No, I never wanted him to go. I didn't want to be alone. I wanted to find out what these feelings were that warmed my entire body every time I was close to him—but not tonight.

"I don't want to be alone, but I don't want you to get the wrong idea."

He ran his hand over my cheek again. "Rachel, I have no intention of seducing you tonight, but, like you, I don't want to be alone either."

I removed his hand from my cheek and kissed his palm before lacing my fingers with his and going into the house.

"Where is your Tylenol?" he asked as I kicked my shoes off in the front foyer.

"I think there is some in the cabinet in the powder room." I walked into the kitchen and filled the glass that I had used earlier.

He came back with two Tylenol, and I swallowed them. Without another word, he took my hand and led me to the couch.

"Do you have a blanket around here?" he asked.

"Yeah, in that chest over there." I pointed to the long wooden chest situated under the picture window. He pulled out two blankets and came back to me. I watched him kick his shoes off and sit back on the couch.

"Come here." Before I lay down, I walked around him and pushed the button on the side of the couch. It started to recline slowly, and his feet rose up. "Wow, I could get used to this."

I gave him a lopsided grin and dropped a blanket on his lap. He spread it over his legs, and I climbed up and put my head on his lap. He helped me to cover myself with the other blanket. His unique scent filled my nose, and I burrowed deeper into his lap.

"You keep that up, and I'm going to think you are trying to seduce me." He stroked my back.

"Sorry, just getting comfortable."

His fingers trailed lightly over my back and shoulders, and I let my mind float. So many images flickered through my mind, like a television that wouldn't turn off.

"Do you want to talk?" Grant asked a few minutes later. His husky voice warmed me.

"No." I sat up and turned to face him. It was dark in the room, and his face was in shadows, but I knew he was looking at me.

"What do you want, Rachel?" he asked as he ran his hand over the side of my head and tucked some hair behind my ear.

"I want to be closer to you." He didn't say another word. He didn't need to. His actions said it all. He opened his arms, and I curled up against his chest; my ear over his heart, my hand over his left pectoral muscle. He wrapped his arms around my back and laid his cheek on the top of my head.

****

That was basically how Josh found us several hours later. "Mom?"

Grant and I both woke immediately. Startled, I sat up and turned to Josh. "Josh, what time is it?"

"It's almost six-thirty. What the hell are you doing sleeping with Jazlyn's father?"

I rubbed the sleep from my eyes, "Josh we weren't sleeping together. Why are you home so early?"

"I woke up early and asked Mr. Stickler to bring me home on his way to work." He crossed his arms, "I answered your question, now you answer mine."

I climbed off the couch as did Grant right behind me. "Josh, give me a few minutes. Please go make some coffee, and I will explain everything."

He gave me the evil eye, and then he turned it to Grant. "Stop looking at us like that, we are adults," I blurted, feeling frustrated and disoriented.

"Rachel, I'm going to get going. I have to do a few things

anyway," he stopped, "unless you want me to stay."

Ha! So he could watch this show? No way. "I'll be fine. Go take care of what you need to do."

"Okay." He slipped his shoes on and turned back to me, "I'll talk to you later."

Josh glared at Grant as he approached. "Josh, it's not what you think."

"Yeah, I'll be the judge of that," he declared and kept glaring at Grant's back as he went to the foyer.

"Start the coffee for me," I repeated. "I'm going to go take a shower, I need a few minutes to wake up and process everything and then I will explain all of it to you."

"Why do I have to wait?" The earlier strength in Josh's voice faded, and his whiny teenage voice replaced it.

I spun on him, "Because I said so, and I'm in no mood for your whining. Do as I ask, please."

"Yeah, whatever," he muttered as he dropped his arms in a huff and went to the kitchen.

Well, could things get any more awkward? Yeah, we could have been sleeping in my bed which had been a thought last night—until I considered the fact that my husband had just died, his wife had been sleeping with my husband, and with us in that bed, it would have been one big happy freaking family! Not.

I grabbed a pair of jeans and a shirt, and took a quick shower. I still had a headache—for many good reasons.

After my shower, I felt a little more prepared to deal with the day. I went downstairs and found Josh sitting in the family room staring at the couch where we had slept, the blankets still tossed off the side.

I poured a cup of coffee and went to fold the blankets. "You're having an affair with Mr. Murphy?" Josh began his interrogation the minute I picked up the first blanket.

I balled the blanket up in my hands and sat down. "No, Josh. I'm not having an affair." I swallowed, "Mark died yesterday afternoon."

I fought back a wave of tears by blinking rapidly while Josh gaped at me. "What?"

"He had a heart attack in court. Grant is the one who came to tell me, and he took me to the hospital to identify his body. I didn't want to be alone, and that is why Grant was here."

"Mark's dead?"

"Yeah, honey, he is." I watched my son grow up right in front of my eyes.

"Oh, Mom," he stood and came to the couch. "I'm so sorry." He pulled me into his arms to hug me in a way he never had before. It was the first time that his arms felt more like those of a man than a child.

I let the tears slide, not just for Mark and all the rest of the messed up things, but for the fact that my son was growing up too fast.

He held on to me for a few minutes, "Why didn't you call me? I would have come home."

"I needed a little bit of time to deal with it. There was nothing anyone could do, anyway."

Josh let go and leaned back. "Well, that sucks," he said and once again reverted back to the level of a teenager. "I guess I owe Mr. Murphy an apology."

"I think he understands why you were upset. I don't think he will hold it against you. It did look rather compromising, I'm sure."

"Yeah, I couldn't believe my eyes. I stood there for a few moments and just stared at you two."

I stood and wiped my face off with my fingertips, then set about folding the blanket. I wondered briefly what we had looked like curled up together.

"Do you like him, Mom?"

"Do I like who?" I played dumb as I folded the second blanket.

"Mr. Murphy, do you like him?"

"He is a very nice man." I didn't make eye contact with my son.

"I know he's nice, that's not what I asked you." He reached over the couch arm and picked up my coffee, taking a sip.

"Since when do you drink coffee?" I plucked my mug from his hand.

"Since I became the man of the house," he said and grinned. "Come on, answer the question."

I blew out a burst air through my lips, "Josh, my husband just died. Why are you asking me if I have feelings for another man?"

"Because Jazlyn and I both knew that you liked each other. We figured it out weeks ago." He shrugged.

"What?" I couldn't believe what he was saying.

He stood up and put his hands on my shoulders, "Mom, you can't tell me that you were happy with Mark. You two never saw each other, you never talked when you did see each other, and you sure as hell never did anything else together."

"Joshua Wilde, watch your language please." Why I chose to pick on his use of the word hell, out of everything he had just stated, was beyond me.

Josh laughed, "Am I right? You were miserable with Mark, and you like Mr. Murphy."

I stared at his expectant eyes and wondered how my child was able to see all that when I had been blind to it. "Fine, yes."

I turned away from him as he chortled and fell back on the couch. "I knew it! Jazlyn and I were just talking about it. That's one of the reasons we decided to break up."

"You broke up with Jazlyn?" I stood next to the chest, blankets in hand, my mouth agape.

"Yeah, we thought it was too strange to be dating when our parents had the hots for each other." He rolled his shoulder, "Besides, we both decided we didn't like each other that much. I kind of have a thing for one of her friends, and she likes one of mine."

I shook my head as it began to spin and opened the chest. I wished there was more room inside for me to crawl in and hide.

"So are you going to start dating Grant now?" he asked as he kicked his feet up on the sofa.

"Get your shoes off the couch. It's Mr. Murphy to you, and can I please bury my husband before you have me marrying another man?"

"I guess. Wait till I tell Jazzy!" he pulled out his phone, and I snatched it from him.

"You will do no such thing. If and when there is something to tell, Grant can tell his daughter."

He rolled his eyes. "Fine, you take all the fun out of things sometimes." Josh stood and pulled me into a tight hug again, "I'm sorry about Mark, Mom, but you deserve better. I never thought he was right for you."

I bit my lip to keep from bursting into tears and handed him back his phone as he turned to leave the room.

I looked at the clock; it was already seven-thirty. Mark's partner would be in the office by now. I picked up the phone to call him to make sure he knew about Mark. Mark's parents had passed away a few years ago, and he didn't have any siblings. That made contacting his family easy; there wasn't any.

I dialed the back line into the office and listened to the prompt for the extensions; I pushed the three digits and waited for Stuart to answer.

"Stuart Kline," he answered on the second ring.

"Stuart, hi, it's Rachel Wilde." I moved to stand in front of the sliding door. I watched two birds take flight into the sky.

"Rachel, hello, Mark's not in yet. I expected him to be here, but he must have gotten tied up on something."

"Stuart, Mark won't be in."

"Is he sick?" I heard his desk chair squeak and could imagine him leaning back in his dark leather chair.

"Mark is dead, Stuart. I'm surprised you didn't hear. He had a heart attack in court yesterday." I clutched the phone in my hand to the point that I thought my fingers might bruise.

"Are you joking, Rachel? Because that's a pretty sick joke."

"I'm not joking any more than you were while you were

helping him hide his affair for years." I didn't know if it was true or not, but I took the chance.

"Uh, Rachel. I'm not sure what you are talking about." I heard the rise in his voice, the nervous energy that courses through the body when caught in a lie.

"Save it, Stuart. I know all about his affair with Ilana Murphy. Her husband and I have been comparing notes."

I waited almost a full minute before he responded. "Rachel, I don't know what to say."

"Don't say anything; it would only be a lie anyway. I'll let you know when the funeral is and make sure all his files are returned to the office." I hung up the phone without waiting for him to respond.

Fury reared its ugly head, and I started to clean.

Chapter 18 – Grant

Well, shit! I climbed into my car and started the engine. That was not supposed to happen.

I had been so comfortable with Rachel wrapped around me that I slept like a baby for the first time in months. I didn't even hear Josh come into the house, and the look he gave me told me exactly how he felt about me holding his mother in my arms.

I hit the steering wheel as I drove down the road. "Nice going, man."

I couldn't wait to see what Jazlyn was going to say about this. There was no doubt in my mind that the minute Rachel was done talking to her son, he would be on the phone to my daughter.

Crap! What was I supposed to say to that? Sorry, honey, I know your mom's not even cold in the ground yet, but I'm crazy about another woman.

Crazy about another woman? Was I really? The answer didn't take long to come. Of course! Just finding out that our spouses had been in love and planned to run away together left us with a strange connection, but that wasn't all. There were other things about her that I found intriguing and got my analytical police mind spinning—like the sound of her laugh, and the way her eyes crinkled at the corners, and how she had fit right in with Beth and

Tom in a way Ilana never really had. It was the fresh clean scent on her skin, and the bright blue shining in her eyes, the intensity in the way she worked, the emotions she let out with the way she loved her son.

I was crazy about the whole package—absolutely smitten. The sound of my groan covered the engine noise for a few seconds.

The real question wasn't how I felt; it was how she felt about me. Obviously, she was attracted me, she had tried to kiss me, but how did she really feel? Last night, she wanted me to stay with her, so in a way she needed me, but what did that really mean?

How would people react if we were involved with each other, especially so soon after our spouses' deaths? Not that I cared what others thought, but I did care about Jazlyn. I braced myself when I heard the front door open.

"Hey, Dad," she planted a kiss on my cheek as she passed by me in the living room. "How was work last night?"

Okay, not what I expected. "It was a long night."

"Oh, anything interesting happen?" she yawned and I saw small circles under her eyes.

"Have you talked to Josh today?"

"No, why would I?" She fell back over the arm of the chair and swung her legs.

"I thought you talked to him all the time."

"Naw, we broke up. We're just friends now."

"You broke up? Why?"

She shrugged and gave me a sweet little grin, "No particular reason, well actually that's not true. He is interested in Rebecca, and I want to get to know his one friend RJ. So we decided it would be better to be friends."

"And you're not upset about that?"

She waved her hand, "Pfft, not at all. I love Josh, but only as a friend. He feels the same."

"Okay," I said slowly. Why did I get the feeling there was something she wasn't telling me?

"Okay, I'm gonna go do some homework that I didn't finish.

You going to work today?" She jumped up out of the chair.

"Yeah, I'm leaving in a little while."

She leaned down and gave me another kiss, "I love you, Daddy." She was almost to the stairs when she turned around, "Oh, and I wanted to tell you something."

Oh, here it goes. "Yes?"

"I know you loved Mom and all, but I want you to be happy, so when you're ready to start dating, you have my blessing. You should find someone like Josh's mom, she's pretty cool. I could see you with someone like her." She blew me a kiss and whisked up the stairs as my heart pounded in my chest.

What the hell? I had expected for her to say something about Rachel, but not like that.

****

Later that afternoon, I sat at my desk, trying to concentrate on the report in front of me and not on what had happened earlier at home.

Tom set a cup of coffee on my desk and pulled a rolling chair over to mine, seating himself in the vacant one. I looked at the coffee and then him. "Yes?"

"So you want to tell me how that went last night?" He drank from his cup.

"About as good as can be expected." I shifted some papers on my desk.

"That's all you're going to say?" He laughed, "Come on, you have to tell me. I've been thinking about this non-stop since I left you at her door."

"There's not much to tell." I wasn't sure I wanted to tell him about falling asleep with her tucked into my arms.

"Did you tell her about her husband and Ilana?" he asked and kicked his boots up onto my desk.

I stared at the tread on his tactical boots. "You're not going to leave until I tell you, are you?"

He gave a slow shake of his head to emphasize the point.

"Fine," I grabbed the coffee he put on my desk and leaned back. "She already knew."

"What? How?"

I thought for a moment, "I'm not exactly sure how she knew, but she said she had just figured it out. I think that is why she was three sheets to the wind, or close to it, when we got there."

"That would make anyone want to drink."

"Yeah, I agree with you on that. I'm surprised I'm not a raging alcoholic right now."

He laughed, "You have too much control to do that. So what else happened last night?"

"Well, after I told her about her husband, she puked her guts out and sobered up pretty fast." Tom winced. "Then I took her to the hospital and she identified the body, after she bluntly told the medical examiner that the guy in the bag was her cheating husband and my dead and buried wife was his mistress."

He burst out laughing, "You're kidding me."

I joined in on his laughter. Now that I had time to think about it, the way she had said it was pretty funny. "She was still buzzing when we got there."

"I bet his face was priceless."

"Absolutely, but right after we walked out of his office, she fell to pieces."

"Right in your arms, of course."

I glared at him, "It wasn't like that."

"It might not have been last night, but I bet you wanted it to be."

"Yeah, well." I swirled the coffee in my cup. "We went back to her place, and neither of us wanted to be alone."

"You slept with her?" he blurted out.

"Not how you think. We fell asleep on the couch together."

"That's not that bad," he stated with a shrug of his shoulders.

"No, that was nice. Best night's sleep I have had in months, until her son walked in and found us."

"No way," Tom threw his head back and laughed, "and let me

guess, he called Jazlyn as soon as he found you."

"Ironically, I don't think he told her. I found out this morning that they aren't dating anymore." I set my coffee down and grasped the arms of my chair. "She also told me that I had her permission to start dating again." I shook my head.

"Jazz said that?"

I nodded with a smile, "Actually, she said I should find someone like Josh's mom."

Tom choked on his coffee as he swallowed, "She said that?"

I laughed, "Yeah, she did."

"You're not going to tell the doc?" He stood up and pushed the chair back to where it belonged.

"I think she has enough to deal with right now. I don't think I need to add my daughter trying to hook us up to the mix."

"True, very true." We talked for a few more minutes before he went to get dressed for his shift.

I logged into our reporting software and typed in Rachel's name looking for a phone number. I had her son's but somehow I didn't think it would be very smart to call him looking for his mom. I found the home phone number in the report from the accident and dialed it from my desk line.

I cringed and almost hung up when Josh answered. Instead, I tried to sound nonchalant, "Hey, Josh, it's Grant. Is your mom around?"

Josh hesitated, "Can I ask you a question first?"

"Um, I guess." I stared at the calendar on the wall above my desk. It was almost February.

"What are your intentions toward my mother?" His voice had lowered a notch, and his tone was serious enough to make me wonder if I really had Josh on the phone or another man.

"Excuse me?" I tensed.

"I asked what your intentions are with my mother. Do you really care about her or what?"

I leaned up to my desk, unsure of how I should be responding. "Yes, I do care about your mother. Why are you asking?"

"Why am I asking? Because I came home and found my mother asleep on the couch with my ex-girlfriend's father, that's why. And then I find out my mom's husband died. Now, it all seems strange to me, but she said you were only comforting her. Is that true?"

"I think we were comforting each other." I paused and rewound the conversation, "Josh, was Mark not your father?"

"Oh, hell no!" he said loud and slow. "That guy was a prick. I couldn't stand him, and he wasn't good enough for my mother. I only tolerated him because she seemed to care about him. She deserves someone better."

Whoa, Mark was his step-father, and Josh hadn't liked him. That was news, and now Josh was worried that I might not be good enough for his mom. Was I?

"I didn't know that, I just assumed."

"My father lives in Texas, he's a surgeon. They met back in high school. She got pregnant and they stayed together until they went to different medical schools. Mom and Dad are good friends, and I see my dad a couple times a year."

"Oh," like that explained everything.

"So, I'm going to ask you again, what are your intentions toward my mother?"

"Josh, I can really appreciate the fact that you are asking this and that you care about your mom enough to worry about these things, but, in all honesty, I have no clue what the future holds for us. I'd like to find out, but I'm not going to push your mom into anything."

"Okay, I can accept that, but know that I stood around and watched Mark hurt her for years, and I won't allow that to happen again."

"I will consider myself warned. Now, may I talk to your mom?"

"No."

"And why not?"

"Because she's not home. She went out with her friend Susan

to the funeral home this afternoon, and they were going to stop for something to eat. I'll tell her you called, though."

"Okay, could you give her my number? I realized that she doesn't have it." He said sure and I recited my cell number to him to pass along.

"One more question," he said just as I was about to hang up.

"And that would be?"

"Do I call you Mr. Murphy, Detective Murphy, or can I call you Grant since you like my mom?"

I chuckled, "You can call me Grant, Josh."

I set the phone down on my desk and realized that in all my years, I had never been asked my intentions toward a woman, and this boy who was almost seventeen felt the need to make sure I was on the up and up.

I liked that kid, I liked him a lot.

Chapter 19 – Rachel

It was too hot, and the cloying scent of flowers threatened to overwhelm me. I glanced over my shoulder at the full sanctuary. Who were all these people?

"You alright, Mom?" Josh leaned in to me and asked quietly.

I turned back around, "Yeah." I stared at the mahogany casket with the brushed-nickel accents. Scattered around the casket and front of the church were dozens of floral arrangements. I didn't know whom they were from. I didn't even bother to look at the cards. I didn't care.

I clenched my jaw as the pastor started the service. I was angry to be here, angry at the whole situation, and furious with Mark.

I should feel guilty for being mad at a dead man, I thought. As hard as I tried to bring a feeling of sadness to my mind, I could not grasp it. I knew that one day I would grieve for the man I had married and with whom I had shared six years. Today was not going to be that day. Tomorrow would not be either. Maybe next year, I could find a day to feel the sadness.

Josh peered over at me. I guess the sigh I released wasn't just in my mind. He reached for my hand, and I accepted his offering. It helped to sooth the seething anger radiating through my body.

The pastor rambled on, coughs echoed from time to time

around the room. Unlike Ilana's funeral, I didn't hear sniffling. I doubted anyone was crying for my now-dead husband. I sure wasn't.

I spent the majority of the service thinking about the fact that I wasn't mad that he'd loved another woman. I was mad that he'd never had the guts to tell me. If he had, we both could have moved on with our lives.

Grant's face came to mind, and the memory of listening to his heart beat under my cheek brought more emotion to me than the death of the man I had vowed to love, honor, and grow old with. Crap.

Was Grant here? I was tempted to turn and look for him, but even I knew that wasn't a very good idea. I returned my concentration to the pastor who had just finished his prayer, and I watched as Stuart walked up to the podium.

Stuart faced me but couldn't hold my eye. Good, he should be embarrassed. He started talking about what a great partner and friend Mark had been, and I tuned him out and wondered how long I would have to take off work before I could go back. I had already been off for four days, and I was bouncing off the walls at home. Another few, and I would be ready to slit my own wrists from boredom.

I could have called either Susan or Jane, but I didn't want to explain to them everything that was going through my mind. They had once said Mark and I were the perfect power couple. I was fitting on the arm of a prestigious attorney, and I should want to go to more of the functions that kept him out late at night.

If I had done that, would he have found Ilana anyway? Had I made it too easy for them to be together by not going to the constant charity events or business dinners? Did he take her with him to those? Of course he did.

I had tuned Stuart out while I stared at one side of the casket.

Two other people stood to speak about Mark, and I tuned them out as well. I wanted this day over.

Finally, several people came to wheel the casket down the aisle, and Josh and I followed behind it. I didn't look at the people in the pews. I kept my focus on the back of the casket. An irrational urge to push the casket out faster welled in me.

We were just outside the sanctuary door when I felt an arm wrap around my waist, and I turned to see Peter. The moment I saw him, tears prickled my eyes. I had not expected him to come all the way from Texas, but he had, for us.

"Josh," Peter nodded.

Josh smiled back at him, and I leaned into Peter as we walked to the limo. Josh climbed in and Peter stopped me at the door.

He lifted my chin with a finger, "You doing alright?" He brushed hair back off my cheek.

"I'm dealing with it," I said.

He pulled me into a long hug, and I was thankful that he was here. The anger I had felt earlier in the church subsided slightly, and I curled my arms around his back and rested my head on his shoulder. He kissed my head. When we stepped back, he placed another kiss on my forehead, and I noticed people watching us.

I wanted to laugh. Peter was comforting me in a very friendly and intimate manner, and people were noticing. Let them think what they want. I turned to climb into the limo without another thought.

Peter climbed in behind me and closed the door.

"Glad you made it, Dad," Josh stuck his hand out to his father.

"I got here after it started and didn't want to cause a scene walking to the front, so I sat in the back," he told Josh. He then turned to me, "Sorry I wasn't up there for you."

"Don't be," I waved away his concern. "Josh gave me all the support I needed."

"How much have you grown since I last saw you? It was only a few months ago," Peter asked his son.

Josh shrugged, "I haven't seen you since August. You were working during the holidays."

"As I recall, you had a girlfriend at the time who you said was going through a tough time with the death of her mother, and you wanted to be close to home to help her."

Color rose in Josh's cheeks, "Yeah, I guess I did say that." Josh glanced at me.

"You still seeing her?" Peter asked as he reached over and entwined my fingers with his.

Josh gave him a lopsided smile, but stared at me, "No, not anymore, but we are really good friends."

I saw Peter glance between the two of us, and felt the limo moving forward.

"Why do I think there is something more to that than you are telling me?" Peter asked.

I gave Josh a look before responding to him, "It's a long story, one that I don't want to talk about right now."

Peter accepted that, and he and Josh chatted about school and swimming while we drove to the cemetery.

When we pulled up, Peter turned to me, still holding my hand. "You ready for this? This is the hardest part." He squeezed my hand.

"I'm ready for it to be over with," I said as I stared out the window.

"I take it things weren't so great between you guys," he surmised, and I shrugged. "Fine, you can tell me later."

The limo driver opened the back door, Josh and Peter stepped out, and I stared at the open door. I didn't want to do this, but I knew I had to.

I slid across the seat and took Peter's outstretched hand. He pulled me close to him.

It was cold out. Being the middle of winter with temps below freezing for the last few weeks had left the ground hard, and I didn't worry about my heels sinking into the lawn.

We followed the men who were carrying the casket to the plot of ground that beckoned right beside his parents' grave. He had told me he had purchased a double plot right beside them when his mother had died and that someday we would be buried beside one another.

141

I snorted and hung my head. Over my dead body would I go in the ground beside my cheating husband, I thought.

Peter wrapped his arm around me, and Josh stood on my other side. As mourners filled in around us, the cold breeze that had been whipping my coat was blocked.

Peter kissed the top of my head again, and I leaned on his shoulder—not because I was sad but because I was tired. The pastor once again started speaking.

I stared at the box in front of me. A snowflake fell and then another. I lifted my eyes to the dark gray sky and the cold flakes landed on my cheeks and eyelashes. When I lowered my eyes, they landed on Grant.

He stood directly across from me, Jazlyn at his side. His eyes searched mine and asked questions that I couldn't answer. I looked away, and distanced myself from Peter slightly.

I knew that Grant was wondering who the man was that I leaned on. Peter wrapped his arm tighter around me, and I didn't have the strength to fight it.

I stared back at the wooden casket for a moment before I let my eyes wander around the people who stood beside the grave to pay their final respects. Some people were looking at me; some were staring at the box.

The ones who watched me would glance away when I met their gaze. Did they know? Did they feel sorrow for a woman made a widow or did they pity me because of what they knew he had done?

My eyes landed on the dark brown rectangular box again, Damn you, Mark! I shouted in my mind.

How could he do that to me for years? If he had told me he was in love with another woman, I would have told him to go. I would not have held him in a marriage he didn't want to be in. He should have said something, should have admitted it when Ilana died.

I lifted my eyes to see Grant watching me again. A snowflake landed on my eyelashes. A tear ran down my cheek.

I would have told him about Grant. I would have told him I had feelings for another man. I swiped the tear away and looked at the pile of dirt off to the side. I had feelings for another man? I was burying my cheating husband. I was no different than Mark.

I stared at the box again and then met Grant's intense gaze. Grant.

I pulled my focus away from him. This was wrong. This was so wrong. How could I have feelings for the husband of the woman who had been having an affair with mine? How could he return the feelings? What kind of distorted reality was this?

The pastor said the final prayer while my head was bowed. I did not listen or follow along with the words he spoke. My mind spun on the realization that there was no way I could follow through with a relationship with Grant. Ilana and Mark would always be there. Looking at one another would always be a reminder of what we had gone through, how we had been wronged.

The pastor finished, and some people came to shake my hand and to offer their condolences. I gritted my teeth and accepted a few before I turned to Peter. "Get me the hell out of here."

Peter took me by the arm and led me back to the limo. Josh stuck close to my other side, and when he opened the door, I stopped and looked back to the site. A handful of people stood in a group talking, all attorneys from Mark's firm. I scanned the rest of the area and saw Grant standing beside the passenger side of his car. Jazlyn was now in the front seat. He glanced my way, and I fought the urge to run to him and hide in the warmth of this arms.

I lowered my face and stepped into the back door as tears filled my eyes again. I felt more loss at the fact that I would not allow my relationship with Grant to grow than I did at the death of my husband. How messed up was that?

Josh and Peter climbed back in and closed the door. The limo started to move shortly after.

"So you want to tell me what's going on?" Peter asked.

I turned to him. "What are you talking about?" Peter crossed his arms over his chest. He was built so differently than Grant. He was tall and lean, no bulking muscle. His shoulders weren't overly wide, but they were strong, and he held them straight. He had always taken care of himself and had been a runner since high school, when we'd met.

"Why don't we start with the man who was shooting daggers at me because I was holding on to you?"

Josh laughed, and I stopped him with a can-it look. "I don't know what you are talking about."

An eyebrow rose. "Yeah? Somehow I doubt that. I saw you two watching each other. He was focused on you the entire time, except when he was putting me in his crosshairs."

"I still don't know what you are talking about." Josh laughed, and I looked away from Peter and out the window at the passing scenery.

"Dad, that was Grant."

"Who is Grant?" he asked.

"Grant is a cop and the father of the girl I told you about."

"The one who lost her mother?" I turned to watch Josh nod. "Okay, so what's up with the looks he was giving your mom?" Peter cast a glance my way.

"Because he likes her," Josh laughed again.

"Were you having an affair with this Grant guy?" Peter asked bluntly.

"No!" I spun on him, "No! I was not the one having the affair, Peter." I saw Josh watching me carefully, his eyebrow raised at my words. I had not told him about Mark's indiscretions with Jazlyn's mother.

I took a deep breath, "How long are you here?"

"I have a flight out tomorrow morning. I'm staying at the Hilton tonight."

"Why don't you stay at our house tonight? I'm sure Josh would like to spend more time with you, and I will explain, later."

Peter accepted the invite, and I leaned back in the seat and wondered what he would think of the whole twisted situation.

Chapter 20 – Grant

"Come on, Dad, we're going to be late," Jazlyn called from the stairs.

"Are you sure you want to go? I know you hate funerals," I said as I made my way down the stairs.

"I do hate them, but Josh was there for me, and I'm going to be there for him. Isn't it ironic that we both lost one of our parents within a few months of each other?" she asked.

Not as ironic as the fact that your mom and Mark were having an affair, and I can't get Josh's mom off my mind, I thought to myself. "Yeah, it's ironic."

On the way to the church, I wondered if I would get a chance to see Rachel alone. I had called her a few times, but she had never returned my calls. I wasn't looking for anything; I only wanted to check on her to make sure she was alright.

Jazlyn and I sat a few rows from the rear of the church. I got a glimpse of Rachel and Josh in the front when we sat down. I had a hard time not getting angry while I listened to Mark's friends talk about what a great guy he was. How many of them knew he'd been sleeping with another woman?

We stood as they walked by with the casket, and Rachel stared straight ahead. I was about to slip out of the pew and attempt to approach her when another man moved out of the last row and put his arm around her.

The other people present followed them out. I stood outside and watched the man tilt Rachel's face up to his. The intimate way he touched her sent a blade of jealousy through my chest, and I turned and led Jazlyn to our car.

Was the man a relative? They didn't look like they were related. I had no idea if she had brothers. Maybe he was a close cousin. I clenched the steering wheel of my SUV while I considered that maybe it was another man that she cared about. Did she have an affair on Mark?

At the cemetery, I stood across from her and watched her. The man beside her had a possessive air about him that irritated me. He met my stare once, and I felt him watching me from time to time after that when he didn't have his attention on Rachel.

Snow began to fall, and I watched the flakes land on her long charcoal overcoat. She lifted her face to the sky and took a deep breath. She looked so beautiful with her face turned up to the sky and the snow drifting down around her.

The man beside her pulled her closer, and I fisted my hands in my heavy coat pockets. I couldn't have cared less about being there to pay my respects to the man who had stolen my wife from me, but I had come for Rachel. Obviously, she didn't need or want me.

I put Jazlyn into the car and turned to see Rachel staring at me. A want I had not felt in years coursed through me at the painful look on her face. She slid inside the limo door, and I turned my attention to the man who stood at the door. His light brown hair was cut short, and he had an authority about him that demanded respect. He had questions in his eyes, and I turned away and entered my car. If he wanted an explanation, he could ask her.

We lived two different lives. Our children were only friends now, so the likelihood that we would meet again was slim. That thought saddened me, but life was about finding and losing people. I would live.

Three weeks later, I walked into an office building and stared at the list of names on the board. The offices I wanted were on the fourth floor, and I moved toward the elevators.

I had no idea why I had been called here. I was only told it was a legal matter and I needed to attend in person. I exited the elevator and walked through a set of glass doors. The name Kline, Rogers, and Milton was written in bright white letters on the door but meant little me.

I leafed through a magazine after I had given my name to the receptionist until a man called my name, "Mr. Murphy?"

"Yes, sir." I stood and held out my hand. He was roughly six inches shorter than I and stocky.

"I'm Stuart Kline, thank you for coming today. Follow me." He turned and walked down a hallway.

He stepped into an office near the back of the building; a large window overlooked a wooded area. In the summer it might look pretty, in the cold of winter, it was depressing with all the naked trees and dingy gray outside the glass.

I took a seat in one of the two dark burgundy leather chairs in front of his desk. He cleared his throat and took a seat.

"Mr. Murphy, we are just waiting for another party, and then we can begin." He appeared nervous and shifted his eyes to the papers in front of him.

"Okay, do you mind telling me what this is about?" I asked as I studied him. He had dark brown hair and a receding hairline. His brown eyes flicked towards mine and then back to his desk.

He cleared his throat again, "If we could just wait until the other party is here, then I will explain. Can I get you some coffee or water or anything?"

"No, thank you." I watched him fidget in his chair. He was about to say something when the phone on his desk beeped, and the voice of the receptionist filled the room.

"Mr. Kline, your other party is here."

"Thank you, send her back please." He glanced at me and at

the phone. He shifted papers around on his desk without looking my way again. When the door behind us opened, he stood, "Rachel, thank you for joining us."

I stood and spun around. Rachel? What the hell?

She locked eyes with me and froze in midstep. "Grant, what are you doing here?"

I turned to the attorney who looked even more uncomfortable. "I don't know. Why don't you tell us why we are both here?"

"Rachel, have a seat, it's good to see you again." The attorney sank into his seat without meeting her gaze or offering her a hand.

"Didn't take you long to change the name on the door," Rachel remarked as she approached the chair beside mine. I stood until she sank into it. She glanced my way then back to the attorney, "I thought we were going over Mark's will, Stuart."

He heaved a breath and cleared his throat yet once again. Either this man had a sinus issue or he was seriously nervous.

"We are," he replied and lifted his head to us. I noticed he never responded to the sign comment.

"Then why is Grant here?" she asked. I turned to her; she wore a black leather jacket over a blue blouse and jeans. Her hair hung straight down past her shoulders, and I followed the line of her jaw as she clenched it.

"Rachel, I know this might seem strange, but Mr. Murphy is part of the will."

I spun around to him. "What?" I said at the same time that Rachel echoed my word.

He lifted a file off his desk and tapped it on the hard wood surface. "Strangely enough, he is part of his will."

"Stuart, he didn't even know Grant. Why would he include him in the will?" I realized as Rachel called him by his first name that this must have been the firm where Mark had worked; therefore, the man across the desk from me probably already knew exactly who I was and that Mark had been sleeping with my wife. The muscles in my body began to tense.

"Look, this isn't easy, Rachel, and I'm sorry it has taken so long to get around to doing the reading of the will, but there were things the insurance company needed to check out before they could issue the check. I have the will here, and I also have a letter from Mark that he wanted me to read to you word for word. It does include Mr. Murphy," he nodded in my direction, "and it will all be explained as I read it."

Rachel and I exchanged a glance. I had no idea what was going on. Of course Mark had known who I was, but why the hell was I a part of his will? Guilt?

"May I begin?" Stuart asked.

"By all means, let the circus begin," Rachel replied dryly.

Of course, Stuart cleared his throat again before he began, "'Dear Rachel, I thought many times about how to start this, but everything I came up with led me right back to this one thing: I'm sorry. I know that it will never be enough, but you did deserve to hear that.'"

Rachel stared at her hands tensely clasped in her lap. I glanced at her face, her jaw once again clenched tight.

"'I know that by now you have probably learned that I was in love with another woman, and that was nothing against you. I loved you, in my own way.'"

I found myself locking my own jaw and shifting in my seat as the lawyer continued.

"'Grant, I owe you an apology, too. Ilana and I never meant to hurt either you or Rachel. We knew each other a long time ago, and when we ran into each other a few years ago, things just happened.'"

Rachel snorted and shook her head as she stared out the window behind the attorney.

"'Both of us loved you in our own ways, but we loved one another more. That is why we were starting to build a life together. I lost Ilana once and never wanted to live without her again.'"

Rachel held her hand up and Stuart stopped. "This sounds like a suicide note. Why?"

Stuart leaned back in his seat again. "I thought the same thing when I first read it." He raised an eyebrow, "In fact, I even questioned him on it. He assured me it wasn't. This is one of the reasons the insurance company took so long to release the life insurance. They wanted a full medical report to make sure he hadn't caused his own heart attack."

"He only had a five-hundred-thousand-dollar policy. Why would they hold that?" Rachel asked.

"No," Stuart shook his head, "about two months ago, he changed his life insurance policy to two million." His words came out slowly, and I heard Rachel gasp.

"Two million?" she repeated softly.

"Yes, and that is why the insurance company had to do some research." Stuart nodded at me, "They wanted to make sure that he didn't kill himself, because if he had, you would have gotten nothing."

Two million dollars, holy crap! That was a lot of money. Way more than the measly amount Ilana had through her company.

"May I continue?" Stuart flicked impatient eyes between us. I nodded and assumed Rachel did too since he picked up the letter and started reading again.

"'I saw you two one day sitting in a coffee shop holding hands.'"

"What?" Rachel blurted out. I remembered it clearly, and wasn't sure if she was questioning that it happened or that he had seen it.

Stuart glanced at her, but kept reading without answering her. "'I also saw you kiss him goodbye, Rachel. Strangely enough, I hope you two get along and things work out. You both deserve some happiness.'"

"What the hell is he talking about?" Rachel leaned forward in her chair, her hands clenched around the armrests.

"Rachel," I said to get her attention, "when you left that day, you kissed my cheek. You were saying goodbye." I stared into her blue eyes, remembering that she had told me goodbye because she couldn't spend time with me because she was married and she felt things she shouldn't. I remembered the whole thing perfectly, and it hurt that she didn't seem to recall it at first.

Her eyes scanned the room for a moment before she spoke softly, "Yeah, I remember that."

Stuart let our little side conversation go and pulled a silk pocket square out of his suit jacket to wipe his forehead.

Stuart cleared his throat and began reading again. The paper in front of him trembled slightly, and I realized that he was extremely nervous and the hairs on the back of my neck rose.

"'Rachel, you remember I told you a long time ago about my past. Well, I never realized how much it would come to mean to me as the years went by. I had accepted long ago that I would not be a part of that life, but, well, sometimes fate steps in.'"

I glanced at Rachel, wondering if she understood what he was talking about. Her jaw was slack now, her eyes wide. The attorney kept his gaze on the paper in front of him.

"'To find her after so many years, to know that I still had time to get to know her, was something I could not pass up.'"

"Oh God, no, please don't say it, Stuart," Rachel's voice was thin and stressed. Stuart blinked at the paper, swallowed like he was trying to swallow a golf ball and kept going.

"'She's my daughter, Rachel. How could I pass up getting to know her?'"

The hairs that rose up earlier stood on end. What the hell was he talking about? "His daughter?"

"Stuart, there is no way that can be true." Rachel moved to the edge of her seat, her gaze never wavering from the attorney's.

"I assure you, it is true." He opened the folder and pulled out a document and slid it over the desk to her. "Mark is her father. This is the paternity test results."

"What the hell are you two talking about?"

Rachel shook her head. She turned to me and reached for my hand, "Grant," tears raced down her cheeks, "Mark is Jazlyn's father."

"No, he isn't," I barked and pulled my hand out of hers.

"Mr. Murphy, Mark Thompson is your daughter's biological father," Stuart said, and a bead of sweat ran down the side of his face.

My stomach rolled, and I thought I would be sick. "You are wrong. My name is on the birth certificate."

I expected Stuart to reply, and Rachel's response threw me for a loop, "He signed off his rights before she was born."

I gulped, "You knew about this?" My blood raced through my veins so fast that I could hardly hear her answer.

"I didn't know it was Jazzy. I knew he had a daughter, but I had no idea it was Jazlyn."

The words reached my ears, but I didn't hear them. It didn't matter if she knew or not. Her husband tried to steal my wife. Now from the grave he was trying to steal my daughter.

"This is bullshit! What the hell does he want?"

The weasel behind the desk coughed and began reading again faster, "'This is where Grant comes in. I don't want anything from him, other than for our daughter to know I was her father.'"

"No…Fucking…Way," I enunciated each word between clenched teeth.

"'In my will, I have left seven hundred and fifty thousand to Rachel and two hundred and fifty thousand to my stepson Josh. I leave one million dollars to my daughter, with the following stipulations.'"

"I don't want the money." I stood as fury roared through me.

The lawyer ignored me and continued, "'Rachel and Grant are to get married within six months of the reading of the will.'"

"What!" Rachel and I blurted out together, and I swore my blood boiled right into my eye sockets because all I saw was red.

"'If they do not get married, Rachel will get nothing. Josh will inherit five hundred thousand on his thirtieth birthday, and Jazlyn will inherit one point five million when she turns thirty.'"

Chapter 21 – Rachel

"What are you doing today?" Susan asked me as I put my stuff in my locker and prepared to head home.

I groaned, "I have to go to Mark's office, they are reading the will today."

"How are you doing with all that?" Susan asked as she picked up her purse.

"Fine," I sat down on the bench in front of my locker to put on my sneakers. "I never told you, but things with us weren't that great."

"They weren't? I thought you guys were the perfect power couple." She sat beside me.

"Nope," I shook my head. Enough time had gone by that I could finally talk about it and not get upset. "He was having an affair."

"What?" Her hand went over her mouth.

"Yep," I stuck my other foot into my shoe and leaned down to tie it, "and, get this, remember that woman who got run over by the van? She was the one he was having an affair with."

Her hand drifted down to her lap, and I glanced up to see her eyes wide, "You're kidding me? Wait, isn't that the wife of the guy you were flirting with?"

"That would be the one." I stood up and reached for my jacket.

"Wow, that is, like, all kinds of strange and maybe fate."

I laughed, "Fate? I don't think so."

Susan followed me out of the locker room. "Why not? You thought he was hot enough to flirt with, and his wife and your husband," she paused, "okay, that's just weird. Anyway, they were together, why would it be weird for you two to be together?"

We walked toward the parking lot. "It is too weird. Doesn't matter if he is hot or not, it's not going to happen." I pushed the door open, and we stepped out into the cold. "I'm so tired of this weather. I can't wait till the end of March when Josh and I get to go to the beach."

"I'm jealous, and you just changed the topic. When is the last time you saw him?"

"Who? Josh?" I knew she was talking about Grant, and I was suddenly sorry I brought it all up.

She rolled her eyes. "Uh, no! The hottie!"

I laughed at her again, "I haven't seen him since the funeral."

"Have you talked to him?" We reached my car and stopped.

I shook my head, "No, not since he left that morning after Mark died."

She raised an eyebrow, "The morning?"

I glanced around the parking lot, "Yeah, after he brought me to identify Mark's body he stayed the night."

She stepped closer to me, her eyes once again huge, "You slept with him the night your husband died?"

"No, I didn't sleep with him like that. We fell asleep on the couch, he was offering comfort." I shrugged, "I took it."

"And you haven't seen or talked to him since?" She put her hands on her hips and stared at me.

"Nope, and I don't plan on it either." I leaned back against my car, "As much as I want to, I can't. He called me a few times, but I never called him back."

"Why not?"

Why didn't I call him back? Because I knew that the way we met would only make things even stranger than they already were. The fact that our kids were friends and our significant others were involved made me wonder if we did get together whether it would be real or not.

"I don't know. I have to go run a few errands before I go read the will. I'll tell you more about it later."

We split ways, and I took off to grab a few groceries before I went to Mark's old office. I almost laughed when I saw the new sign and realized they had already removed all signs of Mark from the firm name. They were so cutthroat, I wondered how long it actually took them to make the change.

The receptionist let Stuart know I was there, and I rolled my neck to release the tension in the muscles as I walked down the hallway. I had not seen him since the funeral, and I had avoided him there. He had never been my favorite person, and knowing he knew the truth did not rate him any higher in my book.

I stepped into the office and froze. Why was Grant here? Was this some kind of sick joke that Mark wanted to play on the two of us. Bring his mistress's husband to the reading of his will? Did he leave Grant money as an apology for falling in love with his wife?

I got over the initial shock of having Grant there only to realize that while I sat beside him, I missed him. How was that possible? I realized as his musky cologne wafted over me that I didn't want to avoid him. One look in his eyes reminded me that I had found him attractive, and that I was a free woman now. He was a free man. Maybe we could make this work, maybe.

Stuart started reading the letter and immediately I felt the anger I had let go of begin to build inside of me again. He was sorry? Screw him! He screwed with so many lives and messed them all up, especially his. Why should I care about an apology or the fact that he says he loved me?

I didn't.

I snorted when Stuart read the apology to Grant. Like Grant cared, give me a break. I never realized that Mark was such a dramatic person before. Huh, I wondered how I had missed that. I had the distinct impression that what Stuart was reading was actually the last words of my husband, and that he had meant for them to be read after he had taken his own life, a woe-is-me kind of thing.

"This sounds like a suicide note. Why?"

When Stuart explained that the insurance policy was actually two million dollars, I almost fell out of my chair. Two million dollars? No, I heard that wrong, no way.

I stared at Stuart as he continued reading the letter, "'I saw you two one day sitting in a coffee shop holding hands.'"

"What?" How did he see us? What was he doing, following me around?

"'I also saw you kiss him goodbye, Rachel. Strangely enough, I hope you two get along and things work out. You both deserve some happiness.'"

"What the hell is he talking about?" I said without realizing I had spoken aloud. Did Grant really think I didn't remember that day? Next he would think I forgot about the fact that I had slept all night lying on his chest. Of course I remembered the feel of his cheek on my lips. The memory haunted me along with the sound of his heartbeat in my ear.

"'Rachel, you remember I told you a long time ago about my past. Well, I never realized how much it would come to mean to me as the years went by. I had accepted long ago that I would not be a part of that life, but, well, sometimes fate steps in.'"

No, oh God, no. As he was reading the words, I was traveling back in time to when Mark and I were dating. We were talking about Josh, and he told me that he had done something stupid. He told me about a daughter he'd had, but at the time he was young and his only goal was to become an attorney. He hadn't wanted to get saddled down with a kid, so he had signed off his rights. He had mentioned the name Jazlyn, and it wasn't until this very moment that I remembered Josh telling me about the girl he liked. Oh God, this was going to kill Grant. Let me be wrong, please let me be wrong!

"Oh God, no, please don't say it Stuart." I would beg if I had to, get down on my knees and beg.

Stuart read the words that I feared the most, "'She's my daughter,'" I thought I would throw up, or pass out. The room began to spin, and I wondered what Grant was going to do when he realized what was being said.

I looked at the paper Stuart thrust at me, and bile filled my throat. It was true, Mark was Jazlyn's father. Would it come easier if it came from me?

I turned to Grant and took his hand. "Grant, Mark is Jazlyn's father."

He jerked his hand out of mine, "No, he isn't." His face was pale, and I wanted to reach out to him.

He turned to speak with Stuart. The conversation that Mark had with me years ago haunted my memory as I watched the anger and pain roll over Grant's features.

"He signed off his rights before she was born."

Grant glared at me, "You knew about this?" The deepness of his voice was a complete contrast to the wildness of his eyes.

"I didn't know it was Jazzy. I knew he had a daughter, but I had no idea it was Jazlyn." I was telling him the truth. All those years ago he had told me about it, but I didn't remember the girl's name.

Stuart went back to reading the letter, and I felt the flood of anger surge through the room as Grant stood up so fast and hard that the chair he had been sitting in moved backwards.

"'Rachel and Grant are to get married within six months of the reading of the will.'"

Mark had lost his mind! Married? Why the hell would we get married?

Stuart continued, ignoring our outburst. "'If they do not get married, Rachel will get nothing. Josh will inherit five hundred thousand on his thirtieth birthday, and Jazlyn will inherit one point five million when she turns thirty.'"

"You have got to be kidding me!" I practically yelled.

Stuart shook his head and peered up at Grant, "Mr. Murphy, if you could sit down, we can finish this."

Grant approached the desk. "We are finished. I want nothing to do with this. My daughter is my daughter, and she will never know differently. You can take that money and shove it up your ass!" He slammed his hand on the desk, "And there is no way in hell I would ever marry that woman!" He turned and pointed at me so hard it felt like he had stabbed me in the heart with a knife.

The color had returned in his face, but not his natural healthy tan. His face was beet red. He stalked to the door and yanked it open.

"My daughter will never see a penny of that money, you got that?" He didn't wait for an answer and the room vibrated as the door slammed closed behind him.

Stuart dropped the papers down on the desk, "Well, that went as well as I expected."

"I can't believe you did that to him. I can't believe Mark did that to him." I shook my head and wiped the tears from my eyes. How could Mark have done that to Grant?

"Rachel, trust me, I didn't want to do this." He rubbed his hands down his face. "Mark and I had an argument over this the day he gave it to me."

I sat there, numb. I didn't care about the money. I had no problem selling the house and moving to a smaller one. My concern was for the man who now felt he had lost everything. I reached down to the floor and lifted my purse. It felt like a fifty-pound load of bricks.

"I'm sorry, Rachel. Do you think he will come around? I would hate for you to lose all that money."

"Are you serious, Stuart? I don't give a damn about the money. I care about that man and the daughter he feels he just lost." I pointed at the door to make a point as I stood up. "I have no interest in that money, so you better start working on the trust funds for the kids, because the money is going to be gaining some serious interest in the coming years."

I left Stuart at his desk and walked to the elevator in a daze.

Oh, the twisted truth that just kept rearing its ugly face. Where did Mark come up with this stuff? How could he think that Grant and I getting married would be good, for anyone? What kind of distorted loyalty did he have? I punched the button for the elevator and waited for the car to arrive as I pondered how sane my deceased husband had been when he had written his will.

Chapter 22 – Grant

What just happened? I was in a disturbed vortex heading straight to hell. The elevator stopped at the bottom floor, and with it, my stomach dropped even further.

I brushed past people as I rushed to the front door. The sudden need for fresh air tightened my chest. I shoved open the front glass door and sucked in the cold winter air.

If I pinched myself, would I wake up and find that this was a bad dream? This couldn't be true. I stopped near the road and turned to look at the building. It was a six-story office building with glass all around. I stared at my reflection in the wall. What had happened to my life?

I turned in a circle. Was the rest of the world just as fucked up as I was? It didn't appear to be. People were talking on cellphones, drinking coffee, carrying on like nothing earth shattering was going on. I wanted to yell, drop down on my knees, and curse the world.

The building door opened again, and Rachel stepped out. She froze when she saw me. Was that pain in her face? Was she upset because she wasn't going to get her money now? She slowly made her way to stand in front of me.

"Are you alright, Grant?"

How could she ask me that? How could she be so calm after

she heard that her husband was my daughter's biological father, and that he wanted us to get married? Wait—

"Did you know about this? Were you in on this?"

She took a step back. "In on what?"

I waved at the building, "In on all that crap. Was the medical form made up? Did you know what your husband had planned?"

She stared at the ground before she met my gaze. Was that sympathy or embarrassment in her eyes? "I did not know that Mark had done any of that," she said evenly. "How could I have been involved? Do you think I knew he was going to die?" Her voice grew louder as she spoke. "I'm as shocked by all of this as you are."

"Don't pretend that you are upset about what I was told in there. You knew! I can't believe you didn't tell me." I turned and stared across the street.

Rachel put her arm on my bicep, and I shrugged her off. "I didn't know it was Jazzy, Grant. Mark told me about his daughter years ago, but he never mentioned her again."

There was so much emotion in her voice, and I couldn't figure out what it all meant. I was so angry that I couldn't think straight. "But you knew." I glared down at her. "You knew, and you didn't say anything."

"Grant, if I had known it was Jazzy, I would have told you. Don't you realize that?"

"Realize what? Ever since Mark died you have been avoiding me. You refused to return my calls. That sure seems like a guilty conscience to me."

"What?" She stepped closer and looked up into my face. I could smell her clean fresh scent, and my stomach clenched harder. "You think I knew that Mark was her father, and that is why I didn't call you? Give me a break!" she yelled. "I didn't call you because I didn't think it was a good idea for us to get involved, not after everything that had happened."

"What happened, Rachel?" I stood over her, watching her bright blue eyes widen and her breath come out in puffs of white.

She opened her mouth to speak, but closed it and stepped

back. "Nothing happened, Grant. Nothing happened then, and nothing will happen now." She spun to leave, and I grabbed her arm and stopped her.

"Aren't you upset by all of this?" I never saw the hand coming until it was too late, and then I only felt the sting from her palm making contact with my cheek.

"Are you kidding me?" She yanked her arm out of my hand, "I couldn't care less about the money or his stipulation, Grant. My concern in all of this is you! You and Jazlyn! I don't need Mark's money! I don't want his money, especially after all of this!" She looked like she wanted to say more, but she didn't.

"You really didn't know about this?" My anger was on a smooth simmer now, no longer trying to boil over.

Moisture filled her eyes and she shook her head, "No, I didn't know anything about it. My God, Grant, if I had, I would have told you. I wouldn't have hidden it to play some evil game on you. I cared about you Grant. I would never have done that to you."

I watched two tears spill over and slip down her cheeks as she turned and walked away. She said she had cared about me, did she not now? I watched her walk down the block before I turned in the opposite direction to walk the four blocks to the station. It didn't matter if she did care or not. There was no future for us.

****

Tom found me buried in paperwork two days later. I had avoided speaking with him since that ugly day.

"You look like you could use a beer, or two, or maybe three," he proposed as he dropped down in a chair next to my desk.

"I could use a dozen, but that wouldn't change the hell in my life. It would only give me a hangover," I grunted out.

"What's going on? I haven't spoken to you since you had that appointment at the lawyer's. Was it bad?"

Was it bad? It was worse than everything else that had happened all rolled into one. "It wasn't good."

"You're not getting sued or anything are you?" he asked as he eyed me carefully.

"I wish." I tossed my pen up on the desk, "I don't want to talk about it here."

"Alright, I get off at six. You want to go grab something to eat?"

"Yeah, let's do that. I gotta get this shit off my chest."

Three hours later, we slid into a booth at a Mexican joint down the road. We put our order in before Tom looked at me pointedly and asked, "So?"

"You are not real good about hinting around are you?" I stared at him and tried to figure out how to get started. "Rachel was there."

"Rachel? As in Dr. Rachel?" The waitress set our beers on the table, and I took a long gulp before I responded.

"Yeah, the wife of the man who was screwing Ilana."

"Blunt as ever, I see. So why were you in a meeting together?" Tom spun his beer on the table.

"For the reading of the will."

"Whose will?"

He took a drink and before he could swallow, I replied, "Her husband's."

He almost spat the beer over the table at me and ended up having to wipe his mouth with a napkin as the cold brew dribbled down his chin.

"What? Why were you there?"

I leaned back on the seat, "Because I was in the will."

"You have got to be kidding me? The man sleeps with your wife and puts you in his fucking will? Was he feeling guilty or something?"

"Or something." I glanced around the bar, "It wasn't the first time he had slept with Ilana."

"Well, I assume they had been seeing each other for a while, so they probably had sex quite a few times." He shrugged a sorry for the comment.

"I'm talking about over seventeen years ago."

Tom stared at me, the wheels in his head turning slowly, "He knew your wife when you guys first got together?"

"Yeah, it seems that they had an affair while I was off at the police academy." I squeezed my eyelids closed not wanting to see his face when I said the next words. "He got her pregnant."

Tom didn't say anything, so I finally opened my eyes and found him staring at me with his mouth hanging open.

The waitress put a bowl of chips and salsa on the table and walked away. Neither of us reached for them.

"You aren't saying what I think you're saying, are you?"

"Jazlyn is Mark Thompson's biological daughter." I couldn't believe I said that out loud.

"There's no way." Tom kept staring at me and I shifted in my seat.

"I saw the paternity test." Well, actually I didn't, but the look on Rachel's face was all I needed to see.

"So what does that mean?"

"It means nothing. I don't care what a test says. I'm her father and the only father she will ever know." I lifted my beer mug. "I turned down a million dollars."

"You what!" Tom sat back. "Wait a second, what million dollars?"

I started to tell Tom everything that happened in the meeting while we ate our dinner. Somehow I managed to swallow the food I was putting in my mouth. Over the last two days, I had come to the conclusion that Jazz would never have to know—well, not until she was thirty and learned she was a millionaire. She would probably be pissed, but I could explain it all to her then. She would be old enough to understand.

"So Mark wanted you to marry Rachel, and then your daughter would get the money, and Rachel and her son would get the money."

"Yeah, the kids will still get it, but when they are adults."

"And Rachel isn't getting anything?" He pushed his empty plate back.

I shook my head, "Nope, she's not. She said she didn't want the money."

"And you believe that?" he asked with a raised brow.

"Doesn't matter, if I did marry her, I'd have to tell Jazzy. I'm not doing that, and I have no intention of getting married again."

"I thought you liked Rachel?" He cocked his head and watched me. I tried not to shift in my seat and met his stare.

"I do, but not enough to destroy my daughter."

"How do you think this would destroy her? You would have enough money that you could send her to the best college."

"If I told her, she would think that I had lied to her for her entire life." I tossed my napkin down on the table and reached for my second beer bottle.

"It was Ilana that lied to you both. This wasn't your fault, and it sure as hell isn't Rachel's either."

I gasped at him, "You think I should marry Rachel?"

"Hell, yeah! You like her, and it's obvious that she likes you, too. Why not? You guys could get married, try it out for a year, the money is transferred, and then you could all split up and go your own way."

"You're crazy, Tom. I'm not going to marry Rachel to get the money for Jazzy to pay for college. I already told you that I have no intention of telling her about this."

He shook his head and scanned the room, "I think you are making a big mistake in not telling Jazz. No matter what you decide to do about Rachel. She deserves to know the truth about her mother and her...her sperm donor."

I knew he had been about to say father, and it pierced my heart. No one was her father but me. I had fallen in love with her the moment she was put in my arms. Through years of diapers, feedings, tears, and play, I had been her father. I was her father, and that was final.

"I'm not going to do it." I set my bottle down hard on the table.

"I think you are going to regret that later, Grant."

I refused to believe that I was making the wrong choice. There was no reason for Jazlyn to know, not now. I could tell her later when she was older. She had been through enough this year.

Yet, as I watched Tom pay the bill, I wondered if he was right and I would somehow regret all of this.

Chapter 23 – Rachel

Pain fades. It will take a while, but eventually it will fade. I kept telling myself that.

Yet, after a month and a half, I still felt the sting of Grant's accusations like they had just sprung from his mouth. How could he have thought I had anything to do with Mark's will? If I'd remembered what Mark told me all those years ago about his daughter, I would have told him the minute I realized it was her. Unlike my dead husband, I didn't keep secrets.

The money was the part that hurt even worse. For him to think I would be more upset over losing the money than over what we learned about Jazlyn thrust a sharp blade right through my soul. He had seen my large house and knew I was married to a prominent attorney, but what Grant didn't know was that my grandparents had left me enough to pay off my college loans and still give me a nice, large nest egg. I would eventually sell the house we lived in, but not until Josh was out of school. Then I could downsize when he left the nest.

I knew in my mind that his accusations only came from the pain of finding out the hard truth. I knew that he hadn't really been trying to hurt me—but the wound in my heart wouldn't listen to the common sense of my mind.

I glanced at the clock on the wall and couldn't wait for my shift to be over. I hadn't slept well in weeks, and working a sixteen-hour shift left me ragged to the bone.

"Dr. Wilde, can you see one more patient before you leave? It's an easy one, a laceration," Dr. Simpkins asked me as he approached the desk.

"Can't one of the physician's assistants stitch him up?" I asked as I dropped into a chair.

"I would, but the patient asked for you. He's in curtain five." He dropped the chart, and I fought not to groan.

Great, just what I needed: a frequent flyer coming in to get patched up again. It better not be that old guy, Ralph, who kept hitting on me and felt like the emergency room was his second home.

I stifled the sigh and snatched the chart off the desk. I could do stitches and be out of here in twenty minutes. I yanked the curtain back just as I glanced down at the chart. My eyes flew up and right into Grant's.

He had a large pack of gauze over the left side of his chest, but the rest of his torso was naked. I forced myself to keep eye contact.

"Detective Murphy, did you request me?" There was no way this man would want me within twenty feet of him, much less have asked for me.

Grant gave me a timid smile, "Actually, I did."

My heart stuttered. "Why?" I asked just as Susan stopped next to me.

"Well, isn't that nice," she whispered into my ear, and I cut her an annoyed glance before she chuckled and walked away.

"Because I knew you would do a good job," he replied.

Of course, it was my skills he wanted, not me. I knew he didn't want to have anything to do with me. The doctor in me should have been proud that he knew I would do a damned good job, but the doctor was tired and the woman was emotional.

I looked over my shoulder. I wasn't sure I should be doing this. I was so tired, and the smoldering look in his eye made me nervous. What if I messed up? I didn't think I could take him looking down at me with anger again.

Susan and two other nurses stared at me with silly grins on their faces. I rolled my eyes and stepped further into the area, pulling the curtain closed behind me to keep the prying eyes at bay.

"Are you sure you want me to do this? There are other doctors that can help you. I know I'm not your favorite person." That was the understatement of the year.

His eyes meandered down the length of my body before coming back to my face, "I never said that."

Did he really just check me out? "You didn't have to. I think the last time we saw each other, you made it crystal clear."

He sighed, "Come here, Rachel. I need to tell you something."

Tell me something? We had been having a conversation already, so why do I need to get closer? I hesitated for a moment, but I finally moved to stand near his gurney. I fought to keep my eyes on his face and not allow them to absorb the toned chest that called out to be caressed.

"I'm sorry," he said when I stopped fidgeting.

"You have nothing to be sorry for."

"Rachel," he shook his head and winced. I glanced down at the gauze and saw blood starting to bleed through. "I should never have taken my anger out on you."

I could do one of two things here. I could accept his apology, sew him up, and send him on his way, or I could sit here and argue with him and fight the temptation he caused within me for a much longer period of time. Okay, there was a third, but while he might be inclined to use my medical services, I doubt he would want anything more from me. I went with option one.

"Apology accepted." I set the clipboard down, "What did you do to yourself?" I washed my hands and dried them.

"That's it? You're going to accept my apology that fast?" He stared at me with surprise on his face.

"What do you want me to do? Argue with you? I'm too tired for that," I pulled out a pair of nitrile gloves and pulled them on, "and by the look of the circles under your eyes, you're too tired for it, too, so let me get you fixed up and you can go home and get some sleep."

"Rachel, I'd like to talk about this with you."

I moved a rolling tray over to the side of his bed and avoided looking him in the face.

"Grant, there really is nothing to talk about." I pulled the gauze back and wiped the remaining blood from his skin. "Hmm."

"Did you just 'hmm' my chest?" he laughed.

Oh, God! I said that aloud? "No," I said quickly, "I was looking at the laceration."

"You were not. I saw you look over my chest, and you said hmm."

I felt my cheeks blaze with heat and knew I was busted. "Okay, so yeah, fine. Unprofessional of me, I know." I turned to throw the soiled gauze away and get a grip on myself. When I turned around, Grant reached out and took my hand.

"Rachel," he said huskily and I met his gaze.

He was only a foot away, and even though I had on gloves, I could feel the heat of his hand racing through my skin and up my arm. Were these the first words and first touch all over again? My heart thumped in my chest, my mouth was dry, and I had quite a powerful, nonmedical urge to ravage the man in front of me. I wanted to feel the anticipation of the first kiss creep from head to toe.

"Rachel, I like that you said hmm." He grinned at me, and my cheeks burned hotter as I looked away and tried not to bounce up and down on my toes.

"How about I sew you up now?" He laughed quietly and I picked up a needle to give him a shot to numb the area. "So how did you do this?"

"A fence jumped out and snagged me." He winced again as I pushed against the wound.

"Jumped out at you, huh?" I peered up at him from under my bangs.

"Yeah, you have to watch out for fences, sometimes they get pissed off and just jump right out in front of you when you are chasing a guy."

"Oh, so this was at work?" I cleaned the area around the laceration. "I didn't realize you worked so late."

"I don't normally, unless I get called in. We had a warrant for a guy who shot a store owner. He took off, and we chased him through some backyards. I got snagged by the fence."

"You weren't wearing your vest?" I straightened my back and stared at him.

"I was. I would never go out for something like this without one. Somehow, I managed to catch it from the side and it snagged my vest at the same time and went under it."

I picked up the needle and stared at the laceration and then beyond. I had laid my head right there in the center of his chest. "You need to stop looking at me like that," he whispered and I jumped.

"Sorry," I muttered and turned to busy myself with something, anything, so I wasn't facing him.

"Don't be sorry," he replied. When I turned back to him, his head leaned back against the gurney and his eyes were closed. His eyelashes fluttered as he held them closed.

Oh, that didn't make this any easier, but at least he couldn't see the desire in my eyes as I allowed them to roam over his taut skin.

"Please stop looking at me like that and sew me up. If you don't, you will find yourself lying on this gurney with me."

I sucked in a quick lungful of air and met his heated blue eyes. "Maybe I should get someone else to do this. I seem to have a problem staying focused this morning."

"No, I want you." I saw the same desire I felt reflected back in his eyes. Good Lord, give me strength.

"Lie back and relax, I will have this done in a few minutes." I forced myself to be professional and put the nine stitches into his chest as quickly and carefully as I could. I stood back to look at my handiwork. "There might be a small scar, but I think most of it will be a clean heal."

He checked out the sutures, "Wow, nice job."

"Alright, well, I'll have the nurses get your papers for you and then one of your buddies can get you home." I stepped back from the gurney and tore my gloves off my hands. "I'll have the nurse bring you some pain meds, unless you are one of those macho guys who won't take pain medication."

He laughed, "No, I'll take the pain meds, if only to get a good night's sleep, for once." He shrugged, "Can I borrow a phone? I don't have my cell. I think I lost it during the chase. I need to call someone to come get me." He swung his legs over the side.

I looked up at the clock on the wall. "Actually, if you can give me a few minutes, I'm getting off. I could give you a ride home."

He eyed me carefully, "Only if you will allow me to buy you breakfast as a thank you for giving me the lift."

"You don't need to do that."

He stood up and reached for his shirt, "No, you're right, I don't, but I haven't eaten all night, and if I am going to take pain medicine, I could use some food in my stomach, and I'm too tired to cook something at home."

I smiled, "Alright, give me a few minutes, and I'll come get you when I'm ready to go."

I walked away trying not to skip as I approached the desk and three pairs of watchful eyes. We were going to have breakfast together. No big deal, people eat together all the time, and it doesn't mean anything.

"And?" Susan asked.

"And what? The guy needed stitches. Stop looking at me like that." I busied myself with notes on the chart and tried to ignore the heat in my cheeks and the snickering of the nurses. We were going to have breakfast together!

Ten minutes later, I grabbed my purse and walked back into the emergency room. Grant leaned against the wall, favoring his left arm.

"You sure you don't want me to take you straight home? You

look like you are in a lot of pain."

"I'd be in even more if I didn't eat something." He winked. "You ready?"

We went out to the parking lot and climbed into my BMW SUV. Grant glanced around the interior of the car, "Nice. I haven't been in one of these before."

"Thanks. I just bought it a week ago, a present to myself." I grinned at him.

"Must be nice to be able to afford a present like this," he remarked and then fell silent. I knew he didn't mean anything by it, but it stung just the same.

I pulled out of my space and asked him where he wanted to go. He mentioned a small diner on the outskirts of town, and I turned the car in that direction.

"Grant, I want you to know something." I didn't take my eyes off the road, afraid of what I would see on his face. Things had been going smoothly, and I worried that his comment about the car would take him back to feeling the anger he displayed the last time I saw him.

"You don't need to tell me anything, Rachel," he said to the side window.

"You're right; I don't need to tell you, I want to." I flicked a glance his way and looked at his profile. Even from the quick lock, I could see how tired he was. "I was not angry with your decision."

"What decision?" he asked.

"The one about taking the money, or should I say, not taking the money. If I were in your shoes, I probably would have done the same thing, and I'm not upset with you over all of that."

"Okay," he replied quietly.

Neither of us spoke again until we pulled up to the diner. As I parked, he turned to me, "Thank you, I was worried you were angry with me about that. I had no idea what your financial situation was, and I wondered if I hurt you by not allowing you to get the money."

"Nope, as you can see, I'm just fine without it. Come on, let's get some food in you and then we can get to bed." I popped the door open and climbed out to meet him on the sidewalk in front of my car.

"Are you coming with me?" he asked, and I stared at him.

"That's normally what buying someone breakfast means, you eat with them."

"I wasn't talking about breakfast," he said huskily, and it took me a moment to realize he was talking about going to bed. My cheeks flamed in the cool air.

I heard his throaty chuckle, and it sent tingles all the way to my toes.

"Alone, not together, I meant go to bed alone." I walked past him to the door, unable to meet his eyes. If he had seen my face, he would have known I had just lied.

How did he cause giddy feelings to course through my body when I barely knew him? I had been married to Mark for years, and couldn't remember one time he'd made me feel giddy—or Peter either. Although I was young when Pete and I were together, the feelings I'd had for him were stronger than with Mark, but nothing like the things I felt with Grant around.

We settled down into a booth and opened menus. The waitress walked away with our orders before we finally looked at one another again.

"Sorry about that comment, I'm tired and I was being silly." Grant gave me a lopsided grin.

The waitress returned with the coffee pot and filled our cups.

"It's alright, I get it. I say dumb things when I'm tired too." I added sugar to my cup.

"I didn't say it was dumb." He looked at me as he set the creamer tin down. "I was flirting with you."

I stopped mid-stir, "Why?"

"Why was I flirting with you? What, did no one ever tell you how it works and why people do it?" He smirked at me over his cup as he lifted it to his mouth. His lips curled around the cup lip, and I shifted in my seat.

"I know how it works, Grant. I want to know why you were flirting with me."

"To be honest, I have no clue." He set the cup down, "What I do know is that I can't seem to help myself when I'm around you, and," he leaned forward over the table, "I can't seem to get you off my mind."

Just like that, my heart tripped over itself, and I knew I was in deep, deep trouble.

Chapter 24 – Grant

Why did I like flirting with her? Because it seemed like the most natural thing in the world to do when she was around.

If you had told me ten hours ago that I would be sitting in a diner eating breakfast with Dr. Rachel Wilde, I would have laughed in your face. Yet, here I sat, and I couldn't think of one other place I'd rather be.

For over a month, I had refused to consciously think about the doctor with the bright blue eyes. After the night I told Tom, I swore him to secrecy and decided then that I would not tell Jazlyn the truth until I absolutely had to.

I went through days where I questioned my decision and woke up mornings frustrated from seeing the anguish on Rachel's face in my dreams. Why had I accused her of knowing the truth? It wasn't fair to do that, and someday, I needed to apologize for it.

I didn't realize that my apology would come while I lay on an emergency room bed waiting to have a gash repaired.

An ambulance had brought me in, and when they had me squared away in the curtained room, I asked the nurse if Rachel was working. The cat-that-ate-the-canary look passed over the nurse's features as she said she was.

The moment Rachel walked into the room, I knew that I was

no longer angry with her. In fact, I doubted my frustration had ever really been directed towards her. She had done nothing wrong, and I had used her as a scapegoat. I was determined to gain her friendship again.

She looked exhausted, and her pale lavender scrubs were wrinkled from a long night of work. How tempting it would be to remove the clothing and curl up with her on my lap again and sleep. I hadn't slept well since the night she had snuggled on my chest.

The vibration that left her throat as she glanced over my chest went straight into my groin, and I fought to keep my hands at my side and not tangle them in her hair. Butterflies took flight in my stomach and tried to tug my heart out of my chest.

It took all my concentration to lie still while she worked on the area above my left pec. Her gloves were cool on my skin, and more than once, they rubbed over the nipple on that side. Each time, it sent a jolt straight down.

She was almost as flustered as I was, but she was much better about putting her feelings aside and doing her job. Could she keep her cool if I reached up and brought her lips to mine? I clenched my eyelids more tightly. Was there a way to get this woman out from under my skin? Did I even want to?

I was happily surprised when she offered to take me home and thankful that a truce had been called between us. From the moment I saw her, I knew that I wanted to continue seeing her. I would do it right this time and find a way for us to get to know each other better. I wanted to see where this connection would take us, and not because someone else wanted us to have one.

I sat in her car and wondered how much money she really had. Small town detectives didn't make enough to drive brand new BMWs off the lot or live in huge houses. Did she think less of me because I wasn't a big shot lawyer and drove a Ford instead of an expensive foreign car?

I guess it didn't really matter, but in my mind I wondered if I could ever be enough for a woman like her.

The money came up again as we arrived at the diner, and I

wasn't sure what to say. So many times I had wondered if by walking away from the stipulations of the will, it would cause her financial worry. Seeing as she had a new car, I didn't think it had.

The fact that she said she probably would have done the same thing meant the world to me, more than she would ever know. She made a comment about going to bed, and I could once again imagine her body curled against mine on the couch. Hunger pains not associated with my stomach gnawed at my insides.

She blushed again and I thought she couldn't be any more beautiful than she was at that moment.

We sat and ordered, and I noted that she put a packet of sweetener into her coffee. "I was flirting with you," I stated and watched her wide eyes flip up to mine.

Why was I flirting with her? Hell if I knew. I was only just now beginning to realize that I really wanted to get to know her better.

"What I do know is that I can't seem to help myself when I'm around you, and, I can't seem to get you off my mind," I said honestly. "I haven't seen you in what five, six weeks, and all that time, you kept swirling back into my mind."

"You were angry with me. Of course I kept coming to mind. Those things can be a distraction." She lifted her mug and held it with both hands.

"You were a distraction, but it wasn't because I was angry." I wrapped my hands around my mug, "Rachel, can I ask you a question?"

"Yes," she said softly.

"Do you feel it? When we are together, do you feel the chemistry between us?" I gestured between the two of us. I knew she had to feel it, but would she admit it?

She set her mug down on the table, "Yes, Grant, I do, and from the moment I met you, it has scared the hell out of me."

"Me, too." We shared a smile and I reached over and pulled one of her hands off her mug to take it in mine. "Why don't we stop being scared of it and find out what it means."

"Grant, I'm not sure we should do that." She took her hand

back. "This whole thing, with how we met and how our spouses were together," she shook her head. "It's weird."

"No weirder than meeting at a bar or on the internet." I thought for a moment, "Besides, it's not Ilana and Mark who introduced us, it was our children."

"True." She leaned back as our plates were set down in front of us.

I went to reach for my plate and forgot about the stitches; I hissed when they pulled.

"Here, let me cut that up for you," she reached for my plate and pulled it over to her side, "that way you can keep your left arm down."

I watched her cut up my sausage and then my omelet into manageable pieces. I could not remember the last time someone had done something like that for me.

She pushed the plate back to me and dug into her own meal. I took a few bites before I set my fork down. "Thank you for doing that."

A tiny bit of color graced her cheeks, "You're welcome. I'm sorry, I probably should have asked you first."

"You're cute when you blush," I blurted. What am I, twelve? The color deepened. "So what do you say?"

She stared at me while she chewed and swallowed, "About what?"

"About us. Can we start over?"

"Do you really want to?" she asked.

"Yes, I do." I shoved my fork into my mouth and chewed. She watched me, and after I swallowed, I looked at her carefully. Maybe she did feel something, but was she embarrassed to be seen with a man like me. "Unless, of course, I'm not good enough for you." I wiped my mouth and leaned back in my seat.

"What?" she spouted. "Why wouldn't you be good enough? Where did that even come from?"

"You're a doctor, a well-paid doctor. I'm just a small-town detective."

Anger flashed in her eyes as they clenched into slits, "You think I wouldn't want to date you, because you're a cop and I'm a doctor?"

I didn't respond. I was too enthralled with the expressions crossing her face. Surprise, indignation, alarm, and fury all ran riot over her features.

"How dare you?" She dropped her napkin down, "Do I really seem like a snob to you? Like I'm better than you? My God, Grant. I can't believe you would say something like that."

I glanced at the table next to us and realized they were listening. I leaned forward so I could speak softly to her. "No, I am not saying you are. I'm asking you a question. If that's how you feel, that's fine, I get it."

"That's not how I feel, at all." She crossed her arms over her chest and glared at me.

"Then how do you feel?" I retorted.

"Honestly?" I nodded at her. "I'm confused."

"About what?"

The waitress approached our table. "Is there anything else I can get you two?" Rachel shook her head and I asked for the check.

"Can this wait until we are in the car? I don't want to talk about this here."

"Sure."

I got the feeling I wasn't going to like what she had to say. I paid the bill, and we went back out to her car.

We were halfway to my house before she finally spoke. "Grant, why do you want to get to know me?"

"I told you that."

"No, you only told me that you felt chemistry with me, not why you wanted to get to know me."

What other reason would there be? I felt something for her, I liked her. I thought she was gorgeous. I didn't think there had to be any other reason. "That's not enough?"

She cut me a glance, "Are you looking for someone to sleep with?"

"What? No. I want to get to know you." She turned on to my street.

"Is it because of the money?" she asked quietly as she pulled up in front of my house.

I tensed, "What money?"

She turned in her seat, "The money from the will. Did you change your mind?"

Anger seeped into my limbs. I didn't want the goddamned money! I wanted her. "That was the last thing I was thinking about."

She scrutinized me for a few moments, "Are you sure?"

"Are you kidding me, Rachel?" I threw my right hand up in the air, "Do you not remember me telling you and the attorney that there was no way in hell that I was going to marry you for the money?"

As soon as the words left my mouth, I knew I'd made a mistake. That wasn't what I meant, not really. I had meant there was no way I would do what Mark wanted me to do. I had played in his game long enough. If things were meant to be, then they would come on their own, not on his timeline.

"Oh, I remember what you said perfectly." She turned away from me, "I hope you feel better, Grant."

"Rachel, that's not what I meant."

"I know exactly what you meant, Grant. I heard you the first time. I sure as hell don't need a reminder of one of the most embarrassing days of my life. Get out of my car, please."

"Rachel, I told you that's not what I meant." I began to reach over to touch her, and she leaned against the door.

"Get out of my car, Grant. We have nothing else to say to one another." I heard the hurt and anguish in her voice and wished like hell I could take back what I had said. I reached for the door handle.

"I'll get out, but not before I say this. That day, when I said I would never marry you, it wasn't because I didn't like you, or the thought of being with you bothered me. Just the opposite, I said that because no one, not Ilana, not an attorney, and not your dead husband are going to dictate how I live my life and who I love." I shoved the door open and climbed out of the car. "Do you understand that?" I asked pointedly from outside the vehicle.

She didn't respond, didn't look my way, and for a brief moment, I thought she was going to break down in tears. Instead she put the car in gear, took a deep breath, and said, "Thank you for breakfast. Goodbye, Grant, close the door."

"Goodbye, Dr. Wilde." I slammed the door shut and stepped back as she pulled away. She had no idea what I was thinking or how I felt, and obviously she wasn't going to listen. I stalked up to the front door, and it opened as I approached it. Why did I even bother?

"Dad, where is your car?" Jazlyn asked as I stepped into the house.

"At work," I stated gruffly.

"Why? Who gave you a ride home?" She followed me into the kitchen.

"I cut myself at work. I got a ride from the hospital." I shucked my jacket off and dropped it on the table.

"Oh, my God! Look at your shirt! Are you okay?" She came to stand in front of me, eyeing the red stain and tear on my clothing.

"Yes, sweetheart, I'm fine. It's only a few stitches." That were lovingly applied by a very sexy and aggravating doctor.

"You sure?" she asked as she studied me. I leaned down and kissed her forehead.

"Yes, I'm fine." I turned to get a glass of water so I could take the pain medication.

"Who brought you home?" she asked as she jumped up on the counter.

"Dr. Wilde. She was getting off work and said she could drop me off." I filled my glass.

"So does that mean that I can talk to Josh again?" her voice lifted happily.

Right after the whole mess in the attorney's office I had told

Jazlyn to stay away from Josh. I was afraid that he would hear about everything and say something to her.

"No, that does not mean you can talk to Josh. It was easier to have her drop me off than to call someone from the station."

"Come on, Dad. I don't get why I can't talk to Josh. He's my friend. I'm dating his best friend, he's dating mine. It's a little hard to avoid him," she whined.

"Jazz, I said to stay away from Josh." I dumped the pills on to the counter from the little packet they had given me at the hospital.

"Why?" she whined again.

"I'm sorry, Jazz, I'm your father, and I'm telling you to stay away from Josh." I popped the pills in my mouth and lifted the glass to my mouth.

Her voice grew quiet, "Are you sure?"

I choked on the water. Was she asking me if I was really her father? Had Josh already said something? I coughed the water out of the wrong pipe and looked at her, "Excuse me? I *am* your father!"

Chapter 25 – Rachel

Damn it! Damn it! Damn it! I slapped my hand on the steering wheel as I pulled out onto the main roadway.

What the hell was I thinking? Why did I push the issue? I didn't really think that Grant had changed his mind about the whole issue, but the thought crossed my mind. How could it not? His daughter stood to inherit a million dollars if he married me.

A million dollars…I didn't want Grant to want me for the money. I wanted Grant to want me! The woman! Me!

What a fool I was to bring it up. Hearing him reiterate that he wouldn't marry me, no matter what the reason, stung deep, but even I knew I didn't want to marry Grant, especially just because we all would benefit. If I did ever get married, it would be my choice, and I would marry whom I wanted, when I wanted.

Wasn't that exactly what Grant had just said? That he wasn't going to allow anyone else to determine whom he would marry?

Yes—and I got pissed off at him, for no other reason than because I could—because I was afraid of what he made me feel, and because I barely knew him. Why would I even think of marrying a man I barely knew?

A little voice inside my mind spoke softly, because you know that you two were made for each other. One look was all it took to break open the dam that closed off my heart. One word spoken, and I was already falling for him.

With Grant, I felt safe. Was that because he was a cop? No, it was because he was a man, who cared. How many men would hold you all night long and not take advantage of you? He hadn't even kissed me, and yet I felt as if our bodies were meant to be together.

I drove home mulling over the whole thing. It didn't matter that my heart thought we should be together. Common sense said differently, and I relied on my intelligence and common sense to get me through my days. Emotions and feelings had no place in my life.

Wasn't that why I had married Mark? It was common sense that got us together, common sense that we ended up getting married and building a relationship on mutual friendship. How many times did I tell him I loved him?

"Huh…" I said to the empty car as I tried to recall the last time I had said those three words. Wait…did I ever say them to him? Had I loved him at all?

"My God, I can't remember ever telling my husband that I loved him." Not even on my wedding day did I remember saying that to him, and I wracked my brain to remember him saying it to me. We married out of convenience. We never spoke about children. We never talked about the future. Or did we? I pondered this for a few moments. We had talked about taking another trip, but that was a while ago. We had never spoken about having children and decided we didn't want any. Was that a clue? A clue to what?

I pulled into the garage and sat staring at the wall in front of my car for a long time.

Josh pulled the inside door open. "Mom, you alright?" he called out to me.

I opened the door and climbed out of the car. "Yeah."

"Why were you sitting in the car?" he asked me as I walked past him into the house.

"I was thinking." I dropped my purse down on the counter and hung my keys on the hook by the fridge.

"Thinking about what?" Josh asked as he pulled a carton of orange juice out of the fridge.

"Pour me a glass of that, please." I toed off my sneakers and pulled out a stool.

Josh poured two glasses and slid one over the granite countertop towards me. "You didn't tell me what you were thinking about."

"Nothing important." And it wasn't really.

"Did you have a rough night?" Josh pulled up the stool next to me and leaned back on it.

I studied him for a moment, "Josh, would you do me a favor?"

He shrugged, "I guess."

"Would you please stop growing up? You are becoming a man right before my eyes, and it depresses the hell out of me."

Josh laughed, "I thought you wanted me to grow up." His cellphone buzzed, and he lifted it to read the screen.

"I wanted you to grow up to a certain extent, but now, you are growing too fast. What am I going to do when you go off to college?" Josh was the one man that I did love, no doubt about it.

Josh typed a response and set his phone down. "Did you have a fight with Grant?"

I stared at his phone: Jazlyn. I climbed off the stool, "Shouldn't you be getting ready for school?"

"I leave for the bus stop in five minutes. What happened this morning?"

"Josh, I'm not going to talk to you about that." I went towards the stairs, "I'm going to bed. Will you be home tonight?"

"I have practice after school, but I plan on being home. Why?"

"Just asking, I'm off tonight." I began to climb the stairs, "Have a good day at school."

"Hey, Mom," he called up to me as I reached the top landing.

"Yeah," I turned to him.

"You know, if you want to talk about it, I could listen. I might not have any advice, but I am a guy you know. I might be able to help you out."

"Josh, you really need to stop growing up." I walked away before he could say anything else or see the tears. I wiped the moisture off my face with two angry swipes and yanked off my shirt, tossing it at the laundry basket. I missed. Who cares!

Josh was going to be off to college in another year, and I would still be alone: no husband, no life, no son. Anyone want to come to my pity party? There is plenty of room.

I turned on the shower and stepped in once the water had warmed. The spray ran over my head, and a sob escaped my chest. Everything came to a head at that moment, and I bent over and wrapped my arms around my waist as I cried.

Tears fell for the man who was dead, the one I had never loved. They poured out for the son who was growing up so fast and would soon leave the nest, and for the loneliness that I felt so terribly deep inside of me.

I cried for Grant, and the knowledge of the secret that had been kept from him for seventeen years. I sobbed harder for the girl who would one day find out about the lie.

The drops streamed down like the spray of the water over my back—but unlike the water, they did not cleanse me.

****

A month later, I stood in the emergency room talking softly to a woman who had been assaulted by her husband. She had marks around her neck from where he had choked her. The whites of her eyes were bloodshot from the strain of the assault. He had choked her until she was almost dead, and I knew the police would be arriving soon to speak with her.

"Betsy, is this the first time this has happened?" I sat on the edge of the bed and rested a hand on her forearm. Black and blue marks were beginning to show there, too.

She shook her head, "No, he choked me once before, but not this bad."

"And you stayed with him?" I asked and saw the pain in her eyes as she looked away from me. "Betsy, I'm not judging you I know how hard it is to get away from an abuser. I'm only asking so I can make sure you get the help that you need."

"That night, he threatened to kill me if I tried to leave. That's what happened tonight. I told him I was going to move to my mom's and he freaked out."

I handed her a tissue to wipe the black streaks from her mascara running down her cheeks. "Have you called the domestic violence hotline?"

"No, I was afraid to." She blew her nose and I handed her another tissue.

"Well, I think that is going to be the next step. I'm going to call them and have someone come here and talk to you. They can help you, Betsy."

She nodded, "I need help."

"We'll get some for you." I patted her hand and stood up. The curtain behind me pulled open, and Betsy's eyes flashed behind me. Her face paled, and I spun around afraid that her husband would be standing there.

"Detective Murphy, can I help you?" I rolled my shoulders back and moved closer to Betsy's side.

"Dr. Wilde, I came to speak with the victim." His voice was curt, but professional.

"May I speak with you for a moment outside?" I asked, and he nodded and stepped aside. "Betsy, I'll be right back." I patted her arm again gently.

I walked past Grant and wondered if he could hear my heart thumping in my chest. Over the last month, I had forced myself not to think about him. Seeing him now sparked all the thoughts I had kept hidden to come to the surface. I took a deep breath while we walked away from her treatment area.

"Is the man in custody?" I asked when I turned to face him.

"Not yet, he took off before the officers got there. That's why I need her statement, so I can file charges."

"Have your officers been to that house often?" I tried to avoid looking at him, and he appeared to be doing the same by scanning the room over my head.

"Unfortunately, yes, at least once a month for the last six or seven months. Did she tell you anything?" he asked and finally looked me in the eye.

The dark blue of his eyes brought a shiver to my spine that I couldn't quite stop. Grant glanced down to my shoulders for a millisecond.

"She told me that he did the same thing a month ago and that he threatened to kill her if she left him." I broke eye contact and watched an orderly wheel a gurney into another treatment area.

"Okay, well, hopefully she will stick to that story, and we can prosecute him. I'll get her to give me a statement, and we will go from there." He turned to walk away, but stopped and looked back. "Thank you for your help."

"Grant, I'm going to call domestic violence and have an advocate come out to see her here. She said she wants help."

He nodded and walked away, a crack made its way down the center of my heart as he left.

The tension eased from my shoulders as he disappeared behind the curtain, and I went to the desk to make the phone call.

Susan leaned down next to me when I hung up the phone. "That man just keeps getting better looking. If you don't want him, let me know."

I almost growled but held it back, "He's all yours." I stood up, grabbed another chart, and went to see my next patient.

Forty minutes later I was writing notes on a chart when Grant walked up to me, "Dr. Wilde, I'm sorry to bother you, but I have a question."

The question—Do you want me?—flashed through my mind, and I heaved it aside. "What can I do for you, Detective Murphy?" I kept writing in the chart.

"Did you get a chance to call domestic violence? If you didn't, I was going to call them."

"Yes, I did call them. They said they would be here within the hour." I stared at the papers in front of me, not seeing a camred thing.

"Okay, thank you." From the corner of my eye, I studied the cream dress shirt and burgundy tie he wore. I refused to look up at him. He began to step away, but paused. "Rachel," he said softly and touched my forearm.

My body froze while every nerve ending burned. I eyed his hand and followed his arm up to his shoulder, right up his thick neck, and over his strong jaw to his wide lips. I flashed my focus up to his eyes and saw the same yearning I felt reflected back.

"Rachel, can't we talk?" he asked.

"I think we are talking, Detective Murphy." I went back to staring at my papers blindly. The only image I saw was the need in his eyes.

"That's not what I meant, and you know it." He stepped closer and leaned down to whisper in my ear. "Rachel, I can't stop thinking about you. Can't we please talk this out?"

The soft flow of his words over the sensitive skin of my ear brought goose bumps to my arms, and I was tempted to throw myself in his arms and say yes.

"I don't believe that would be a good idea." I forced myself to make eye contact, "Grant, no matter how we might feel, things would never work with us, not with all the twisted events of our pasts."

Sadness flitted through his eyes, but he kept contact. "We can get past all that." He reached up to touch my cheek and I knew if he did, I'd melt to the floor at his feet.

"Dr. Wilde," Jane called out from behind me, and I turned away from Grant with a wildly-beating muscle in my chest.

"We have a gunshot victim coming in, four-minute ETA." She rushed off to one of the trauma rooms.

I picked up my clipboard. "I have to go. Take care of yourself, Grant." Before he could open his mouth to reply, I walked away and dropped the chart down on the desk as I headed to the trauma room.

Chapter 26 – Grant

I did not believe that we couldn't get past all the fucked up things that had happened to us. To us! We didn't do them. They were done to us, by people we cared about. We were the victims here and as such we had the right to move forward with our lives without feeling guilty.

Thinking of being a victim reminded me I still had work to do. I walked back to the curtain and slipped inside with Betsy. She had given me a full statement, not just of the events of the night, but a complete history of all the times he had abused her. She also gave me all the hospitals and doctors that had seen her with injuries.

I had already talked to the district attorney's office, and we were going to move forward with attempted homicide charges.

A few minutes after I returned to the curtain, another woman walked in. She nodded at me and immediately focused on Betsy by moving to her side and telling her she was from the local domestic violence center. I stood off to the side as they talked, keeping one ear on them and one ear on the commotion on the other side as the gunshot victim was brought in and treated.

I heard nurses rushing around and a few doctors throwing out medical jargon that I didn't understand. Every so often, I would catch a word or two from Rachel.

I moved to the edge of the curtain and pulled it back a few inches to watch all the movement. I could only imagine that this was what happened when they had brought Ilana in. The room across from us had eight people in it from what I could see. All of them using equipment or handing things to the doctors. Rachel's shoulders were hunched down as she worked on the patient's chest.

I assumed it was a man, as the boots that were facing me were large and had heavy tread. On the floor under the gurney was a blue rag. I stared at it for a moment longer and realized it was a bandana. It dawned on me that Rachel very well might be working on a gang member.

She was elbow deep in her work along with all the other people in the room. No one cared that he belonged to a gang, to them he was a life, and they were trying to do everything they could to save him.

I observed for a few more minutes and absently wondered who had shot him. Was it a rival gang attack? Did he piss off one of his buddies?

The domestic violence advocate pulled me from my spying when she asked me a question. I turned from the curtain to speak with her and the victim for a few minutes as I learned what safety plan they were going to put in place, and how I would handle the charges and prosecution.

We were just finishing up when a scream pierced the emergency room and multiple voices started to yell. I spun around and moved towards the curtain as another scream rent the air and shots were fired.

I yanked my gun from my holster and peered out from behind the edge of the curtain. A man with a black shirt and a red bandana tied around his head stood in the door of the trauma room firing rounds. I stepped out and took aim at his back.

My eyes made contact with the front sights at the same time that my finger found its place on the trigger. I pulled, once, twice, three times in quick succession and watched the subject jerk and arch his back as each bullet entered him from behind. The gun he held was still clenched in his hand, and when he tensed, he fired one last round into the ceiling above him. The fluorescent light exploded. Sparks and glass rained over the emergency room area.

He fell to the floor, and for four seconds, there was almost silence. Only the sounds of the hospital equipment beeping and chirping around us could be heard.

I held my firearm out in front of me as I approached the subject while carefully scanning the area to see if anyone else would pop out and surprise me. I stepped on a piece of glass and felt the crunch as I heard a scream come from the trauma room.

My eyes left the subject to look deeper into the room, and my heart stopped. There on the floor, with blood spreading over her back, was Rachel. I froze.

People rushed around me trying to get into the room with Rachel. "Can you move him so we can get to her?" A nurse called out as she raced past me.

"No, I can't move him." I stopped beside the gang member and felt for a pulse. He was dead. I stood and moved to Rachel's side.

"We need to get her up to OR stat." A doctor stated as he tried to work on her on the floor. "We need a gurney in here so we can move her."

"You can't move that guy. Put the gurney outside the door, I'll carry her out." I shouted and leaned down to scoop Rachel up.

The doctor grabbed my arm, "Be careful moving her, we don't know what the bullets hit."

I nodded to him, and together we rolled Rachel over as gently as possible. Her face was pale, almost as white as Ilana's had been the last time I saw her in the hospital.

No! No fucking way was I going to lose someone else. No I lifted her while the doctor supported her neck, and within a few seconds we had her on a gurney and they were racing away with her. I watched them disappear on an elevator that an orderly had been holding open. The door closed and my knees almost went out from underneath me.

I took in the scene around me. Some people were silent, staring at the body, or at me. Some were crying and consoling others. A shout echoed through the area and some of the bystanders screamed as several officers came in holding their firearms out in front of them.

"This part of the scene is secure, one perp, he's on the floor over there. I don't know if he had anyone else with him on the outside." I put my hands up in case they didn't know who I was and saw alarm cross some of their faces. I glanced at my hands and found them covered in blood, Rachel's blood. My stomach heaved. I turned and dashed to the closest treatment area where I bent over the sink and vomited.

Someone handed me paper towels, and I wiped my face and hands after washing them. I turned to find one of the nurses I always saw Rachel talking to. I stopped drying my hands and stared at her.

Please God, don't tell me she died. Please! I prayed.

"Do you by chance have Josh's cellphone number?" she queried. "I wanted to call him and have him come to the hospital."

"I do, but I don't think it's a good idea to tell him over the phone. I'll have an officer go pick him up and bring him in."

She put her hand on my arm, "I'm so sorry. She's gonna make it, we have to believe that." She blinked away tears and turned to leave. I reached out for her arm and stopped her.

"Thank you. I can't lose her."

She put her hand over mine as I held her forearm, "I pray that you don't. I'll bring you a shirt to change into so you can go upstairs and wait."

"Grant! What the hell happened?" Tom turned the corner into the treatment room. "Are you alright?"

"I'm fine." I sank down on the empty gurney behind me as my knees began to shake.

Tom put his hand on my shoulder. "What happened?"

"I was here interviewing a victim from a DV incident. They had a gunshot victim come in, he was Crip. I didn't see the other guy come in, a Blood, but when he started shooting, I fired on him. I was standing over there." I pointed to the curtain I had been in. "Casings are probably scattered now with all the movement in here. I think I shot him three or four times, I don't remember."

"Okay, you know the drill." He held his hand out, and I unholstered my weapon. I slipped the gun out of the leather holder and placed it carefully in his hand.

"Tom, he shot Rachel." My stomach rolled again and I fought to keep the acid down.

"What? Is she alright?" He set my gun down on the gurney and grabbed both of my shoulders. "Grant? Is she alive?"

I swallowed, "I don't know. They rushed her up to surgery. She took at least one, if not two into her back." I clenched my eyes to try and stop the image.

"Okay, she'll make it. She's right here at the hospital, she'll make it."

Tom called another officer over and told him to get a gun box for my handgun. When the officer got back, I looked up at Tom.

"I need a favor."

"Anything, whatever you need."

"I need someone to go get Jazlyn and Rachel's son Josh."

Tom looked confused, "Why Jazzy?"

"Because they are good friends, and if anyone can help him through this, she can." I swiped my hands down my face, "Jesus, Tom. What if she dies? I can't deal with that again."

Tom searched my face for a few moments, "You really care about that woman, don't you?"

"Tom, I didn't know how much I cared about her until I saw her lying on the floor." I thought for a moment, "This is different than when Ilana died. I don't know why, but this hurts worse. It's like a piece of me is being ripped out of my chest."

"You have to believe that she's going to make it. I will personally go get the kids and bring them to you."

A few minutes later, Tom rushed out the door to get the kids while I changed into a light blue scrub top and tossed out my blood-soaked shirt.

She has to make it. Please, God, don't take her from me. I need her. I don't know why I need her so much, but I do. Please do not take her from me.

The nurse who was Rachel's friend came to me a few minutes later and directed me to the fifth floor to wait. I sent Tom a text with the information so he could bring the kids up there and not through the circus in the emergency room.

I turned to watch the coroner take a few photographs of the body. Was Rachel going to be the third victim in this gang-related incident?

No! I spun around and took the elevator up to the fifth floor to find the waiting room.

I paced around the room for a few minutes wondering how I was going to tell Josh what had happened. It was like déjà vu in reverse. I sat down and dropped my hands between my knees.

"Dad? What's going on?" Jazlyn's voice broke through my worry, and I stood up and looked between her, Tom, and Josh. My focus stayed on Josh.

"Mr. Murphy, what's going on?" I sent Tom a silent thank you for not telling him on the way.

I stood before Josh and put my hands on his shoulders, "Josh, your mom was shot tonight."

Jazlyn gasped and Josh's face paled before he spoke, "You're kidding, right?"

"No, I'm not kidding, Josh." I took a deep breath, "She was working on a patient, a guy who came in with a gunshot wound. Another man came into the ER and shot her while she was working on the patient."

"Is she still alive?" His eyes were wide, and I felt his body trembling under my hands.

"She's in the operating room right now. They are doing all they can." Jazlyn wrapped her arm around Josh and cried silently.

For a minute, Josh stared at me, and then he glanced at Jazlyn before he moved away to sink down in a chair. Jazlyn followed him and rubbed circles on his back as he stared at the floor.

"The guy who shot her, where is he?" Anger contorted his features.

"He's dead."

He studied me for a long moment. "Did you kill him?" He finally asked, and Jazlyn stilled beside him.

I gave him a single nod. "Good," he answered.

Tom moved to stand beside me. "Any news?"

"No, I haven't heard anything." I took a seat on the other side of Josh and leaned back. Tom seated himself across from me.

"I need to go make a phone call," Josh said and stood up.

"Josh, do you want me to make the call?" I asked him and he turned to me.

"Thanks, Mr. Murphy, but I have to do this myself. I'll be down the hall if you hear anything."

That was a very strong young man, a very mature young man. I couldn't have been more proud of him if he were my own son.

Jazlyn scooted over to my side. "Are you alright, Daddy?"

I took a few seconds to study her. Her hair and the way she spoke reminded me so much of her mother. She was going to grow up to be even more beautiful. "Yeah, I'm alright."

I sat quietly with Jazzy until Josh came back. "Mr. Murphy, did she say anything after it happened?"

Yeah, she said that things weren't going to work between us, but if that woman lives, I am going to make it my mission to make sure she realizes that we were meant to be together. "No, she was unconscious as soon as it happened."

"Where did she get shot?"

I sighed, "She was shot at least twice in the back."

We both remained silent for a few moments, "Do you think she's gonna make it?"

I met his direct look with one of my own, "We have to believe she's going to make it. I know I personally don't want to think about losing her, not before we have even had a chance to get to know each other."

"You really like my mom, don't you?"

I didn't hesitate, "Yes, Josh, I care a great deal about your mom."

"Thank you," he said.

"For what?"

"For a lot of things: for caring about my mom, she needs someone to care about her—I mean really care about her. She deserves to be loved and to be happy. I've never seen her happy with anyone, and I'd like to see her with you," he paused, "and for killing the asshole that shot her." Josh clenched his fists.

His words shocked me. "You're welcome, Josh, and thank you." I put my hand on his shoulder and squeezed just as the doctor walked in.

"Are you Dr. Wilde's son?"

Josh and I stood up, and I kept my hand on his shoulder for support. He stepped closer to me. He might seem mature, but I knew that at that moment, he was a petrified child.

"Yeah, I'm Josh Wilde."

Jazlyn entered the room and stood beside Tom. He put his arm around her shoulders.

"Josh, your mom was shot twice." I felt Josh tense, "Once in the hip and once in the lower back."

"Is she alive?" he asked in a strained voice.

"Yes, sir. It was touch and go, and we thought we lost her at one time, but she is stable for now. We have put her into a coma for a while, but she is in recovery right now."

I spoke over the top of Josh's head, "Why did you put her into a coma?"

"Who are you?" the doctor asked.

"Detective Grant Murphy."

"Detective, you know I can't pass along medical information about a patient without the family's permission."

Josh straightened his shoulders and answered before I could, "Grant is her boyfriend, and you have my permission to speak with him."

The doctor acknowledged him and explained that the bullet went into her back and very close to her spine. There was a lot of swelling in the area, and they wouldn't know if there was any damage to the spinal cord until the swelling went down and they could do more tests. For the time being, they were keeping her in a drug-induced coma so she wouldn't move.

Josh's shoulders sagged and I pulled him into my chest I didn't know if he would be receptive to a man giving him a hug, but the moment his face touched my shirt, his bravado fled and he sobbed onto my chest. I let the tears finally flow as I clung to him and let him release his fear.

"I'll have a nurse come get you when she's in a room." The doctor nodded to us before he walked out.

Josh pulled away and wiped the tears from his face. "Sorry about that," he said and looked away embarrassed.

I gripped his arm and waited for him to look up at me. "There is nothing wrong with having emotions for the people you care about." I wiped my own damp cheek and gave him a lopsided grin. "I'm glad I was here for you."

"Me, too, now we just have to get Mom to realize that."

"That might be the hard part." We both laughed and sat down to wait for the nurse to come get us.

Chapter 27 – Rachel

I needed a trauma to get my mind off of Grant. I rushed into the trauma room, "Jane, what do we know?"

"All I know is that we have a gunshot wound to the chest coming," Jane said.

"See who is available to help." One of the aides grabbed a gown and helped me to get it on.

I was pulling my nitrile gloves on when they wheeled the gunshot victim to the trauma room. He was a young black male with a large-caliber gunshot wound to his chest. By the size of the wound, I wasn't sure if he was going to make it, but I would do everything I could.

Within seconds, the conversation I'd had with Grant disappeared into the far recesses of my mind. There would be another time and place for the conversation.

I was elbow deep in the patient's chest when I heard a woman scream in the other room. Another doctor and I were trying to clamp off an artery that had been struck and neither one of us could turn and look. Whatever the problem, somebody else would have to take care of it.

I didn't realize the gun had been fired at me until I was already falling to the ground. The sound echoed off the ceramic tiles in the small room, amplifying the blast from the gun. I gasped for breath as the pain traveled through my back. I sucked in three painful breaths before my vision darkened.

I knew as things started to dim that I needed to hold on. I didn't want to die. What would Josh do if I did? I was in the prime of my life, and I wanted to live it. I wanted to work, to watch Josh grow, and I wanted a chance to love and to be loved like I deserved to be. Was Grant the one who could do that? Could he love me the way I wanted to be loved? Despite all the craziness in our lives, were we really meant to be together?

Unconsciousness took over. I began to feel weightless, as if I were floating in water or a feather in the breeze. I heard nothing and saw nothing. I drifted until peacefulness extended over my mind and body.

For a few brief moments, I felt the pain return, but then it vanished. The darkness around me began to lighten, and I felt the urge to embrace the light. I had heard people speak about walking towards the light, but I had never been sure I believed it. Now, the light was right in front of me, and I could no longer deny it.

I hesitated, not sure if I should walk forward or turn around. I found my feet moving before I decided to go. A shadowy figure emerged from the dazzling light, and I hesitated. I could tell by the gait of the walk that it was a man and within a few steps I recognized Mark. My own steps faltered.

Did I really want to come face-to-face with Mark again? Could I deal with him knowing what I did, the truth about his affair with Ilana, the knowledge that Jazlyn was his daughter? Was I able to turn around and leave or was I destined to move forward into the warmth?

My steps shuffled forward while his gained momentum. Maybe I could ask him the questions that I needed answers for and then I could go back.

"Rachel, we didn't expect you so soon." Mark held his hand out for me.

"And I didn't expect to be here." I glanced around me

hesitantly, but I could only see shadows to my sides. Behind me, darkness loomed. The brightness of the light behind Mark gave him a haloed looked and made it hard to see his features.

Mark reached for my hand, and I allowed him to take it. His touch seemed so unfamiliar even though we had been married for almost six years. His hands, while never calloused from physical labor, felt softer now. The shadows that I remembered underneath his eyes were now gone and replaced with a healthy glow to his cheeks. He leaned down and kissed the side of my face, and in that moment I wanted to feel the anger that he had left me with. I wished that I could have yelled at him, but the emotions would not rise. Anger and pain did not exist here.

"I bet you have a lot of questions," he paused and slipped his hands into the pockets of his khaki slacks. "I kind of thought I would have more time before I had to answer them."

I shook my head, "Sorry to disappoint you."

Mark reached for me again, this time with both hands to my forearms and pulled me to stand directly in front of him. "I'm sorry, Rachel. I never meant to hurt you. I really did care for you, and my feelings for Ilana had nothing to do with you."

"Your feelings for Ilana had everything to do with me and with Grant—and also with your daughter." I shrugged out of the hold. I might not have been able to feel angry, but I could still voice the words.

Mark glanced over his shoulder again, and I followed his line of focus, but I still didn't see anything. He turned back to me as he spoke, "I think that the reason you're here is to make a decision."

"If my choices are between life or death, then I choose life."

"Maybe that isn't the decision that you need to make. Is there another choice that you have to decide on?"

I didn't want to answer him because he already knew about Grant. I wondered if he knew how Grant felt about the stipulation in the will, or if he knew that Grant refused to tell Jazlyn that he was her father, sorry, make that biological father.

"Are you trying to tell me that you're going to give me

relationship advice?" I laughed, "Because I don't know if I trust your advice."

"Rachel, I know that everything that happened before I died is upsetting and confusing, but like I told you, I never meant to hurt you."

"It's not me that I'm worried about hurting." I glared at him for a few moments, "It's Grant and Jazlyn who concern me. Do you have any idea how he felt when he found out that Jazlyn was not his daughter? He felt like he had been totally taken advantage of for his entire adult life."

"How do you think I felt when I found out that Ilana and Jazlyn were living right here, right under my nose all these years, and I didn't know about it? I mean, I hadn't thought about my daughter in years, and to one day walk into Ilana's office and see a picture of a young girl, it took my breath away. She looked so much like my mother that there was no doubt that she was my daughter."

"I get that you were surprised, but you knew that you had a daughter. You gave up those rights years ago. Grant had no idea. His name was on her birth certificate. How would he have known that Jazlyn wasn't his daughter?"

"That would be my fault," a woman's voice came from behind Mark. She was still too far back in the light. I couldn't make out her features, but I had no doubt that it was Ilana.

As she grew closer, Mark turned to her and held his hand out, she took it as soon as she could. Their fingers intertwined as they stood shoulder to shoulder. I stared into her face, a face that I had memorized the day I tried to save her life. There was no paleness now, only vibrant color on her cheeks and radiating from her eyes.

"I'm probably the last person that you want to see or talk to, but I thought I might be able to answer some of your questions."

"Ironically, I think I'd rather talk to you than him." I jutted my chin out in Mark's direction.

Ilana turned to Mark and smiled, "Why don't you give us some time to talk?"

Mark gave Ilana a gentle smile and a kiss on the cheek that

showed me a passion I would have never believed coming from him.

"Let's take a walk," Ilana suggested.

I glanced between the light in the dark, "A walk? Where are we supposed a walk to?"

Ilana's eyes scanned the area, and she turned to me, "That's right, you don't see what we see. Let's just walk here."

We turned and walked a parallel between the two sides. I had no idea what she could see, I only saw day and night.

"I think it's important for you know that I loved Grant with all of my heart."

I held back the laugh that threatened to erupt, "You did a good job of showing that."

"I'm sure that you think I'm a terrible person for what I did. I know I've made mistakes, but I never meant to hurt anyone, especially not Grant or Jazlyn."

"I can think of a few mistakes that you made." We continued to walk, and for a time neither of us said anything.

"Let me explain, and then maybe you'll understand. Grant and I were dating back in high school, and he decided to go to the police academy which was a couple hours away, and he had to stay there for three months." She took a long deep breath and released it before she continued. "I went to a party one night with my cousin and ran into Mark. He was in college, and I'd had a crush on him for years. He used to live next door to my cousin, and every time I would go to visit, I would sneak peeks at him with his friends. That night, we were drinking and Mark was paying attention to me. One thing led to another, and I was so in awe that he was paying attention to me that I ended up sleeping with him." She sighed, "Have you ever met someone that made your heart beat faster, that could take your breath away with one look?"

I turned my face away so that she couldn't see the answer in my eyes. Of course I felt that, but I wasn't going to tell her that her husband had that effect on me.

"Mark always made me feel that way. From the very first

moment I saw him, he had a way of making my heart go mad in my chest. When he was around, it was all I could do to keep from making a fool of myself. Anyway, of course I ended up getting pregnant. I honestly did not know if it was Mark's or Grant's."

"How could you not know?" I slid my hands into the pockets of my lab coat, realizing only then that I wasn't wearing the yellow gown from the trauma room.

Ilana stopped walking and turned to me, "I was drunk that night, and it was only a few days after Grant had left. I told myself that it was Grant's. I never wanted to tell Grant what I had done. I didn't want to hurt Grant. I did tell Mark, and he said he didn't want anything to do with the child even if it was his. He signed a form stating if the child was his, he gave up his rights. He was starting law school and as much as it pained me to hear that he wouldn't want our child, I knew that Grant would."

"How old was Jazlyn when you realized Mark really was her father?"

"I think I always suspected, but it wasn't until she was about five or six that I started to see pieces of Mark in her. By that time, Grant and I were married and Mark had moved away. Over the years, I thought about telling Grant, but what was I supposed to say?"

Really? "How about the truth?"

"I wanted to tell him the truth, but what if Jazlyn really was his? I would've ruined my relationship for nothing."

"If you loved Grant, you would have told him the truth. You don't keep something like this from someone you love."

We turned in unison and began to walk again. "How long have you and Mark been together now?" I asked her.

"Mark came into my office one day looking for one of the other attorneys, and the minute I saw him he took my breath away, again, and my heart raced in my chest. He says that he felt the same way, and I think he did because he kept staring at me." She turned to me. "Right then, at that moment, I knew that Mark was the one I was supposed to be with. We started to have lunches together, and then that turned into some dinners here and there. Before we knew it, we were going away on business together."

It was a good thing that I had already realized my relationship with Mark wasn't all that great, because if I was hearing this without already knowing the information, it would hurt. "So you would travel together a lot?"

"No, not often, but we did get away once in a while."

We walked in silence for a while, and I looked between the light and the dark, the black and the white. Some decisions were that easy, they were yes or no, for good or bad. Ilana had made her decision and whether that was the light or the dark, I didn't know.

"Were you going to tell Grant the truth?"

"Yes, the day that I died, I had decided to tell Grant that I wanted to divorce. I was going to tell him I was in love with another man."

What would have been worse, watching your wife get struck by a vehicle, or having your wife strike you down for another man? "I'm glad that you never got to tell him."

"Rachel," she stopped and put her hand on mine, "and I'm glad that you're there for him."

But I hadn't been there for him, I had pushed him away because I was afraid of the feelings I felt for him. I tried to look into the light, but it only burned my eyes.

"I don't know if I can, be there for him, I mean."

"Yes, you can. You two are meant to be together, I know that deep in my heart." She placed her palm against her chest, "He needs you, Jazlyn needs you."

I shook my head at her, "I'm finding this very strange, a woman who cheated on her husband and lied about the parentage of her daughter is now asking me to take care of the man she was about to leave, and the fact that you were in love with my husband only adds to the absurdity."

"It does seem strange, I know."

"Are you aware that Mark stipulated in his will that Grant and I were to be married?"

She bit her lower lip. "Actually, that was sort of my idea." She explained, "When Mark and I talked about getting together, we joked about the fact that you and Grant would probably get along perfectly and that maybe we should just swap partners. I was joking at the time, but I guess Mark took me a little too seriously."

Chapter 28 – Grant

Three hours later, I sat alone by Rachel's bed. Josh had had a chance to sit with his mom for a few minutes, but I asked Tom to take Jazzy and Josh home. There was no reason for all three of us to sit at the hospital and wait.

Tom had tried to talk me into going home, but I refused. It didn't matter how long it would take for Rachel to wake up, I wasn't going anywhere. I wanted to be the first thing that she saw when she opened her eyes. I wanted her to know that I was going to be here for the future, our future.

I leaned back in the hard blue vinyl chair and kicked my feet up on another chair. I allowed my mind to dwell on all that had happened. I had already given my statement as to my recollection of the incident. I knew that my kill was justified and that I would be cleared soon, but being put on administrative leave had its advantages right now. It meant that I could sit by her side and not have to worry about missing work.

I turned my head so that I could see Rachel lying in the bed. She was on a ventilator to help her breathe; wires and tubes emanated from all parts of her body. A nurse came in every fifteen minutes to check on her and take her vitals. I closed my eyes and tried not to remember Rachel lying on the hard tile floor of the trauma room earlier.

When I had seen Ilana on the asphalt after she'd been run over by the van, I had been horrified. I compared that feeling to what I felt when I saw Rachel unmoving on the hard floor. With Ilana, I had been scared and confused. When I realized that Ilana had died I was sad, but I was able to move on, especially when I learned of the lies.

One glance at Rachel's prone body had thrown me for a loop. The thought of never seeing her face again or having a chance with her made me weak in the knees. I had gotten over the death of my wife relatively quickly, but I knew that if Rachel did not make it, my grief would last for a much longer time.

If Jazlyn could believe that she saw her mother after her accident, then I could believe in love at first sight. I opened my eyes and stared at Rachel. Please, wake up. I don't want to live without you. I want to find a way to live with you. I want to build a life, raise our children.

Of course there was no answer to my plea, or prayer, or whatever it was that I was doing. The machines kept beeping and a ventilator kept whooshing. I closed my eyes and allowed myself to drift off to sleep.

Throughout the night, I woke up with each visit of the nurse. Sometimes I would ask if there was a change, sometimes I would pretend to be asleep.

I stood before the window as dawn approached and the sky changed. Would the swelling go down enough so they would allow her to wake to see if there was any damage to her spine? Or would another day come and go before we knew?

The door behind me opened; I turned as Josh entered.

"Any change?" he asked as he approached his mother.

I shook my head, "No. Did you get any rest last night?"

Josh picked up his mother's hand and held it, "Not really, you?"

"Probably about as much as you." I sank down in the chair next to the bed.

Josh took a seat on the other side of the bed, "Do you think she can hear us?"

"I would like to think that she could, but I don't know."

Josh nodded absently as he stared down into his mother's face, "I called my dad last night."

"I kind of figured that's who you called." I paused for a moment, "What did he have to say?"

Josh met my gaze over the bed, "He asked if I wanted him to come, but I know how busy he is, so I told him that it was all right and I would keep him updated."

I studied Josh for a few seconds. "Are you sure you don't want him here with you?"

He gave me a one-shoulder shrug. "I figured there was nothing that he could do, and since you're here it would just be too many people around."

"Josh, if you'd like to have your father here with you, that doesn't bother me."

Josh set his mom's hand down and stood up to stretch his back, his arms over his shoulders. "No, that's okay. I'll let him know if anything happens."

"Are you close with your father?"

"I guess. We talk once a week, sometimes more often, and I visit him on holidays. He lives in Texas with his wife and two kids. Sometimes we all meet at his house on the beach in North Carolina." Josh chewed on his lip as he looked down at his mom. "We're supposed to be going there next week."

"You might still be able to. Your mom might wake up and be okay. Going to rest at the beach might be good for her."

"Yeah, maybe you're right." Josh looked up at the clock on the wall, "I'm going to head off to school. Can you give me a call if anything changes?"

I stood, "Are you sure you want to go to school today? I mean, not that I'm telling you not to go, but I think your mom would understand if you didn't today."

"Yeah, she would understand, but I have a big test and I need something to keep my mind busy. It's not like I can do anything while I'm sitting here. Unless, you don't want to stay here with her and then I will."

I walked around the side of the bed, "I have no intention of leaving until your mother wakes up, and even then she's going to have to tell me to leave."

"Okay, give me a call if anything changes." Josh held his hand out for me to shake, but I put my arms around him and gave him a short hug. He smiled, picked up his backpack, and left.

I returned to my chair and flipped on the television. I needed something to fill the silence.

Jazlyn and I texted for a few minutes, and I told her nothing was new but asked her to keep an eye on Josh today. Tom stopped by midday and brought me a large cup of coffee and a sandwich from my favorite deli. "How is she doing?"

"Pretty much the same. They took her for another MRI today. I'm just waiting to hear what the results were."

"So you plan on staying here until she wakes up?" Tom asked.

"That's the plan."

"Then what are you going to do?"

I considered Tom's question carefully, "I'm going to do everything that I can to make her understand that we were meant to be together."

"How can you be so sure that you are meant to be together?"

I took a sip of my coffee before I replied. "Tom, I don't think I've ever been so sure of anything in my life. It's just this feeling that I get, a feeling I've never had before telling me that it's right."

Tom took a drink of his own coffee as he scanned the room. "I know what that feels like. I still feel that with Beth every time I look at her." He studied Rachel for a moment before he continued, "If you have those feelings for her, then don't let her go."

"I have no intention of doing so." I took a bite of my sandwich, and we both watched television for a few minutes.

"What if that's not what she wants?" Tom broached.

I set my sandwich down and dusted the crumbs off my fingers

over the deli paper. "I know she wants it, Tom. She might not know that, but I do. I'm not going anywhere and will do whatever I have to do to make her understand that."

Tom gave me a brief nod and turned his attention back to the television. A few moments later the doctor appeared in the doorway.

Anxiety rippled through me as I stood up. "What did the test results say?"

The doctor flipped open his chart and scanned through some information before he answered. "Her latest MRI shows that the swelling is going down."

The tension in my shoulders relaxed slightly. "That's good, right?"

"Yes, that's very good. In fact, that's good enough that we're going to stop the medication and allow her to wake up on her own."

Tom and I shared a relieved look. "How long will it take her to wake up?" Tom asked.

The doctor gave a brief shrug, "That will all depend on her. It could be an hour or it could be six hours."

"Okay, thank you. I'll let her son know." I pulled my cellphone out of my pocket and sent Josh a text message as the doctor checked on Rachel's vitals and a few other things.

Josh responded to my text message a few moments later. He would come to the hospital as soon as school was out.

Tom left a few minutes later for work, and I found myself once again staring out the window lost in thought.

Rachel was such a strong woman, and I had a feeling that she would fight this, but, like I told Tom, I would do anything I had to do.

I was reading a magazine two hours later when I heard the sheets rustle. I looked at the bed and wondered if I had just imagined the noise or not because she was so still. I was just about to return to the article in front of me when I saw her fingers flutter at her side.

212

My heart quickened in my chest, and I stood so quickly I felt lightheaded. I moved to the edge of the bed and reached for her hand, "Rachel, wake up, honey."

Her fingers flexed in my hand and then curled around my fingers.

"That's it. Rachel. That's it, sweetheart. Wake up." Her eyelashes flickered against her cheek, and I realized the color in her face looked better than it had since she'd been shot. Thank you, God.

I perched on the edge of the bed and held her hand with both of mine. Her head shifted to the side, and I wasn't sure if I wanted to yell or cry, I was just so happy she was waking up.

"Rachel," I brush my hand against her cheek, and her eyes opened.

"Grant," she said softly.

Tears came to my eyes, and when her eyes closed again my head drooped in relief. I took a few deep breaths to control my emotions, and when I felt strong enough, I lifted my chin off my chest to find her watching me.

"Welcome back," I smiled down at her.

"Good to be back." She shifted and winced.

I stood up. "Let me go tell the doctors that you're awake. I'll be right back."

She gave me a jerky nod, "I'll be right here."

I squeezed her hand one more time before I rushed out the door. A nurse and the doctor came in to check on her, and I sent Josh a quick message to let him know that she was awake.

Rachel answered the doctor's questions and asked a few of her own. Over and over again, I found her staring at me, and I wondered what was going on inside her mind. While she had been sleeping had she thought about me, about us? She didn't seem to be upset that I was here, in fact, just the opposite.

It was another twenty minutes before we were alone again, and I sat on the edge of her bed as soon as they all left.

"Why are you here?" she asked. I felt a little disappointed that she asked me that.

"I'm here because I care about you Rachel. I have no intention of leaving until you admit that you care about me, too."

"You know that I care about you. That has never been the problem." She squeezed my hand.

"As far as I'm concerned, there is no problem," I confirmed.

Her gaze left mine and she scanned the room, "Okay, so that's not the problem."

I smiled down at her, "See, there is no problem."

She seemed to be contemplating what she wanted to say next, and I waited patiently for her to say something, anything.

"Grant, I need you to do me a favor." She held onto my hand harder.

I realized that this was the moment I had been waiting for. "Rachel, I'll do anything you want, anything."

I watched her swallow, "I need you to tell Jazlyn the truth."

I felt like I had just been punched in the gut. "What?"

"If we are going to have any kind of relationship, then it has to be based on the truth. That means no lies, between us, or the kids."

I felt cold, as if someone had just poured ice water over my head. I pulled my hand slowly from hers and stood up, "I would do anything for you, Rachel, but I can't do that."

"Grant if you can't tell her the truth, then we can't be together."

I was at a loss as to what to do or say. My hands hung by my sides, numb, while my heart beat an irregular cadence in my chest. I scanned the sterile hospital room, the beeps filling my ears, but no other sounds.

"Rachel, there has to be another way," my voice hitched as I spoke.

She shook her head slowly, and the sound against the pillow was almost like a hiss in my ears. "No, Grant, there isn't."

I stared at her, unable to think of anything to say to change her mind.

"I can't do that, and you know it. I refuse to do that." I felt my frustration build. I turned from her so she wouldn't see it, but I knew she could feel it in the room.

"If you can't do that, then there's nothing else to say."

I stared down at the woman that I had come to care about more than I could've imagined, and realized there was no way I could do as she asked.

"I guess not." I turned and walked out of the room. I would've done anything for her, just not that.

Chapter 29 – Rachel

"That is twisted. You do know that, right?" I asked Ilana.

She gave a small shoulder shrug and looked into the brightness. "I guess once I died, Mark took my comment seriously."

"By shocking the hell out of Grant and telling him he had to marry another woman?" I shook my head at her.

"I wasn't trying to shock Grant. I wanted him to know the truth, and I think Jazlyn needs to know, also. She is old enough now to understand."

My mouth hung open, "Old enough to know that you lied to her for her entire life? That both she and Grant had been lied to by the one woman that they loved, that they trusted."

At least she had the decency to look embarrassed as her eyes fell away to the ground. "I never meant to hurt either one of them. For the last two years, since Mark and I have been together, I wanted to tell them both," her voice lowered, "I just didn't know how."

"And Mark took it upon himself to explain this in your absence. Nice touch." I looked between the light and the dark, I didn't want to be here anymore. I didn't want to hear more excuses or lies, but I didn't know how to go back.

"Rachel, I know that Grant cares about you, in a way he never did for me." She turned to stare at me.

"And how do you know that, Ilana?" I put my hands on my hips.

She grinned at me, "It's true that we can watch out for people from here. I've watched him, and I see the way he looks at you, I hear what he says. Grant never looked at me like that."

"You two were together for seventeen years, how can you say he never looked at you like that?" How did he even look at me?

Ilana reached out and touched my arm, "Because he looks at you like I look at Mark, like he couldn't live a day without you, like you're the very air he needs to breathe."

Did Grant really look at me like that? Could he possibly feel that way about me? I knew that I felt things for him that I had never felt before with any man, and I was afraid of those feelings.

I tried to stare into the brightness and closed my eyes before I turned back to the darkness to escape the intensity.

"I want Grant to have the love that I was never able to give him. I want him to know how it feels to be cherished and taken care of in a way he never was. I know you can do that for him, Rachel," she chewed on her lip for a moment before she continued, "and I know you will take care of Jazlyn, too."

"This doesn't make any sense." I began to walk again, feeling the urge to move towards the darkness but staying right on the line between the two.

"It makes complete sense, Rachel. Both of you feel things for each other, and that's huge. The two of you could have a wonderful life together and watch our children grow up, watch their children grow up."

I laughed, "I don't want to think about our kids growing up much less having children of their own."

"But that's what happens, people are born, they live, they grow up and have lives, and then they die. You and Grant have the opportunity to love one another and have a wonderful life, don't let that go."

"But he refuses to tell Jazlyn the truth. How do I get him to do that?"

Ilana was quiet for a few moments as she thought over the question, "I'm not sure how to get him to do that, but I know that the sooner he does the better. I learned a valuable lesson being here and watching the pain that I caused between all of you. I know that the sooner he tells her, the sooner they can move on with their lives. I'm not sure how she would react if she was older and learned that Grant had known for so many years."

"I think you're right. I think he should tell her, but I can't force him—and I can't be with him if he doesn't tell her the truth." I gazed toward the brightness one more time, and felt the tug of the darkness at my back. "I do care about him, but I can't force him to do something he doesn't want to do."

"All you can do is try. I think in time he will realize it is the right decision."

"I'll try, but I can't promise anything."

Ilana turned to me and said, "Will you promise me one thing?"

Her image was starting to blur, and the brightness began to fade. "What?"

I saw tears come to her eyes as she began to speak, "Tell them both that I did love them and that I never meant to hurt either of them. I did what I thought was right at the time, and I know that I made mistakes, but they were never intentional. Love Grant the best way that you can, and promise me this, promise me that on my daughter's wedding day, you'll tell her how much I love her and how proud I am of her."

Her words touched me profoundly, and I tried to hide my own emotions. I didn't want to like her or even understand her, but I did. I nodded, unable to voice a response.

"You know she wants to be a doctor, right? She's got a good role model to look up to."

The darkness behind me drew me more strongly. It was time to return to life and try to find love and happiness, whether that was with Grant or not, only time would tell.

As the color faded, I watched Mark walk to her side and wrap his arm around her waist. As strange as it was, I felt happy for them, happy that they were together.

The clear images faded, and noises that I hadn't noticed before became apparent. Machines hummed and beeped in the background. The realization that I was back in the land of the living made me feel good, even though pain radiated through my body.

I lay for a while on the verge of consciousness, contemplating all that Ilana and I had talked about. I knew that I wanted to be with Grant, but I also knew I could not if he didn't reveal the truth.

The low sound of the television broke through the last barriers. I heard rustling and felt the bed dip on the side, a large warm hand took mine, and I knew without looking that it was Grant.

"Grant." I squinted and tried to get his face to come into focus. I'd never been so happy to see anyone. I felt so much for the man sitting beside me holding my hand, I knew that I was falling in love. If he couldn't tell Jazlyn the truth, I knew that it would be a long time before my heart healed.

We spoke softly to one another for a few moments and then the doctors and nurses came in. I had been very lucky that the surgeons had removed the bullet near my spine without any permanent damage. I could wiggle my toes and feel the sensation in my legs. A full recovery would take a while, but I would get there.

I saw the way Grant looked at me, and I loved every moment of it, but I had to do this. "I need you to tell Jazlyn the truth."

The transformation that came over Grant was immediate; his body tensed, his face became stern. "What?"

"If you can't do that, then there's nothing else to say." My heart was tearing apart inside, but I knew myself well enough to know that I would never be able to live with that lie on my shoulders.

"I guess not." His back was rigid as he turned and stalked towards the door.

As the door closed slowly behind him, I knew that as much as it hurt, it was the right thing to do. Maybe someday he would understand, maybe someday he could forgive me.

Tears rolled from the corners of my eyes into the pillow, and in the recesses of my mind I pictured Ilana and Mark together. I tried, I said to them both and allowed the exhaustion to pull me back under.

When I woke the next time, it was to find Josh sitting in the chair beside my bed doing homework. "Hey, kiddo."

Josh snapped his book closed quickly and set it aside, "Mom, you're awake."

I tried to shift in the bed, but no matter what I did, everything hurt. Josh helped me move to my side and lifted the bed slightly so I could see over the railing.

"I'm sorry, honey."

"What are you sorry for? You're the one who got shot." His eyes sparkled in the boyish way that I loved.

I gave him a very small smile, "I'm sorry for worrying you." I watched the expression change on his face from one of joy to one of concern.

"Mom," he hesitated briefly, "what happened with Grant?"

"What do you mean, what happened with Grant?"

Josh took a seat next to me on the bed, "Do you know that Grant was here from the moment you were shot. He never left your side. I saw him leaving when I was coming in, it looked like he was upset."

"I'm sorry, Josh, things are just not going to work out between us."

"Why not?" he asked staring at me hard.

I sighed more because I didn't know what to say. "It's complicated, Josh."

He thought for a moment, "You know, Mom, I'm almost a man, I could probably understand."

There was such a serious look on his face that it kept me from laughing. "Honey, I know you're growing up—and I wish you'd stop, by the way—but this is between Grant and me."

"Mom, whatever the problem, I'm sure you guys can fix it.

You know he really likes you, and I think he's pretty cool."

"I wish it were that simple, Josh. Sometimes life is just a little bit more complicated, and when there's something that is between two people that can't be resolved, you just need to let it go."

Josh reached down and took my hand, "I'm trying to pretend I understand what you just said, and I don't really get it, but, if you ever want to talk about it, I'm here."

"Thank you," I squeezed his hand in return.

Josh stayed until the early evening and then went home to get a good night's sleep. I dozed on and off all afternoon, each time waking with the hope that Grant would have changed his mind and returned to my side. He never did.

Several of my coworkers from the emergency room stopped in to visit, and it was Susan who asked the question.

"So where is that gorgeous detective?"

"I sent him away." I looked away from her when I saw her eyebrows rise.

"Why the hell would you do that? That man carried you out of the trauma room and never left this hospital after you were shot, and you send him away? I don't get you."

I groaned, "I didn't want to send him away, Susan, but I had to."

"Would you please explain to me why you have to send a man like that away?"

I needed to tell somebody about this, needed to get this off of my chest. "Susan, remember when I told you that Mark and Grant's wife were having an affair?"

"Sure."

"It wasn't the first time that they'd had one." Her left eyebrow rose. "They had one about eighteen years ago, but it was more like a one-night stand."

"Okay," she said slowly.

Rip the band aid off, just rip it off. "Grant's daughter is really Mark's daughter."

"You are kidding me." Her eyes went wide as she spoke slowly.

I shook my head, "I wish I were. Grant refuses to tell Jazlyn, and I think that's wrong. I don't want any more lies in our life; we had enough when Mark and Ilana were alive. I told Grant that if he couldn't tell Jazlyn the truth, then we can't be together. He said he couldn't do that."

Susan reached out and squeezed my forearm, "I'm so sorry, Rachel. If it means anything, I think you're right on this. I think I would want the same thing, too. You can't build a relationship when there is a loaded bomb in the room."

"Exactly," I squeezed my eyes closed to fight the tears, "and as much as I care about him, Susan. I can't sit back and wait for the bomb to explode."

Chapter 30 – Grant

What the hell just happened in there? My mind spun like a top on steroids. I stood outside the door and stared at everything, seeing nothing.

I thought I had been prepared to do anything I could to build a relationship with Rachel, but the one thing that she asked me to do, I couldn't.

As I walked to the elevator, I felt like I was the one that had been shot, right in the center of my chest. My whole life seemed to be falling apart around me, and the one chance I thought I had for happiness had just disintegrated in a few minutes.

The world moved in slow motion as I pushed the button for the elevator. The door slid back and I entered. As I leaned my shoulders against the back of the cold metal wall of the elevator, I looked at the door to her room. There was no way that I could do what she asked, and I knew she was right: It was over.

The doors opened two more times to allow other people on, but I paid no attention until we landed on the bottom floor. I followed the strangers off the elevator and moved towards the front door.

"Grant!" I cringed at the sound of Josh's voice as he tried to grab my attention in the crowded lobby. How was I supposed to explain this to him? I turned slowly to face him as he approached, trying my hardest to neutralize the expression on my face.

"What's wrong?" he asked as he reached me.

I closed my eyes and tried to come up with something to say, but all I had was pain.

"Is something wrong with Mom?"

I shook my head, "No, you're Mom's fine."

"Then where are you going?" He scrutinized me, and I felt as if I were about to break into pieces.

"Josh, I have to go. Your mom can explain it to you." I reached out and squeezed his shoulder briefly before I tried to move away.

"Grant." I paused when he didn't continue. With as much energy as I could muster I turned to face him again. "Are you all right?"

I saw the concern in his eyes and the father in me wanted to assure him that everything would be okay, but I couldn't. "No, but I will be." I took a few more steps and heard the glass door close behind me.

I knew I would be all right, that I would heal from this like I had from the death of Ilana and all the lies that I had been told. It would take time, and I would hurt for a while, but I would survive.

****

Beth and Tom came over for dinner a week later, and we were sitting in the living room talking after we ate.

"I know you don't want to talk about this, but have you tried to speak to her?" Tom asked from the couch.

I glared at him, "You're right, I don't want to talk about it."

Beth and Tom shared a quick glance, and then Beth leaned forward and rested her elbows on her knees. "Grant, we're both worried about you."

I shrugged and took a long pull of my beer. They could worry all they wanted, I didn't care.

"Have you thought about doing what she asked?" Beth was the

one who questioned me, but it was Tom that I stared at. I had spoken to Tom in confidence and hadn't expected him to tell Beth.

"Grant, don't get mad at me. Beth and I have no secrets." That comment alone made me angry, and coupled with the question that she had just asked, I was ready to take somebody's head off.

I let my glare move over to Beth, "I'll tell you the same thing I told your husband, I'm not telling her."

"You can stare, glare, yell, and be angry with us all you want." Beth's eyes met me head on, "You won't intimidate me, Grant. I think Rachel is correct, and you should tell Jazlyn."

"No." I looked away and finished my beer. "You can think what you want. She's my daughter, and there is no one who is going to tell me what I should do or what I should tell her."

Tom spoke up next, "We aren't telling you what to do, Grant. Beth and I talked about this for a long time, be both agree with Rachel."

"Didn't I just say I didn't care what you all thought?" I stood and clenched the bottle so hard, I was surprised it didn't break. That would be great. I'd need stitches in my hand, and I would end up back in the emergency room reliving the demons of the last few months.

I stalked off to get another beer from the fridge and tossed my old bottle into the recycling bin by the garage door. Why the hell did everyone think I should tell her? So I could lose her, too?

I wasn't going to let that happen.

I twisted the cap off another beer as Tom and Beth walked into the room. I refused to look at either one of them. Why did they even have to bring it up? We had been having a good night, and it felt great to unwind and not dwell on it for a few minutes. Jazlyn had taken off for a friend's house right after dinner, and we had retired to the living room to kick back and relax. I was beginning to wish I hadn't even invited them over.

Tom leaned back against the counter, and his arms crossed over his chest. He was in deep thought, I knew that look. Beth stood on the other side of the counter, her fingers playing nervously on the Formica.

"Grant, we aren't trying to tell you what to do. We care about you." Tom lifted his chin so he could see me. "Ever since Rachel woke up, you've been so low. We know you're hurting. Shit, with everything that you have gone through these last few months, I'm surprised you're even standing up straight," he shook his head, "but Rachel's right. You need to tell Jazlyn the truth."

"Why the hell do I need to tell her? Huh?" I asked loudly. "She doesn't need to know I'm not her father."

"You're not my father?" Jazlyn's soft voice filled the room and everyone spun in her direction.

Adrenaline shot through my body, and my heart began to pound against my chest plate. "Jazlyn, that's not what I meant." I straightened up to walk over to her.

"Not what you meant? What did you mean? What does, 'She doesn't need to know that I'm not her father,' mean?" she asked shrilly.

Beth approached her and she side-stepped her, "Jazzy, calm down."

She threw Beth a heated glance, "I'll calm down after he answers the question. Are you or are you not my father?"

"Of course he's you're father, Jazzy," Beth affirmed and Jazzy threw her another venomous look.

"I didn't ask you, Beth, stay out of this."

She turned her face towards mine. I read pain, anger, confusion, and fear in her features.

I came to stand in front of her, "Jazlyn," I tried to calm her as I reached out to put my hands on her shoulders, and she slapped my hands away and jumped back.

"Answer the damned question!" she shouted.

Why? Jazlyn had left the house, why had she come back home? Why did Beth and Tom have to be pressuring me on this? Why did we have to be talking about it when Jazz walked in? Why the hell was this happening to me?

I wanted to scream all of those questions, just like Jazlyn had done, but I took a deep breath and realized that I had no choice but to tell her the truth.

"Jazlyn, my name is on the birth certificate. I raised you, so yes, I am your father, but," my voice faltered and I watched her visibly shake, "but, I am not your biological father."

Her hands went to her mouth and tears began to stream down her face. "What?" she squeaked out.

I reached for her again, but she shuffled backwards. She bumped into the wall and bounced around the corner into the hallway. She was in flight mode.

My God! If Ilana were here right now, I'd strangle her. I hope you see what you have done! I shouted in my head.

"Jazlyn," I called after her, "the fact that I'm not your biological father doesn't change anything."

"I heard Uncle Tom say Rachel's name, does Josh's mom know about this?"

I nodded, not sure what was about to happen or what to say.

"Why does she know, and I didn't?" She had stopped moving backwards, and I was afraid to approach her again. What if she ran out the door? What if she ran away and never came back? Oh, Jesus!

"Rachel and I found out at the same time," I said softly to her, trying to calm the situation with quieter words.

Her eyes darted all over the place, searching for something just out of her reach. They finally landed back on me. "Who is my father?"

A stake going directly through my heart would not have hurt as much as hearing her ask those words. "Rachel's husband, Mark. Mark was your biological father."

Her face wrinkled in agony. "What? The man who died? We went to his funeral; we were there for Josh and his mom. Why didn't you tell me he was my father?" she sobbed around her words, and I felt tears leaking out of my eyes and spilling down my cheeks.

"I didn't know, honey, I didn't know until after he died. Your mom kept it a secret from all of us."

"Mom?" she cried. "Why would she do that?" She put her face into her hands and sobbed hysterically. I approached her and began to pull her into my arms.

"Let go of me! Don't touch me!" she shouted.

"Jazlyn, calm down, honey, calm down. It's going to be alright." I tried to hold onto her, but she was hitting me in the chest and struggling to get out of my grasp. I let her go, afraid that she would hurt herself if I didn't.

She fell back against the front door. "You can't tell me what to do! You're not my father!"

The words entered my ears, and the fear I had felt at just the thought of telling her multiplied by one hundred.

"Jazlyn, don't you talk to him that way," Beth interjected as she rushed around me and tried to get to her.

"I can talk to him any way I want, he's not my father." She yanked the front door open and ran out, leaving it wide. I watched her run across the front lawn and jump into her friend's car. I heard her scream as she got in the car, "Go! Go! Go!"

Her friend stepped on the gas. At that very moment, my feet unthawed from the floor, and I bolted out the door and down the porch. "Jazlyn!" I screamed as I saw the taillights of the car turn the corner.

"She'll come back, Grant," Beth consoled from behind me, and I whipped around to face her.

"See! Do you see why I didn't want to tell her?" I shouted at Beth, and Tom moved to put himself between Beth and me.

Tom grabbed me by the shoulders, but I was like a bull seeing a red cape, I shoved his arms off of me. "Do you see why? Do you?" I shouted into his face.

"Grant, you need to calm down," Tom said as he met my glare.

"Get off my property," I sneered at him and stalked around him to go back into the house. I didn't look back as I slammed the door so hard, the windows rattled. They could all shatter, I wouldn't care. My life had already done that, into a million pieces, and the only good part I'd had left was now destroyed, too.

I went up to my room and threw myself on the bed. I didn't want to see Tom or Beth again, not now. I couldn't face them. I couldn't even face myself. I threw an arm over my face and cried into my elbow.

I lay awake all night, staring at the white ceiling and praying Jazlyn would come home. She didn't. She didn't answer her cellphone or her text messages, either.

"Do you see what you have done, Ilana? Did you hate me so much that you had to destroy everything that meant something to me?" I spoke to the quiet room in the early moments of dawn and jumped when I heard something in the closet.

I scooted off the bed and pulled back the door. Maybe I would get lucky and someone with a gun would shoot me dead. I flipped on the light and looked down to see Ilana's jewelry box lying on the floor.

I stared at it. I knew I had put it up on the shelf and had not taken it down since I had cleaned out the room. What was it doing on the floor?

I bent down to pick it up, and as I lifted it, I noticed a ring lying on the carpet beside it. I reached for it and as my finger closed around the gold of the band, I felt warmth, as if it had just come off of a finger. I stared at the ring and realized it was Ilana's engagement ring. What the hell? I walked out of the closet and sat down on the bed still staring at the ring.

"Is this your way of telling me something?" I said aloud to the empty room. "Because if it is, I don't get it!"

I waited to see if something else would fall down or strike me dead, but nothing else happened. I went back to the closet and dropped the ring in the box before putting the box back on the shelf. I stared at it for a long time.

I went into the bathroom and pulled my shirt over my head. My eyes went to the pink scar on my chest and I ran my finger over it. Rachel.

I could call her now. I could tell her that Jazlyn knew the truth.

Would she talk to me? Would we be able to take off where we left off?

I lowered my head as I placed my palms on the counter. I couldn't face her, and I couldn't take the chance of losing her, yet again. I'd lost enough already.

Chapter 31 – Rachel

"You sure you feel alright to go? We can stay home," Josh asked as he carried my suitcase down the stairs.

"I'm fine, Josh, and I could use the fresh air right now." I descended the stairs gingerly, putting one foot down and then the other. My stitches had been removed, but I still needed to move slowly. "Are you sure you are going to be able to drive for six hours? You've never driven that long at one time," I asked him when I finally reached the landing.

"Sure, although I'm not crazy about being on the highway for most of it. All those semi-trucks whizzing down the road freak me out, but I need the experience."

I opened the front door so he could carry the two suitcases out. "Sorry I can't help you carry those. I feel like an old lady."

Josh laughed, "You are an old lady." He grinned, "I'm just kidding."

"You better be," I smirked back at him. "Let me just make sure the doors are locked, and we can go."

"Mom, get in the car, I'll check the doors. If you check them, it will be another hour before we get on the road."

"You trying to tell me I'm slow?" I joked.

"As molasses," he yelled over his shoulder as he reached the car with the bags.

The car ride was anything but fun. I didn't load up on pain medication or muscle relaxers. I wanted to remain clearheaded in the car if there was a problem. By the time we arrived at the beach house, I was ready to cry or poke someone's eye out; it didn't matter which.

The house was a large two-story stone and cedar construction set on the high dunes of the beach area. Josh pulled into the circular driveway and stopped as close to the front door as he could. Peter stepped out of the house as Josh climbed out of the driver's door and stretched.

"Hey, Dad!" he called out over the roof of the car.

Peter pulled the passenger door open. "Hey, son," he called over the roof of the car. Then he bent down to me, "How are you doing, Rachel?"

"I need drugs," I grunted and tried to roll out of the car. Peter helped me as much as he could, and I winced and sucked in air several times before coming to stand upright.

Peter helped me into the house, and Christina met us in the foyer. "Rachel, you look terrible."

"Thanks, Christina," I snarked at her.

"That's not what I meant, silly woman. I was talking about how much pain you look like you're in. Come on, let me take you to your room and get you in bed to rest for a while. I put you in the other master suite down here so you wouldn't have to walk up and down the stairs.

Christina was Peter's wife, and I loved her like a sister. We had been friends since college, and she had never batted an eye about Peter having a son with me. At the time, they were only friends. After we broke up, the two of them got together. She was always the first one to jump on my side with issues over the years.

"Josh, ask your sister to get Rachel a bottle of water so she can take her medicine."

Christina led me down the hallway. There was no way I could respond to her; my pain level was a fifteen on a scale of one to ten.

Christina and Peter got me to the room, and the bed was already turned down and ready for me. I tried to sink down onto the bed, and Peter went to lift the back of my shirt.

"Hey, I'm so not in the mood," I growled, trying to be funny, but feeling like shit.

"I want to check your incisions before you lie down." He tugged at my shirt again.

"There will be no difference in them between now and later this afternoon. Let me take my drugs and get a nap." I pulled away from him, and he helped me to sit down.

"I don't want to fight with you because in the mood you are in, you'd tear me a new one. I'll wait until later."

Christina pulled the vial of pills from my purse and handed them to me as Melody came in with the water.

"Wow, Rachel, you do look terrible," Melody said, and I glared at Christina. "Sorry, it's nice to see you again, I'm glad you are alright." She put a kiss on my cheek, and I winked at her before I took the water bottle.

"Come on, Melody, let's let Rachel get some rest," Peter said as he pulled her from the room.

I lay back and the urge to cry hit me as I slowly released each tense muscle. Christina pulled a blanket over me and sat down on the edge of the bed.

"Looks like we have a lot to catch up on," she said quietly. I stared at her, unable to speak. I felt a drop of moisture roll down the side of my face. She wiped it off with a finger, "Get some sleep, and when you are ready to talk, I'm here."

"Thank you," I said as I turned my head away and allowed the pain to pull me under.

Four hours later, I woke up and felt like a new person. I still hurt like a bitch, but it was tolerable. My stomach growled as I got out of bed.

Everyone was on the back deck when I walked out. "She lives," Peter called out as he stood to greet me.

"Yes, I live. Sorry about that."

Peter gave me a gentle hug and then passed me on to Christina who held me tight enough to make me wince.

"Don't worry about it. Josh called us about an hour before you got here and warned us what kind of shape you were in. He was worried about you."

I shook my head as I sank down into a large cushioned chair.

The three kids were all in the pool even though it was only sixty-something degrees out. The pool was thermally heated and the water was in the seventies.

I watched Josh drag Melody, his thirteen-year-old half-sister, under the water and Trey, his eleven-year-old half-brother, climbed on his shoulders and tried to dunk him. Josh was getting close to being seventeen, and his shoulders were filling out. His jawline seemed to be strengthening, too, and I glanced at Peter. He looked so much like his father, and I was happy for that.

"I can't believe how much he has grown. I saw him just a few months ago, but he looks a year older already," Peter commented as he watched them roughhouse in the pool.

"I know. I see changes in him on a daily basis, and it surprises me. I can't imagine how much he has changed to you."

For an hour, we sat around and chatted. Peter got up and put steaks on the grill while the kids put together a salad and set the table. A little after five, we sat down for dinner. By the six o'clock hour, I was ready for bed again.

Peter came back to my room with me and lifted my shirt to check the incisions. He pulled the bandages off of them, "They look good. A little inflamed, but that is probably because you were sitting in a car and stretched them for hours."

"Probably," I concurred as he prodded one of the patches of healing skin.

"I'm glad you came down, you could use some TLC," he said as he turned me around and put his hands on my shoulders. "You alright?"

"I'm fine. I couldn't control the fact that a shooter came into the ER, and I'm not having any PTSD from it. It happened, I got shot, I got fixed, and now I'm healing."

"That's not what I meant." He searched my face, and I realized that he must be talking about Grant.

"What did Josh tell you?" I asked him softly.

"He didn't tell me much, but he said enough for me to know that something is going on. Why don't you tell me about it?"

I turned away from him, "I can't."

"Then if you can't talk to me, talk to Christina. Obviously, something is bothering you, and you need to get it off your chest. Holding emotional things in delays the healing, and you know it."

"Yes, Dr. Galloway."

He chuckled at that. "Why don't you take a shower? I'll have Chrissy make you some hot tea and come in and visit with you in a little while."

I didn't want to talk about it, but, then again, I did. Since I had sent Grant away, I had hidden the pain inside of myself. The conversation I'd shared on the celestial plane burned a hole in my memory, and maybe if I let it out, I could move forward.

I climbed in the shower and kept my back out of the water so I could rinse off with a washcloth. I needed to let go and move forward. There were no more choices now. Grant had made his decision, and neither of us was going to change our minds.

Christina came to my room with cookies and tea, and she snuggled up on the other side of the bed. I felt like a college dormer being comforted by a roommate.

"Peter says I need to talk about it," I stated after we had chitchatted about the kids for a few minutes.

"You know that Peter isn't always right. If you're not ready, we can hold off." She picked at the blanket with her fingers.

"I think Peter is right on this one, sadly." We both snickered. "I need to get this all off my chest."

Christina sat and listened as I ran through all the events from the moment I had met Grant until the time I'd said we had nothing else to say. She'd handed me tissues when I needed them, and squeezed my leg or my arm once in a while to give me strength to continue.

"Did I do the right thing, Christina?"

She contemplated her answer. "Do you think you did the right thing?" she countered.

"Oh no, put the shrink back in her box. I'm talking to my friend, Christina, not the psychologist." I shook my head. I didn't want to be analyzed, and I didn't want her to make me think deeper than I needed to. I only wanted someone to tell me I'd done the right thing.

She threw her head back and laughed, "You know me so well, but I'm serious. From one girlfriend to another, do you think you did the right thing?"

"I don't feel like I had any other choice. I couldn't live with any more lies in my life," I responded honestly.

"Then you did the right thing. I think I would have done the same exact thing that you did. No matter how much you love a person, you can't build a life on lies."

I looked away from her, "I'm not in love with him." Was I? No, I didn't know him well enough to love him.

"You aren't?" She tilted her head to look into my face. "From where I'm sitting, if you didn't love him or weren't on your way to loving him, this wouldn't be such a big deal."

Damn, she was right. Maybe I wasn't head over heels in love with Grant, but I was well over halfway there, and the knowledge did nothing but rip my heart just a tiny bit more.

"Christina, can I ask you question?"

"Sure."

"Do you believe in life after death?"

She eyed me curiously, "You mean people coming back to life or the heavenly place in the sky?"

"The one beyond the bright light."

"Of course," she shrugged lightly. "I wouldn't want to think that when we died that was all there was. I believe that good people go to a special place and can watch out for their loved ones. Why? Wait...Did you see it? The tunnel? After you were shot, did you see it?"

"I think I did."

"Oh, my God! That's incredible. I have only ever spoken to one person who saw the light and returned. You have to tell me all about it." She looked like a kid on Christmas morning as her green eyes sparkled.

"On no, you're going to analyze me again, aren't you?"

"What? No, okay, maybe a little, but this is so cool, Rachel, you have to tell me everything. What did you see? What did you feel? How did you come back?"

She rattled off the questions, and I watched the glow brighten in her eyes. I hope I don't disappoint her with my answers, I thought.

"Well, I didn't feel any pain, and I couldn't feel anger while I was there—which was strange because I wanted to be angry."

"Why would you be angry? Because you thought you'd died?" She shifted to get more comfortable on the bed.

"No, because the first person I saw was Mark."

"Oh, damn. Wait, who else did you see?"

"I had a long talk with Ilana, too."

Her eyes grew round. "No wonder you wanted to be angry. So what happened?"

For the next few minutes, I relayed to her all that we had talked about, and everything I had felt and seen. She asked a lot of questions and on this, I didn't mind. I knew that it was rare for someone to visit this place and to come back to talk about it. Maybe, it would help her in the future with her patients.

By the time we got done talking, I was trying to stifle my yawns and needed to take more medicine. Christina gave me a hug goodnight and tucked me into bed. I felt worlds lighter now that I had finally had a chance to talk to someone about everything.

When my head hit the pillow, I realized that I could look back on everything with some good thoughts, and that I was ready to move forward.

Sunlight streamed through the windows when I woke up, and

the calls of the seagulls carried through the closed windows. I took a few minutes to stretch then took a quick shower, dressing in yoga pants, a t-shirt, and a long button-down shirt.

I could smell the coffee when I entered the kitchen, and heard voices outside. I poured myself a cup and found Peter and Christina sitting on the stone patio enjoying the fresh morning air.

"Good morning," I called out as I joined them. "Where are the kids?"

"Morning," Peter stood up and kissed my cheek, pulling my chair out for me. "Did you sleep alright?"

"Yes, actually I slept great, better than I have in a long time." Christina winked at me as I got comfortable in my chair.

"Trey is playing video games, I think, and Melody is still asleep. Josh ran out for a few minutes, said he needed to go pick something up." Peter sat down and pulled a Danish off the platter in front of him.

We chatted for a few minutes, and I heard the front door close. I assumed Josh was back from his errand and took a sip of my coffee.

"Mom?" Josh called out to me from the back door. I glanced up and saw the look on Peter's face, I snapped my neck around and saw Jazlyn standing beside Josh holding his hand and looking scared to death. "I think we need to talk."

Chapter 32 – Grant

Where the hell was Jazlyn? I had called four of her friends and they all told me they hadn't seen her. The girl I had seen her with last night wouldn't answer her phone.

I paced the kitchen. I had no idea where the girl lived, or I would have been knocking on her door. I knew Jazlyn was angry and hurt, but I also knew that I needed to explain everything to her. She couldn't possibly have run away, could she have?

I heard the front door open. "Jazlyn," I yelled and ran to the hallway only to find Tom standing there closing the door slowly.

"She hasn't come home yet," he answered his own question.

I fought the anger that rushed through me. "No," I stalked back to the kitchen and heard him follow me down the hallway.

"You know that we never meant for her to hear us talk about that," Tom said as he joined me.

I wasn't angry with Tom or Beth. It had been an accident that Jazlyn had walked in on the conversation. I knew that they cared about both of us and only wanted the best for us.

"I know. I'm sorry about last night." I crossed my arms and leaned back against the counter.

"Don't apologize, we know you were angry. Beth was so upset last night, she tried calling Jazlyn a dozen times."

"She didn't pick up?" I asked and Tom shook his head.

"I don't know where she is. I called all the friends I could think of, but no one knows anything."

Tom came to my side and put his hand on my shoulder, "She'll come home, Grant. She needs some time to absorb it, and then she will come home and have a whole slew of questions for you."

"I'm not sure I'll have the answers," I sighed.

"Well, you tell her what you know, and the other questions she asks, you tell her that neither of you will ever have the answers," he paused, "but whatever you say, you must tell her the truth. You owe it to her now."

"I know." I let my arms drop to my side, sighed, and reached into a cabinet to pull out two coffee mugs. "I know I need to tell her the truth, and maybe all of you were right. Maybe it is better that she knows."

"Have you thought about calling Rachel?" he asked while I handed him his mug. I shook my head. Of course I had thought about calling her, but I wasn't ready for that.

"Now that Jazzy knows, maybe you two can work things out." He blew on his coffee and took a sip.

"I'm not sure about that." I moved to sit at the kitchen table.

"You didn't think telling Jazz was a good idea either. Look how that turned out."

"Thanks for that reminder," I barked out.

Tom was about to say something when my cellphone rang from the kitchen counter. I stood up so fast that I knocked the chair over behind me.

I didn't recognize the number, and a chill ran down my spine as I punched the button, "Hello?"

"Grant? It's Rachel."

I turned to look at Tom. Had he called Rachel and told her what had happened?

"Rachel," I said slowly and I watched Tom's eyebrows rise in surprise. I took a deep breath, "Rachel, I'm surprised to hear from you."

"I'm sure you are, but I needed to tell you something," her voice whispered over the line and I closed my eyes to imagine her face.

"I need to tell you something, too. Jazlyn knows."

"I know," she replied.

I stared at Tom, maybe he had called Rachel. "How do you know?"

"Because Jazlyn is here, with me and Josh in North Carolina."

"What?" I yelled. "How the hell did she get to North Carolina?" Tom stood and stepped closer. I angled the phone so he could hear the conversation.

"She called Josh last night, he borrowed his father's credit card and bought her a bus ticket. He just picked her up from the bus terminal and brought her here."

My daughter had run away from me. Anguish ripped through me for a moment and then resolve took its place, "Where is here? I need the address. I'm coming to get my daughter."

Rachel gave me the address, and we hung up without saying anything else. I was furious and scared to death at the same time. The thought of her getting on a bus alone and traveling over six hours freaked me the hell out.

I threw a change of clothes in a bag and grabbed my keys. Tom pulled the door closed and told me to drive safe and let me know when I got there. I was already climbing into my car when I replied that I would.

Three hours into the drive, the anger was gone, and the fear of what she would say began to gnaw at my bones. Did she ever know that Rachel had called me? Would she run again before I got there?

I had to believe that Rachel would keep her there until I arrived. I couldn't believe that her son had purchased her a bus ticket to go all the way down there. I didn't know whether to be angry with him for doing that, or proud of him for bringing her someplace she felt safe.

I pushed the speed limit the whole way and prayed that any officer who pulled me over would be lenient. The GPS on my dashboard started giving me more directions, and before I knew it, I was driving down the coastal highway and only a few minutes away.

Butterflies flew around in my stomach the closer I got—or that could have been hunger pains since I had refused to stop and I was starving. I hadn't stopped because I wasn't sure I would be able to hold anything down.

It was late afternoon when I pulled up a long driveway and eyed the house. It was huge and sat right on the beach. I could hear the waves crashing on the shore as I exited my vehicle. I stood staring at the massive stone house, my heart hammering in my chest from the unknown.

The front door opened, and there stood the man I had seen standing beside Rachel at Mark's funeral.

"I assume you are Grant." He stepped down the three stone steps and approached me with his hand out, "I'm Peter Galloway, Josh's father."

I took his hand and immediately saw what I hadn't noticed before. Josh looked exactly like him. I had been too busy wondering who he was that I never looked between him and Josh.

"Peter, I'm sorry if this has caused you any problems, I'll pay you back for the bus ticket." I shook his hand.

"Don't worry about that. I'm glad he used the money for something useful. I'm glad your daughter came here and didn't end up someplace else."

I glanced at the house, "You and me both." If she was going to hide from me, at least she was doing it in a nice safe place. "Where is she?" I asked as I tried to look into the front windows.

"She's out on the beach sitting with Rachel. Come on, I'll take you back there." He motioned for me to follow him into the house, and I tried not to let my jaw drop when I saw the inside—and I had thought Rachel's house was amazing.

We exited to the rear of the house, and I scanned the back patio. A large pool and hot tub took up most of the porch. A stone wall ran along the back edge, and beyond that was an endless view of the ocean.

Peter and I walked to the stone wall, I felt my hands trembling as I scanned the beach. "They are over there." Peter pointed over to the right, and I saw Rachel and Jazlyn sitting in the sand staring out over the water. My breath hitched in my chest. There were the two most important ladies in my life, side by side.

Peter put his fingers into his mouth and let loose a piercing whistle. The ladies turned to look over their shoulders, and both of them slowly turned back to the water. I saw Rachel look at Jazlyn and thought she was saying something, but I couldn't be sure.

Jazlyn leaned over and hugged Rachel, and my eyes filled with tears. Jazzy had turned to Rachel when she couldn't come to me. I was torn on being happy she had someone and sad that it wasn't me.

Jazlyn stood and moved slowly towards the house. I watched her slow progress and ached to meet her halfway.

"Mr. Murphy," I heard Josh's voice behind me, and I turned to him. "I'm sorry. I know that I should have called you and told you, but she was so upset, the only thing I could think of was getting her someplace safe where she could calm down. I had no idea why she was upset, she was babbling and crying and said she had to talk to my mom. I thought maybe something had happened to you."

Peter walked to stand beside his son, a proud gleam in his eye.

"Josh, I'm not upset with you. I'm thankful that you did what you did. I'm glad that she had you two to come to, and you too, Peter. I appreciate the fact that you allowed her to come here."

"I'd never turn down family, Grant, never." Peter turned to Josh, "Come on, let's go inside and help Christina with dinner while they talk."

Josh and Peter walked away, and I realized that what I had said was the truth: I wasn't upset with Josh. I was very proud of him. He was going to be a very fine man, and hearing Peter say those words to me, I realized from where from Josh had inherited his good traits.

"Dad?" I spun around and held my breath as I stared at Jazlyn.

"I'm so sorry, honey," I finally said, and she ran to me and threw her arms around my neck. I picked her up off the ground and held her as close to me as I could. "I'm so sorry. I love you, I will never stop, and I might not be your real father, but—"

She pulled away and looked at me through her tears, "You will always be my real father."

I choked on what she said and could barely see her through all the emotions that whipped around me.

"Rachel explained a lot of it to me. She said that there would be more that you needed to explain, but she told me most of it." I clenched my jaw. "Don't you dare be angry with her, Dad. I asked her, and she told me she would never lie to me. She told me the truth, and that is what I needed."

"You're right, you do need the truth." We sat down and she told me what she knew. Josh came out of the house once with a soda for Jazlyn and a beer for me and then quietly disappeared back inside.

We had talked for almost an hour when she looked at me and said slowly, "She saw Mom."

"Who saw Mom?"

"Rachel, when she was shot and she was in the coma, she was with Mom." She watched me carefully.

"Is that what she told you?"

"Yeah, she told me all about the conversation she had with her."

Had Rachel really seen Ilana? Had she been that close to death that she had walked through the tunnel and then returned? I glanced out towards the beach. I wasn't sure if Rachel had returned and entered the house a different way.

"You need to go talk to her. She loves you, Dad."

I stared at Jazlyn. "She told you that?" I asked, surprised.

She grinned, "No, she didn't tell me that, but I can see it in her eyes when she talks about you. You need to go to her, tell her how you feel." She stood up and came to stand beside me, "It's your turn to be happy, and I know that Rachel can make you feel that way." She leaned down and kissed my cheek before she walked away.

I stared above the stone wall for a moment and wondered if I could do it. Could I fix things with Rachel? Did she love me as Jazlyn said?

There was only one way to find out. I stood and stared over the wall. Rachel stood in about the same place she had been sitting with Jazlyn. The sight of her hair blowing in the breeze set off emotions deep within me, and I knew at that moment that I needed her in my life.

She had brought Jazlyn back to me. I was sure that Rachel had enlightened Jazzy in a way I would never have been able to. Women were good at explaining the details. I hesitated another moment before I made my final decision. If Jazlyn could trust her and care for her, then I could, too.

I strode down the wooden steps and kicked off my shoes when I hit the sand. I held a fast pace until I got a hundred feet from her and then slowed to take her in.

Her face was tilted up to the sky, and the wind whipped her hair around her head. Her eyes were closed, and her arms were crossed gently over her chest. She was beautiful, and in that moment I knew I loved her.

I walked up behind her and whispered in her ear, "I'm not sure I like your son buying bus tickets for my daughter." I felt her tense at my words.

Chapter 33 – Rachel

"Jazlyn, what are you doing here?" I stared at the kids. She looked exhausted and scared to death.

"I bought her a bus ticket. I just picked her up from the terminal." Josh glanced at Jazlyn. "She needs you to tell her about her father."

"Grant?" I asked confused.

"No, my real father, Mark," Jazlyn said softly.

Oh, shit! She knew the truth. Had Grant decided to finally tell her or had something happened and she found out another way?

"Jazlyn, did your father tell you that?" From the corner of my eye I saw Peter sit back down.

Her long hair flipped back and forth when she shook her head, "I walked in on a conversation he was having with Tom and Beth."

Oh, God! Poor Grant. "Does he know you are here?" I stepped closer to her.

She looked down at the ground and shook her head again.

I pulled her into a hug, "Jazlyn, oh, honey. I'm so sorry. Look, I'll tell you what you want to know, but I need to call your father and tell him you are safe. He's going to be worried sick."

"I know he is, but I couldn't face him. I said some awful things to him, and I needed to know more before I talked to him."

I pulled back and held her at arm's length. "Like I said, I'll answer your questions, but I need to go call your father first."

Josh and Jazlyn sat down at the table and picked out some food. I made my way into the house and dialed Grant's cellphone from memory. I'd never called him before, but I knew every single digit as if they were mine.

He answered on the second ring, and my heart pulled tight in my chest as I heard his worried voice. Our conversation was short, and I hung up after I gave him the address.

I returned to the porch, and Christina and Peter excused themselves to go run a few errands. I figured Josh had every right to know the truth, too, so I invited him to stay while we talked.

I explained to her about the relationship with her mother and Mark and how they had known each other so many years ago. She sat silent for the most part and listened, sometimes wiping a tear or two from her face.

I also clarified how Grant and I had learned the truth, without revealing any information about the money in the will. I had only told her that some money had been left to her. I was not going to put that kind of stress on a child. It was also the first time Josh heard that money had been left to him.

I figured that if Grant wanted to explain that part, he could. Jazlyn yawned, and I suggested we both lie down and rest for a little while. We both knew that once Grant arrived, it was going to be a long emotional night.

A few hours later, I suggested to Jazlyn that we take a walk on the beach. Josh wanted to come, but I told him we had some girl talk to do, and he laughed and told us to have fun.

I didn't want to walk far, but I needed to feel the wind in my hair, the sun on my face, and smell the sea up close. We wandered down the beach a little bit before Jazlyn suggested we sit.

"Your dad told me that after your accident, you saw your mom." I stared out over the water.

"I did."

"I saw your mom, too—after I was shot." I turned to her and

noticed a tear escaping from the corner of her eye.

"You saw my mom? What did she say?"

"She told me she wanted me to take care of you," I replied. I was not going to lie to the girl. We had all been through too much, and none of us needed more lies.

"She did?" She glanced down the length of the beach, "What did you tell her?"

"Actually, she made me promise that I would take care of you and your father."

Her gaze snapped back to mine. "But you broke up with Dad."

"I had to make a decision, Jazzy. I told your father that he had to tell you the truth and if he couldn't do that, then we couldn't be together."

"Why didn't he want me to know?" she asked as she cupped sand into her hand and let it sift back to the beach.

"He was afraid you wouldn't love him anymore and that you would run away from him."

She dropped the sand and wrapped her arms around her bent knees, "And that is exactly what I did, I ran away."

"But you did it because you were scared, not because you don't love him. I get why you did what you did, and I'm so glad that you came to me." I brushed my hand down the side of her head. "You have no idea how much that means to me."

"Do you love my father?" she asked in a voice that seemed so much older than her sixteen years.

"I care a great deal about your father, but I couldn't be with him without you knowing the truth."

"What about now? I know now, so will you two be able to fix things?"

I shrugged and looked away. "I don't know." We watched two seagulls glide a few feet down the beach. "Your mom told me something else."

"What?"

"She said you wanted to be a doctor." I raised my eyebrows in question, and she grinned.

"I do, I'm not sure what kind yet, but that's what I want to do."

"Good, if you ever need any help, I'm there for you, no matter what happens between your father and me."

We heard Peter whistle and turned around. Grant stood beside Peter, and my heart skipped a beat.

"Time to go face the music and be honest with your father. I think he will tell you anything you want to know now."

"Yeah, I guess." Jazzy stood up and looked down at me. "Remember, you promised my mother that you would take care of me and my dad. If you really made that promise, I'm going to hold you to it. He's been miserable this last week. I know he loves you. I think it's time you guys were honest with each other."

She walked away, and I was left with only the roar of the waves and my thoughts.

I dwelled over everything we had talked about for a while, and finally thought over her last words. Could Grant love me like she thought? Would we be able to get over all of this and build a life? My back began to ache from sitting so long, and I stood and stretched it and my legs.

The sun was beginning to lower in the sky, and my stomach rumbled, but I couldn't find the energy to walk back to the house. I lifted my chin to the breeze and inhaled, allowing the fresh air to revive my senses.

I was lost in my thoughts or the dreams of what could be when I heard the deep soft timbre of his voice in my ear.

It was time to find out what would happen. I turned to him slowly and looked up into his teasing eyes. The blue of his irises looked brighter out here and took my breath away.

"I'm sorry about that. I hope you aren't too mad at him."

He shook his head, and I felt the rest of my tension float away, "No, I'm glad she had him to call," he paused and searched my face, "and you to come to."

"I'm glad I could be here for her." I wanted to reach up and wipe away the shadows under his eyes. "I want to be here for you, too."

"Jazlyn told me about your conversation with Ilana." Grant took a step closer. "I want you in my life, Rachel. I need you in my life."

My heart beat like crazy, and I remembered the first time we met, the day in the store when we flirted with each other over firsts.

"It feels like the first time again," he remarked.

"It's like everything that happened before doesn't matter. That you, me," I motioned between our two chests, "is all new."

"Our first words," he said softly.

I reached out and touched his cheek, "And that first touch that sends electrical pulses right through your skin."

Grant put a hand to my stomach, "And the butterflies that fill your insides."

"The same ones that steal your heart and fly away with it." I placed a hand over his heart and felt the steady, fast thumping inside his chest that matched mine.

"But," he slid both hands onto my hips, "nothing compares to the anticipation of the first kiss."

I stared at his lips and knew that I was ready to take that next step. I was ready to move forward, and so was he.

He lowered his lips to mine, and I felt a ray of the fading sun shine down on us. I wrapped my arms around his neck and kissed him with everything I had in me, and when we finally pulled away, he rested his forehead on mine.

"I think I love you, Rachel," he whispered.

"I think the feeling is mutual," I replied, and we held on to each other. I looked around us and noticed that the beach was mostly shaded, except for where we stood.

I smiled up at the sky, I made you a promise, Ilana, and I'm going to keep it. Thank you.

***

Six months later I stood in front of a mirror and looked at my image. Jazlyn stood peering over my shoulder with a huge smile on her face.

"I can't believe you are about to marry my dad." She bounced on her toes.

"Neither can I," I agreed with a grin.

Over the last few months, a lot had happened. Grant had sold his house, and he and Jazlyn moved in with us. There was no doubt in either of our minds that we would spend forever together.

We had briefly discussed having a quick wedding, one that would fall within Mark's terms, but after only a few minutes, we both decided we were going to do it our way and in our time.

Jazlyn was my maid of honor, and Josh stood by Grant's side at the end of the short aisle. Our wedding was taking place on the beach outside of Peter's home. It seemed fitting that we join in the place where we had solidified the start of our lives together.

A handful of friends joined us, including Tom and Beth, and Susan and Jane. We didn't need many witnesses to this moment, we only needed those closest to us.

Peter walked me down the aisle and handed me off to a dashing Grant. He wore dark brown linen pants and a cream silk shirt. My dress was a short but flowing ivory strapless gown, and I knew that we made a beautiful couple, inside and out.

The service was short and exciting, especially the moment when the official pronounced us man and wife, and a beam of sunlight rained down on us. All four of us looked up to the heavens and knew that Ilana and Mark were smiling.

As crazy and twisted as all the lies had been, that distorted path had led us to be together, and as Grant picked me up and spun me around before he kissed me, I realized that I finally knew the love that they had shared. The love that you could never stop, no matter the amount of time or distance between two people, Grant and I now shared that.

We were halfway through the reception when Peter came to my side, "Rachel, you have a phone call, the man said it was important. You can take it in the study."

Grant followed me into Peter's study at the far end of the downstairs hallway and I picked up the phone. "This is Rachel."

"Rachel, this is Stuart Kline." I stared at Grant for a moment.

"Hold on, Stuart," I hit the speaker phone and set the handset down. "I put you on speaker, Grant is here with me. What do you want?"

"I hear that congratulations are in order," he began and cleared his throat.

"Thank you. What can we do for you?" I watched Grant clench his jaw and knew he was remembering the day we had sat in his office for the reading of the will.

Stuart cleared his throat again, and Grant and I smiled at each other. We had talked about his annoying habit and both found it funny.

"You remember when I was reading Mark's letter to you, and he said you all had to be married within six months."

"Yes, we remember, but it's been longer than that, so it doesn't matter."

"Actually, it hasn't." Grant and I stared at each other, confused. "Mark stated in his letter six months, but the actual will, the legal one, stated one year."

"What?" Grant asked as he stepped around the desk and put his arm around my waist.

"Mark had the will drawn up first and then wrote the letter, he must have forgotten that he put one year in the legal version."

Grant and I stared at one another. "What does that mean?" I asked.

"It means the money will be turned over to you as originally stated and not held in trust until the kids are thirty."

We talked for a few more minutes and then disconnected. Grant pulled me into a kiss, "I guess he got us after all."

"No, we got each other. It's a good thing we didn't sell my house," I said as I wrapped my arms around his neck.

"Why is that?" He cupped my cheek.

"Because we are going to need that extra bedroom."

Grant searched my face. "What are you saying?"

"Yeah, what are you saying?" Grant and I turned to the door

where Josh and Jazlyn were standing. Josh had asked the question. Jazlyn was grinning, she knew, she had seen the test wrapper in the bathroom when we were getting dressed.

"She means we are going to have another addition to the family," Jazlyn blurted out.

Grant grabbed the sides of my face and turned me to him. "Is she right?"

"Yes, she is, we're going to have a baby." His eyes sparkled with moisture as he leaned down to kiss me, a kiss that told me that this was what life was about.

"I should have given him my box of condoms," I heard Josh say from the door, and Grant and I broke the kiss and started laughing.

I knew as we walked back to the reception on the back patio that we had all that we could ever wish for and more. When we stepped outside, Grant and I both saw the shooting star over the ocean, and we knew it had been sent from above to say they approved.

The End

About the Author

Stacy Eaton is a police officer by profession. Currently, she is working as the department investigator and enjoys digging into cases and putting the pieces of the puzzles together.

Stacy resides in southeastern Pennsylvania and is the wife to a police officer and the mother of two. She is very proud of her son who is currently serving in the United States Navy and equally proud of her younger daughter who works hard in her Tae Kwon Do studies.

When Stacy is not working her demanding job, or spending time with her family, she works on her business and volunteers with the World Literary Café. She is also on the Board of Directors of her local Domestic Violence Center. When there is time, she writes.

Be sure to visit www.stacyeaton.com for updates and more information on her books.

Check out Chapter One of "Six Days of Memories"
Releasing June 30, 2014

Chapter 1 – Natasha

"Ms. Barnes, I know that someone told you that you would be arrested, but I promise you, they were lying. You were a victim of a scam, and they are not going to contact you again. If anyone was going to be making an arrest, it would be me and you have done nothing wrong." *Besides being naïve*, I thought.

I paused to allow the inconsolable woman on the phone to repeat, one more time, how upset she was. Of course she was upset. She sent five thousand dollars via Western Union to a scam artist whom I would never be able to locate. It wasn't that I couldn't do my job. The money was wired to a remote location and immediately wired again, if not a few more times before it landed in a bank outside of the United States.

These particular cases frustrated me to no end. Internet scams were a dime a dozen these days, and for the most part, all I could do was make a record of the information. I'd send the victims over to the Internet Crime Complaint Center and tell them to file a report there. More and more people were becoming victims of scams, but no matter how much I preached to our residents or posted warnings on our social media pages, more victims called in each week.

My desk was strewn with papers and I scanned the surface as she repeated the story as if I hadn't already heard it four other times. I had three cases I needed to type follow-up reports for and two people to call in for interviews on a theft investigation. I sighed quietly and tapped my pen on the beige Formica top of my desk as I forced myself back to the one-sided conversation.

The portable police radio crackled on the corner of my desk and I glanced at it. They were calling one of my patrol officers.

"Unit Sixteen Sam Four, I know you are busy, but we have an accident, serious, pending for you." The female voice came through the air along with static. I tuned out Ms. Barnes and listened to see if the officer was able to break off from what he was working on, or not.

"Sixteen Sam Four, I copy, can you see if another unit can assist on that. I'm going to be tied up here for a little while," Sergeant Jerry Johnson, one of the two officers working the street this afternoon, answered. I snatched the portable radio off my desk. I was saved.

"Sixteen David Sixty-One, I'll take that," I replied as I put the microphone to my mouth.

"Ms. Barnes, I'm sorry to interrupt you, but I have to go. We have an emergency that I need to respond to." I heard her say okay, but the phone was already on its way back to its rest. I could apologize for my abrupt end later.

I stuck my arms into the sleeves of my patrol jacket while I made my way to the exit door, and heard the dispatcher advise that it was one car in a ditch with two occupants. I acknowledged her transmission and jumped into my silver unmarked Chevy Impala.

If you saw the vehicle drive by you'd have no idea it was a police vehicle, even the antennas were hidden and not bubbled up on the roof or trunk like many patrol cars. I snapped my red and blue lights onto my visor and flipped it down before turning on my rear and flashing headlights. A black sedan swerved to the side when he saw my lights and heard my siren and I sped off around him.

The accident was only a few miles away and as I pulled up to the scene, there were four cars blocking traffic. People milled along the edge of the roadway looking down the embankment. What idiot said this was a ditch? This was a thirty-foot drop down to a creek, not a ditch.

"Sixteen David Sixty-One, I'm on location. Would you please get our on-call tow company en route?" I asked my dispatcher as I swung my car door open and climbed out. I heard her acknowledgement as my mind switched gears..

A man wearing dirty work pants and heavy boots ran to me.

"They were driving too fast, a deer ran out in front of them, and they couldn't make the curve."

I nodded, not particularly caring how the accident happened at the moment, only concerned with the occupants of the vehicle. "Are the people inside all right?" I questioned as we approached the edge of the asphalt. The guardrail had been peeled back as if it was made of tin foil and not steel.

"Don't know. No one has gone down to check on them. It's a long way down," he stated.

Crap, it was a long way down, and muddy. I searched the embankment for a path that would allow me to work my way down without killing myself. A thin tree about five inches in diameter had been plowed over by the car, but it still looked as if the roots were secure. I grabbed a hold of it and started to descend.

As my hands gripped the damp tree bark, I realized I should have put my gloves on before I started down. I almost fell a time or two, but finally managed to get to the bottom and to the black sedan that was nose first in the creek.

With the angle of the car, I couldn't see into the driver's side window, so I approached the passenger side and realized that the only way I'd be able to reach the door was to step into the creek. *Damn it! There goes my brand new boots,* I growled to myself.

I shuddered as my foot sank into the current. The cold water gushed over the top of my boot and down inside and I was tempted to turn around and go back to the edge, but I didn't. Duty first, comfort second.

The rear passenger door was locked and I banged on the window to get the attention of the two occupants. "Shit," I muttered when neither of them moved. I moved closer to the front door, and a female passenger with shoulder-length brown hair, around my age, was staring sight unseen out the side window. I didn't need the coroner to tell me that the glazed look in her eyes was caused by death. Blood trickled from a cut on her face, but since she was no longer alive, the drops that ran over her skin looked more like slow tears than a serious head wound.

Beyond the female, a man sat in the driver's seat. His head back against the headrest made his Adam's apple protrude further than normal. I scrutinized his throat, just before his jaw line. Right under his ear I saw the flesh moving with his pulse. "Thank God," I said as I wiggled the passenger door handle and found it locked, too.

My key ring had this handy-dandy little yellow tool that when you slammed it the right way against a car window it would shatter it. At least that was what it was supposed to do. To my knowledge, no one in my department had ever used theirs before. I guess this window was going to be the guinea pig.

I gripped the small tool tightly in my fist. I thought about the fact that I didn't have gloves on again, and took a deep breath as I focused on the window. Sirens grew closer as I brought my hand back and slammed it against the glass. The window shattered down onto my feet and the inside of the car.

"Holy crap, it really does work." With my keys back in my pocket, I used my elbow to clear away enough glass so I could put my hand through and open the door.

"Child locks, of course," I muttered as I tried the handle inside and it lifted without doing anything. I used my elbow to clear away the rest of the glass and glanced up the hill. More people stood there, a few of them holding out cell phones—probably videotaping the whole thing. Great, my ass was about to be on film.

I half-dove and half-shimmied through the window, trying to ignore the remnants of glass that dug into my legs. I would have a dozen cuts on my thighs when this was over.

Once inside, a large black duffle bag sat haphazardly on the seat and I shoved it out of my way so I could sit behind the driver's seat. The man groaned as I touched his neck. Groaning was a good thing. My chest pressed up against the back of his seat and I gripped his head slowly on both sides to straighten his neck. I was stuck doing c-spine until someone else got down here with a collar. Something wet touched my fingers and I twisted to see around the side of the headrest. Great, now I had blood on my hands. I absently wondered if I had any cuts to be concerned about.

A mixture of adrenaline and wet feet brought shivers to my body. With a long inhale, I forced myself to calm down. By the time emergency personnel got down to the car, near convulsions racked my body and I fought to control them while keeping the guy's neck straight. Why couldn't it have been June instead of March?

"Hey, Foster, what do you have in there?" one of the firemen yelled from outside of the car as he peered inside.

"Passenger is DOA. Driver is still alive, been unconscious since I got here." He nodded and turned to yell up the hill.

The driver tried to shift his head but I held it tightly. "Stay still, you're gonna be all right. You just need to stay still." My tone was soft while I leaned around the headrest and got closer to his ear. He tried to lean his head toward my voice; that again was a good sign, but I didn't let him complete the action.

A few firemen slid down the hill and began setting up ropes to bring down the tools and pull the medical board back up.

One of the EMTs came around the passenger side and started unwrapping a collar. "You gonna be able to get this on him? Or do you need to me to get in there with you?"

"No, Atkins, I can get it. The car was unstable when I was climbing in. I think if you tried, it might shift the car further into the water."

He nodded his acknowledgement and leaned in to get the collar ready to hand to me. I was going to have to do this one handed, but it could be done. While I was putting the brace around his neck, Atkins felt for a pulse on the passenger. I heard his sigh and knew I'd been correct in my earlier assumption.

The brace was secured and other than a few moans escaping from the driver, it was silent in the car. I watched the heavy equipment coming down the slope and being set up. The driver's door must be damage if they were going to cut the car apart to get the occupants out.

Clanking came from under the car and I stiffened. Atkins turned to me and yelled that they were going to stabilize the vehicle with a winch and pull it out of the creek so they could cut into the car.

I blew out a breath and a visible plume rose in front of my eyes reminding me how cold it was. My feet didn't need the reminder, they were now numb.

I glanced around the inside of the car. The dark leather interior was impressive. I peered over the driver's shoulder, a Mercedes. First time I'd ever been in one. I scanned the interior. "And I thought my Ford Explorer had a lot of gizmos in it."

My gaze landed on the passenger and I wondered who she was. Was this his wife? Had they been away on a holiday or rushing off someplace else? What did she do for a living? Did she have children?

That question stopped me in my tracks. I didn't want to think about there being children out there who no longer had a mother. I returned my gaze out the window and passed the next few minutes watching the firemen. At the top of the hill, two patrol guys spoke to bystanders; at least they could take it from here. Once the motorist was out of the car, I could turn the scene over to them and allow them to do the investigation.

Atkins turned to me. "You ready?" he asked from the far side window. In his outstretched hand was a sheet.

"Yeah." I took one hand off the driver's neck and grabbed the sheet, shaking it out and draping it over the two of us. This was not the first time I had been inside a car while it was being cut apart. The last time, I'd been in the driver's seat and someone else had been sitting where I was now, holding me so that I wouldn't jerk when the loud noises started.

I yelled out that we were ready after I'd secured the cover to protect us from flying glass and pieces of plastic. I let my head fall against the headrest and stared down at the floor. The edge of the sheet lay over the duffle bag. Something was poking out of the open zipper. I strained my gaze in the late afternoon light to see what it was.

I was about to pull the zipper back a little further when the

Jaws of Life roared outside the car and I jumped. The guy in the front seat did, too, so I clamped his head with both of my hands. "It's okay, stay still. It will be over in a minute."

A loud screech of the metal tearing was like someone running nails down a chalkboard. For someone who hated not knowing what was going on around them, being hidden under a sheet while others worked with loud tools had my heart hammering against my rib cage.

The firemen kept working on the vehicle, and a few moments later, they popped the roof off and removed the door. Several people converged on the motorist and I was finally able to release my hold.

Without a thought, I wiped the blood off my left hand onto the sheet and reached for the duffle bag. I pulled the zipper open about five inches and leaned down to look inside.

"Hey, Foster," I heard over my shoulder, but I didn't turn around. I was staring wide-eyed into the bag.

"Tasha." The sound of my first name brought my head up. "You all right? We can take it from here."

"I think I'm going to stick around, Jerry," I said as I met his familiar eyes.

"Why's that?"

I nodded down to the bag near my feet. "Because there are several thousand dollars in hundreds in this bag and it's going to need to be counted and put into evidence for safekeeping."

"Several thousand?" he said, and stretched to look down into the foot well beside me.

"Maybe more like several hundred thousand," I said as we both gawked at the bundles of money inside the bag.

www.ingramcontent.com/pod-product-compliance
Lightning Source LLC
Chambersburg PA
CBHW030121180626
46812CB00002B/508